FALLEN KNIGHT

USA TODAY BESTSELLING AUTHOR

T.K. LEIGH

FALLEN KNIGHT

All rights reserved. No part of this book may be reproduced or transmitted in any form without written permission from the publisher, except by a reviewer who may quote brief passages for review purposes.

This is a work of fiction. Names, characters, places, and incidents either are the product of the author's imagination and any resemblance to actual persons, living or dead, business establishments, events, or locales is entirely coincidental or, if an actual place, are used fictitiously. The publisher does not have any control over and does not assume any responsibility for author or third-party websites or their content.

The author acknowledges the trademarked status and trademark owners of various products referenced in this work of fiction, which have been used without permission. The use of these trademarks is not sponsored, associated, or endorsed by the trademark owner.

Published by Carpe Per Diem, Inc

Cover Design: Cat Head Media, Inc.

Cover assets:

© 2023 willeecole

Used under license from Deposit Photos.

Copyright © 2023 Tracy Kellam
All rights reserved.

BOOKS BY T.K. LEIGH

ROMANTIC SUSPENSE
The Temptation Series
Temptation
Persuasion
Provocation
Obsession

The Broken Crown Trilogy
Royal Creed
Fallen Knight
Broken Crown

The Inferno Saga
Part One: Spark
Part Two: Smoke
Part Three: Flame
Part Four: Burn

For more information on any of these titles and upcoming releases, please visit T.K.'s website:
www.tkleighauthor.com

For a free eBook, sign up for T.K.'s newsletter.

https://www.tkleighauthor.com/newsletter-signup

Or scan the code below

PART I

Sacrifice

*"Let us sacrifice one day in order
to gain our whole lives, perhaps."*

~ Victor Hugo
Les Miserables

CHAPTER ONE

Esme

Nine Years Later

"Aren't you going to come for a swim?"

I open my eyes and take in the sight of the man hoisting himself out of the pool. Every inch of his bare skin glimmers with water droplets, clinging like dew to the hard edges of his sculpted torso.

The rays of the sun high in the cloudless sky warm my bikini-clad body as I enjoy one of the last summer-like days now that September's nearly over.

"The water's beautiful." He sucks in his lower lip as he rakes his gaze down my frame, heat flaming in his chestnut eyes.

It doesn't matter that we've been together for five years now. He still looks at me like I'm the only person who matters. The only person in his universe.

"And miss watching the show?" I raise my sunglasses to

ogle Tristan's physique. Wet and muscular. Tan and solid. "Not a chance in hell."

His eyes darken, the desire in his appreciative stare lighting me on fire.

It's not the same as when Creed looked at me this way, but I've stopped comparing every man to him. I had to. Otherwise, I don't know how I would have survived. I needed to distance myself from the constant reminders of everything I lost that summer.

For the past nine years, I've done exactly that.

Upon moving to Paris, I focused all my attention on studying the culinary arts.

But in the quiet of night, my thoughts always returned to Creed.

To his touch.

To his love.

It was torture to lie awake craving him. I've lost count of the number of times I dreamt he came to me, only to wake up to the reality that he could never be mine. If he ever was.

After months of restless nights, I knew I couldn't keep living this way. Couldn't continue loving a memory. Like my mother often said during her life… *We can't live in the present if we're still held captive by the past.* So I decided to leave the past behind me.

Even if that meant leaving Creed behind.

Enter Tristan Emerson Hughes.

It was as if the world knew he was exactly what I needed. And I like to think I'm what he needed, too.

The son of a former U.S. President, he knows how trying it can be to be part of a powerful family. The path that led him to Paris was similar to mine. His father hoped he'd follow in his footsteps and go into politics. But Tristan always hated everything about the American political machine, preferring to use the influence that came with his last name for good.

Much like me.

I think that's why I was drawn to him. While what we share isn't remotely as explosive or consuming as it was with Creed, I'm okay with that. Tristan was one of the first people to look at me and not see my title.

He sees a person. He sees *me*.

I can't say with certainty Creed ever did.

It took me years to come to terms with the truth that it never would have worked between us, no matter how hard we fought for it. Not when we weren't the only people in our relationship. From the beginning, the crown was there, too. If I've learned anything throughout my life, it's that nothing is powerful enough to overcome the crown.

Not even love.

A deep chuckle rumbles from Tristan's throat as he stalks toward me. Each step he takes causes my pulse to kick up, his eyes gleaming like a wolf on the hunt, dark with danger. Like the predator he is, he cages me against my lounge chair and settles between my legs. When I feel his hard length rub against my core, I don't even care that he's dripping water all over me.

"Why watch when you can be part of the show, beautiful?" he croons in that subtle American drawl I find so incredibly sexy.

He presses his lips to mine, his kiss consuming me as I lose myself in him.

It's been a while since we've been together like this without any distractions. Tristan's spent the majority of the past several months on the set of his next big picture, hence why we agreed to get away to Saint-Tropez.

While he may come from a political powerhouse of a

family, he chose a different path in life. After attending Yale, he headed out to California to try his hand at acting, something he'd grown interested in while earning the degree his father insisted he obtain. Now he's one of the most popular actors in the world.

"And what part will I be playing?" I murmur against his mouth, running my fingers up and down his back, savoring in the ripples of his defined muscles.

"Maybe the dutiful student who'll do anything to raise her grades."

I laugh, succumbing to the infectious playfulness in his expression. But my laughter turns to moans when he peppers kisses along my neck before slowly traveling down my body. His warm breath caresses my skin like a tender breeze, each touch of his lips sending a shiver down my spine.

"Or maybe you can be the nanny hired to take care of some brooding billionaire's only child, who in turn ends up not being able to keep his hands off you once he sees you in a bikini."

"Should I be worried you're listing off popular tropes used in romance novels? Professor/student. Nanny/employee."

"Just trying to keep things interesting, darling."

He flashes me a sinful grin before he returns to me, brushing his mouth against mine in a sweet kiss. When our eyes meet again, his expression is more serene. Resolved. Thoughtful.

"Or how about you play the part of a beautiful princess who just so happened to attend the same charity gala as some no-name actor and they hit it off, both of them smiling for the first time in years?"

My heart swells with happiness as the memory of that night comes rushing back.

I'd given up hope of meeting someone who made me feel the things Creed had. Instead, I was content with the occasional passing fling. A date here and there, none of which ever went anywhere.

Then Tristan entered my life. He had no idea who I was. Sadly, I had no idea who he was, either. I had to Google him after that night. He did the same, and both of us shared a laugh. Still, the fact we were ignorant of who the other was is why we work so well together, even to this day. We liked each other before we knew the truth. We fell for who we were. Not what.

"I think that may be my favorite trope," Tristan finishes.

I scrunch my nose. "I'm not sure that's a trope. Sure, there are celebrity romances, but they usually involve some playboy actor who runs around town sticking his dick into anything with a pulse, so they bring in a glorified babysitter to make sure he stops sleeping around to improve his image, and they end up falling for each other."

He pinches his lips together, a contemplative expression crossing his brow. "I like my version better." He dips his head toward me, smoothing a few tendrils of hair behind my ear. "It may not have the elements of a blockbuster in the making, but it's our story. And I love our story." He touches his mouth to mine. "I love you, Esme."

I sigh as I wrap my arms around his shoulders. "I love you, too."

It took me quite a while to actually tell him that. Being the understanding man he is, he didn't get upset when I didn't immediately return the sentiment after he first shared his feelings with me. We both came into this relationship with baggage, most of which the world knew about.

But we also came into this relationship with secrets.

At least I did.

Despite the fact it's been years since I've spoken to Creed, it felt like a betrayal to say those three words to anyone other than him.

But after months of Tristan telling me how much he loved me, I relented, repeating his declaration to him.

I'm not sure what I feel for him is love. I'm not sure I'm capable of loving him the way he loves me, not when a huge part of my heart is missing. It has been for years.

But I do care deeply for Tristan. My feelings for him are strong. Stronger than they've been for anyone else I've dated since Creed.

He makes me smile. Makes me laugh. Makes me feel appreciated. Respected. Loved.

That should be enough for me.

I want it to be enough for me.

Most days, it is.

But there are still those days I can't help but long for what once was, despite the impossibility of ever having that again. I learned the hard way that the heart doesn't listen to reason.

Tristan deepens the exchange, rocking his hips against me in a slow, steady rotation, his need for me thick and heavy. I pull him closer, surrendering to the moment.

Until my mobile cuts through the silence with its shrill, abrasive ringtone.

"Don't answer it," Tristan pleads against my lips, sliding his thumb across my hipbone. "Whoever it is can wait until I'm done with you." He flashes a wicked smile. "Although I don't plan on being done for quite some time."

He snakes down my body, trailing his tongue along every inch of exposed skin. The heat emanating from his lips ignites a fire in its wake, making me tune out everything except how talented his mouth is. Including my ringing phone.

He takes his time, slowly building my pleasure until I'm desperate for him.

"And what is it you plan on doing?"

"Everything, beautiful. I'm going to do everything you want me to." He spreads my thighs, hunger flashing in his gaze as he pushes my bikini bottoms to the side. He brings his mouth to my center, my muscles growing taut with anticipation.

Then my bloody cell rings again.

"For fuck's sake," I exclaim, swiping it off the table to silence it so there are no more interruptions.

But the name on the screen sends my heart skyrocketing into my throat.

I bolt upright, staring at the phone as if it's a ticking bomb.

It's been nine years since I've seen his name appear on my mobile.

Nine years since I've heard his voice.

Nine years since I've peered into his eyes.

Since I left Belmont, Creed and I have successfully avoided each other. A feat, considering he's my brother's chief protection officer. Anytime Anderson paid me a visit, a different member of his team accompanied him. I'm not sure if it was a directive from the General of the Royal Guard because of our history, or simply Creed not wanting to interfere with my time with my brother. Not wanting to add any awkwardness to his visit.

Why is he reaching out now?

It would have to be serious for him to call after all this time.

Dread instantly settles low in my stomach, turning everything to acid.

"Are you okay, Esme?"

At the sound of Tristan's voice, I snap my eyes toward his, struggling to get my jumbled thoughts and emotions under control.

"It's my brother's CPO. He…" I shake my head. "He never calls."

"Then you should answer it." Tristan climbs off me, brushing a kiss to my temple. "To be continued later, beautiful." Then he retreats, disappearing into the house to give me privacy.

I'm about to unlock my cell and ring Creed back when he calls once more. I do my best to push down the anxiety coursing through me as I hit the answer button. Holding my breath, I lift my phone to my ear, unsure how I'll react to hearing Creed's voice again after so long.

"Esme…," he exhales.

In an instant, every single memory and emotion I tried to lock up and pretend didn't exist rushes forward, especially when he says my name in that soft, raspy way he always did when it was just us.

That's when I know something must be wrong. Because there's no formal greeting of Your Highness.

He's not calling as part of his official duties as my brother's chief protection officer.

He's calling me as a friend.

At least as my brother's friend.

"Creed," I manage to say, my pulse racing faster than it has in years. "What—"

"It's Anders."

CHAPTER TWO

Esme

A hand squeezes my leg as I peer out the window of the private jet. The familiar landscape of my home country of Belmont comes into view — rolling hills dotted with lakes, giving way to jagged mountain peaks toward the south, pristine ocean to the north. A queasiness settles in my stomach that has nothing to do with the plane descending toward earth.

Instead, it has everything to do with having to face the one man I've avoided for years.

It's fitting, in a way.

Tragedy tore us apart when Adam died.

Now another tragedy has forced us back together.

Although, I'm trying not to view it as a tragedy. Still, nothing could have prepared me for this news.

My brother has multiple sclerosis.

The same disease that took our mother from us when she was my brother's age now plagues him.

The past several weeks have been trying, to say the least. From receiving Creed's phone call telling me Anderson had lost consciousness during a public event while in the States. To Anderson telling me he was diagnosed with MS. To him wanting to keep it from Creed for a little while longer so he could drive across the country, something he feared he may not be able to do much longer, not if his progression ended up being as rapid as was the case with our mother.

To him meeting a girl.

To him falling in love.

A part of me wanted to tell him there was no way he could fall in love with someone so quickly, especially someone he just met. Someone who didn't even know his real name, that he's heir apparent to the crown of Belmont.

But I know better than anyone that the heart can't be reasoned with. I tried to control my heart all those years ago. Tried to contain the fire that burned between Creed and me, growing stronger and more out of control with every passing moment.

In the end, it was as futile as trying to control the weather.

Just as it was for Anderson, his own short love affair while traveling across America ending in heartbreak.

Just as mine had.

I'm starting to think my grandmother has a point.

Maybe there truly is no room for love in a monarchy. Not when who we are is such a heavy burden.

"Are you okay?"

My gaze drifts away from the window and onto Tristan's face. His chestnut eyes, framed by thick lashes, flicker with uneasiness.

"Just…worried."

I can't bring myself to tell him the truth. While I am

concerned about my brother, what has my stomach in knots is the idea of coming face-to-face with Creed Lawson again.

"He'll be okay." Tristan presses a reassuring kiss to my temple.

I have no doubt Anderson will be okay. I'm just not sure *I'll* be okay. Can't shake the feeling in my gut that this trip is about to change everything.

We step off the plane and are immediately enveloped in a sea of flashes and shouting reporters, all of them hungry for their next juicy photo. There's no question in my mind someone from the palace PR team tipped them off about our arrival, hoping to put the royal family front and center in the headlines. What better way to accomplish that than to have photographers snap photos of me with my handsome actor boyfriend?

As we navigate through the throngs of people, Tristan's hand is warm against my own, his grip reassuring. My heart beats loudly in my chest, my unease increasing as I'm scrutinized by strangers behind their cameras. It makes me feel more like a circus animal than a human being.

Then again, as a royal, that's precisely what I am. A thing used to entertain the masses. Nothing more.

It's a reminder of how much I loathe this part of who I am.

But Tristan helps me through it, keeping my hand enclosed in his as he waves to photographers, smiling that charming smile of his. The one he reserves for the public. After all, he grew up around this kind of thing, too. He was ten when his father was first elected as President of the United States, forcing him to leave the relatively simple life they were living on a ranch in Texas.

Much like my uncle's death forced me to leave the relatively simple life I was living.

All the more reason Tristan is a good match for me. His life was shaken up when his father won that first election, putting him and his brothers in the spotlight. And while he now seems to enjoy the spotlight as an actor, he's shared how difficult those first few years were, the country seemingly obsessed with him and his brothers.

Just like all of Europe seemed to be obsessed with Anderson and me, the new heirs.

After successfully navigating the short walk from the plane to the waiting SUV, I duck inside, Tristan sliding in beside me. Within seconds, Archie, my chief protection officer, pulls away from the tarmac, driving down the familiar roads of Montrose, the capital city of Belmont.

The streets are filled with people — tourists posing for photos in front of the historic square, locals zooming by on their bikes, children playing in one of the many parks.

I once loved the beauty and spirit of this place. Now, I struggle to see it as anything other than an extension of my former prison.

A heaviness settles in the car as we continue through the city. Even Tristan doesn't attempt to fill the silence with conversation. He simply holds my hand, brushing his thumb against my knuckles in a reassuring manner. This gesture once helped relax me. Now I doubt anything can stop the anxiety from bubbling inside me, especially as we approach the gates of Wintervale Manor, the official residence of the heir apparent my father gifted to Anderson when he turned thirty. I can't help but feel like an inmate who's been absolved of her crimes, only to be sent back to prison for the same crime years later.

I remind myself I'm here for my brother. That I'm not staying forever. Just a short while to help him with the adjustment period. Then I can go back to Paris.

The SUV comes to a stop outside the sprawling estate, and I look up at the three-story building, green vines snaking along off-white stones, the grounds pristine and well-kept. My brother's butler appears out of thin air to open my door. He extends his hand, helping me to my feet before dropping his hold and bowing toward me.

"Your Highness."

I force a smile at his greeting. A reminder of who I am after being away for so long.

Outside of this country, no one really knows me as the Princess Royal of Belmont. Hell, these days, most people only know me as Tristan Hughes' girlfriend.

I like it that way.

Like my identity not being tied to this place.

"Good afternoon," I say to Richard as Tristan sidles up behind me. "Allow me to introduce Mr. Tristan Hughes." I look at Tristan. "This is my brother's butler, Richard."

"Wonderful to meet you." Tristan extends his hand, smiling as they shake.

"Likewise, sir." Richard turns to me once more. "His Highness is expecting you. This way, ma'am." He spins and makes his way up the steps.

As I enter the high-ceilinged foyer of Wintervale Manor, it feels like I've stepped back in time, the décor exactly as I remember from the brief period my family lived here after my uncle's death. That was short-lived, though. Mere months later, my grandfather passed away, making my father king, which required us to move yet again. This time to Lamberside Palace.

Over the past several years, I often wondered why Anderson always insisted on visiting me in Paris instead of trying to encourage me to come home to see him. But as I follow Richard up the sprawling staircase and along the familiar corridors leading to what was once my parents' suite — now Anderson's — I know why. He needed the escape. Needed to go somewhere he wasn't reminded of who he is.

Or, more accurately, *what* he is.

That's the thing about this life. We're not allowed to be people. Not allowed to display emotion. Not allowed to show weakness. Instead, we're merely objects for the people of this country to worship from afar, like rare works of art on display in a museum. Nothing more.

As we walk in silence along the carpeted hallways, the papered walls adorned with portraits of important figures in Belmont history, including one of my family mere days after my father's coronation, Tristan leans close, his shoulder skimming against mine.

"I probably should have brushed up on my royal etiquette rules before coming," he whispers upon noticing every staff member bow or curtsy toward me along with a murmured greeting of "Your Highness." "Should I be bowing toward you like that?"

"Don't you dare even think about it," I admonish. I notice Richard's posture stiffen at my response. "I like that you don't treat me that way. That you treat me like I'm a nobody."

He pulls me to a stop and loops an arm around my waist, dragging me into his chest. "You've never been a nobody to me, beautiful." He inches toward me, breath warming my mouth. "You've always been somebody, even if I didn't quite know who that somebody was."

His lips touch mine, and I melt into him, tuning out the rest of the world for a moment, not caring about any of my brother's household staff seeing us. I never quite understood why public displays of affection were frowned upon. If anything, they should be encouraged, prove we're not these uncaring objects incapable of love.

But when the sound of a door closing echoes in the hall-way, the noise loud in the typical solemnity of this place, I startle, jumping back.

When I do, I'm met with a pair of familiar dark eyes.

CHAPTER THREE

Creed

I stare, pulse steadily increasing, jaw tight as heat rushes through my body.

It was inevitable I'd see Esme, considering her sole reason for being here is because of Anderson's recent diagnosis. Still, I hoped *he* wouldn't be with her.

As luck would have it, the first time I see her, he's not just with her.

He's *kissing* her.

I thought I'd gotten over her. Thought I'd moved on from those few short weeks we spent fooling ourselves we could be together.

I *should* have moved on from those few short weeks.

All it takes is a few seconds in her presence, a few moments of peering into those haunting green eyes, and I'm reminded why I fell so hard for her in the first place.

I didn't think she could get any more beautiful than she was all those years ago, but I was wrong. She's no longer a twenty-five-year-old young woman trying to find her way in the world. She's more mature. Sophisticated. And so bloody sexy it makes my chest ache.

Her golden blonde hair falls to her mid-back in gentle waves, eyes lined with a touch of shadow, full lips tinted red. She wears a form-fitting blue dress paired with pearl jewelry, everything about her style timeless and classic. I always thought she had the look of a Hollywood starlet from the 1940s, reminding me of a modern-day Lauren Bacall.

Beside Tristan Hughes — his tall, fit body clad in a three-piece suit, dark hair perfectly groomed — she looks even more so, considering he *is* Hollywood royalty.

They look like they belong together. Like they were made for each other.

I could never compete with that. I was foolish to think I could. Not when we come from two different worlds. She's sophistication and grace where I'm simple and rough.

Remembering my place, I step back and bow. "Your Highness."

I meet her gaze, the tense air between us palpable. Her eyes are two chips of ice, narrowed in annoyance at my formal greeting. But it's protocol.

After everything I lost the last time I broke the rules, I refuse to make that mistake again. I need to address her this way. Need the reminder of who we are to each other.

Need the reminder that any lingering feelings I may still have for her can never come to fruition.

"Lieu—Captain Lawson," she responds.

It's not the first time I've heard her voice since she left for Paris.

At first, I tried to avoid everything to do with her, always scrolling away or changing the channel when a story involving her came on, the pain of everything still too raw.

But as time went on, I started paying attention. Watched interviews. Stayed up-to-date with her life in Paris.

No amount of interviews or phone conversations could have prepared me to hear her voice in person. That throaty voice that once moaned my name.

What I wouldn't give to hear her moan my name one more time.

But that ship has sailed. I won't allow myself to succumb to my desires. Not anymore.

And not because I'm now a member of the royal guard and swore a duty to serve and protect the royal family above all else. But because of the price we paid the last time we gave in to temptation. The last time I allowed lust to cloud my judgment.

Adam tried to warn me that falling for Esme would be dangerous. And when I found his notebook detailing Jameson Gates' relationship with the missing woman, Callie Sloane, I knew why, especially when I learned it was possible that Callie was seen as a threat to Jameson's potential marriage to Esme and was made to disappear, although no evidence was ever found to support that theory.

Still, this was why he begged Esme to end things. I should have known my brother wouldn't betray me like he did without a good reason. He did it to protect me.

I returned the favor by all but telling him I wished he were dead.

Hours later, he *was* dead.

I may not have struck the match that lit the car on fire, but I feel just as responsible. Which is why I've spent the past nine years trying to make things right.

Falling back into my old habits — namely, this insane pull I still feel toward Esme — won't make things right.

"May I introduce Mr. Tristan Hughes," she continues,

affection warming her eyes as she looks at the man standing beside her. "Tristan, this is Captain Creed Lawson, my brother's CPO."

Tristan extends his hand my way, his charismatic smile displaying his perfect teeth. "It's a pleasure," he says in an American accent that holds a subtle Texas drawl, hinting at what I know to be his roots from all the research I conducted when I learned he was dating Esme.

It may have been overkill, but there's no such thing when it comes to her. I tried to rationalize my actions by claiming Anderson would be spending time with him whenever he visited her.

That wasn't why I endeavored to learn everything about Tristan Emerson Hughes, though.

I did so because I needed to know she was safe with him.

And secretly because I'd hoped to find something that would make her want to break things off with him.

But I didn't.

Everything I've found on him supports the general opinion that he's just a really good guy. He's routinely spoken out in favor of gun control and against the health-care-for-profit system currently in place in America, despite his own father being extremely pro-gun and against socialized medicine. To that end, he's founded several charities to bring an end to gun violence in the country, particularly in schools, as well as founded his own pharmaceutical company where he manufactures a couple hundred different types of generic drugs, selling them to consumers at cost.

As much as I want to hate him for the simple fact that he gets to touch Esme, kiss her, build a life with her, I can't.

Not when I chose this path.

"How's Anders?" Esme asks.

"He's…okay. It's been a difficult few weeks, but I think

he's getting better. He only fired me once in the past twenty-four hours," I attempt to joke. "And only because I told him he shouldn't drink with all the drugs he's taking right now."

"And Nora?" she asks, referring to the woman Anderson met during his cross-country road trip.

I push out a long breath, shaking my head.

I tried to warn him it was a disaster waiting to happen.

Although I'm not sure if I did it for Anderson's sake or Nora's. I'd like to think it was for Anderson. After all, he was once my friend. My best friend.

But I know from experience how devastating it can be to give your heart to a member of the royal family. To be willing to give up everything for them, only to learn it'll never be enough to overcome centuries of tradition.

"How's he dealing with the way things ended?"

"I can't say he's made his peace with it," I admit. "He may have anticipated it would go this way, but I get the feeling he still held out hope for a happy ending."

"Just because she walked away doesn't mean they'll never find their happily ever after." She steps toward me. "Despite all the obstacles facing them, they could still find their way back to each other. Don't you think?"

I study her, unsure if she's asking for her brother's peace of mind… Or hers.

Ours.

But I refuse to entertain the notion. I can't.

"Some obstacles are just too big to overcome. The *crown* is too big to overcome."

She peers into my eyes for several protracted seconds, as if searching for something deep inside me.

As if attempting to peel back the hard outer shell I built around myself years ago.

My pulse increases as Tristan's curious gaze darts

between us with a touch of suspicion. Does he know about our past?

If I know Esme like I once did, I can say with near certainty she didn't tell him.

Just like I haven't shared our past with anyone. Not like I've been with anyone with whom I'd need to share my past. Even if I had been, I doubt I would have told them. Doubt I would have wanted to relive it.

I clear my throat, posture stiffening. "I'll be on my way. Give you some time with His Highness."

"Of course." Esme's response comes out clipped, lips pinched into a tight line.

"Nice to meet you," I direct Tristan's way before turning back toward Esme, bowing slightly. "Your Highness."

"Captain."

I take one last look at her, trying to ignore the prickling sensation in my chest. Then I turn from her, pushing down the emotions stirring to the surface after being in her presence again.

It's been nine years. She shouldn't have this effect on me anymore. I shouldn't crave her kiss. Shouldn't get jealous at the thought of Tristan tasting what was once mine.

But I still do.

It may have been nine years, but even the strongest recovering addict sometimes has an occasional relapse.

I just pray I can be strong enough to resist the temptation this time around.

CHAPTER FOUR

Esme

"There she is!" Anderson slurs when I step into his private suite.

His hair is disheveled, the scruff on his jaw indicating he hasn't shaved in a few days. Typically, my brother follows the rules regarding his appearance, keeping his hair neat and face clean shaven.

That seems to have gone out the window.

"The future queen." He lifts his rocks glass, the amber liquid sloshing around in it.

Apparently, Creed wasn't successful in keeping alcohol away from him. I can't be angry at him, though. I know how difficult my brother can be when he gets like this.

While I don't condone his excessive drinking, I can understand it. This life can be a tremendous burden. Sometimes the only thing that can lessen the weight, even for a little while, is to escape. To have a few hours you don't feel like yourself.

Alcohol has always helped Anderson not feel like himself, and I said nothing.

But I can't stay quiet now. Not when everything he puts in his body can affect him.

"Should you be drinking like that, Anders?" I ask in as calm of a voice as possible, not wanting to sound accusatory.

He has enough people in his life telling him what to do. How to dress. How to behave. The last thing I want is for him to hear it from me, too.

"What are your plans for this space?" he presses on, ignoring my inquiry. "You'll probably do some mid-century modern motif, right? That seems to be your style. You definitely won't be needing this anymore."

He staggers to a portrait of him in his full military uniform, the gold plate below bearing the title, "The Crown Prince".

"Considering I soon *won't* be the Crown Prince anymore."

He pulls the portrait off the wall and smashes it over a chair, the canvas ripping.

I gasp, not in horror that he'd destroy the original artwork commissioned by the royal household. I never quite liked it myself. Doesn't remotely resemble the Anderson I know.

Instead, my surprise is from the helplessness consuming every inch of him. I anticipated he'd be in rough shape. I just didn't expect him to be in such a dark place.

Swallowing hard through the lump forming in my throat, I turn around and meet Tristan's sympathetic eyes.

"I'll give you some space," he offers without me needing to ask him. "I have a few phone calls I need to make anyway, especially now that they're starting to wake up in California. I'll just head to your apartment and get settled."

I pass him a grateful smile. "Thank you."

"I'll see you later on." Our lips touch briefly before he pulls back.

He glances Anderson's way, but doesn't linger, sensing now isn't the time for pleasantries. Then he slips into the hallway, requesting the butler outside to arrange for someone to take him to my apartment, his tone full of confidence.

Once the door closes, I head to the couch and sit, retrieving several articles from my bag, spreading them across the table.

"I've been doing some research. There are a lot more treatment options now than when Mum was diagnosed. You can even control possible relapses with diet and exercise. I've spoken with your private secretary. He says you're scheduled to see a neurologist tomorrow. I've requested he also bring in a nutritionist and physical therapist. You're lucky. According to my research, your form of MS isn't severe."

He barks out a laugh. "Lucky?"

Stumbling toward the wet bar, he recklessly sloshes more scotch into his rocks glass until it overflows and spills onto his hand.

"Not sure I'd call having the same disease that killed our mum lucky." He throws back a large gulp, wincing through the burn as it slides down his throat. "Not sure I'd call having a medicine cabinet full of drugs lucky. Not sure I'd call possibly never being able to get a bloody erection again lucky, Esme."

I square my shoulders, trying to remain as composed as possible when I'd love to break down and get drunk with my brother.

"Have you had difficulty getting an erection?" I ask hesitantly.

I typically don't talk to Anderson about the details of his

sex life. It's different now. I need to know if he's been experiencing any of the effects of his diagnosis.

"Definitely not." A hint of a smile curves on his lips before his expression falls. "Not like it matters anymore since there's no one I need to get it up for." He walks toward the couch, collapsing beside me.

"I'm sorry, Anders," I offer, placing my hand on his arm.

He squeezes his eyes shut and sucks in a gasp of air. His heartache is so palpable, it rolls off him in visible waves.

Despite the fact they only spent two weeks together, I have no doubt he loves Nora.

Over the past few weeks, I heard a change in his attitude during the daily phone conversations I insisted on, especially when I learned he decided to drive across America instead of returning home upon receiving his diagnosis.

At first, our conversations were filled with frustration as he brought up removing himself from the line of succession to save the royal household from doing it anyway. As time went on, as he spent his days with Nora, as he fell in love with Nora, there was no more frustration. No more despair. No more desolation.

Instead, I heard something I didn't think I would after that first phone call…hope.

"I thought…," he begins, his voice shaky with emotion. "I thought if I told her the truth myself instead of waiting for her to find out on her own, she'd see I didn't mean to hurt her."

"Maybe she just needs some time," I suggest. "Needs to work things out in her head. We're not exactly the easiest people to love." I playfully shove him, trying to cut through the tension.

"That may just be the understatement of the century."

He blows out a small laugh, a ghost of a smile tugging on his lips.

It's not his normal laugh or smile that lights up his entire face, but I'll take the small victories where I can. Considering the state Anderson was in mere minutes ago, this sliver of happiness is a huge victory.

"But you and Tristan have made it work." He sets his rocks glass onto the coffee table, then leans into the couch, resting his head on my shoulder.

I sigh, snaking my arms around him and pulling him close.

"Probably because he's infinitely more well-known than I am. At least everywhere else." I pause, biting my lower lip. "Hell, probably even here, too."

It's silent for a moment before Anderson pushes out of my embrace. "Well, I hope you're ready to step into my shoes."

"That's why I'm here," I tell him, ignoring his insinuation. "To help you out while you take some time for yourself. Get a handle on this new normal."

He shakes his head, resting his elbows on his thighs. Then he fixes his stare back at me, any remnants of hope vanishing. "That's not what I'm talking about, Esme. You remember what they did to Mum. This monarchy eliminates anything that can be seen as a sign of weakness." He swallows hard. "Eliminates any*one* who can be seen as a sign of weakness."

I grab both of his hands. "You are not weak, Gabriel Anderson. You're the strongest person I know."

"Not strong enough to fight the royal household. You know better than anyone how it is with them." He gives me a knowing look.

"And thanks to you, I stood up for myself. You gave me the strength and courage to give myself a voice. Now it's my turn to give you the strength to stand up for *your*self. And you can."

"We both know this isn't remotely the same thing as them deciding who you should marry. There may come a day when I'll need a cane to walk. When I'll be stuck in a wheel-chair. Do you really think the royal household will allow a bloody cripple to lead the country? Not to mention, there's the referendum to worry about."

"Referendum?" I furrow my brow.

"To turn the monarch into more of a ceremonial role, like in the U.K."

"And like every year before, it will fail to garner enough signatures to even make it onto the ballot."

He shakes his head, his expression grave. "Not this time, Esme. It got the required signatures. It's on next year's ballot."

I blink, my stomach sinking.

I'll be the first to admit that the monarchy system of government is antiquated and outdated. While no political system is perfect, giving people a say in who represents them is important. The people serving in our unicameral legislature are elected, but the person leading this country is not. The only thing that's kept the anti-monarchist movement from gaining any meaningful traction over the years is the fact that each monarch has been independent, never siding with one political party over another. It also helps that there's an unspoken rule that each monarch will voluntarily abdicate when they reach the age of sixty-five, which my father is only a few years away from.

"That doesn't matter, Anderson," I say, doing my best to remain positive. "While you may be frustrated now about all the changes, you'll get through it. You just need to show them that this won't affect how you do your job. You were *born* for this role. And not because you just so happened to be born before me," I add quickly when I sense he's about to make some joke that he technically *was* born for this.

"I've watched you over the years. Seen how you interact with the people. They adore you. I have no doubt they'll see your diagnosis for what it is. A strength. You're one of the strongest people I know, so I need you to be strong now, too. We'll take the next few days and see what course of treatment your medical team recommends. Get you on a new diet. With all these advances in medicine, you'll go on to live—"

"A long and happy life?" he scoffs, all the positive ground I thought I'd gained evaporating. "Happiness isn't in the cards for us, Esme. We're not allowed to be happy. Just to... Just to be, I suppose. To serve a purpose. And when we no longer serve that purpose..." He sighs, collapsing back into the couch. "They'll eliminate us using whatever means necessary."

He rests his head against my shoulder once more and closes his eyes, the combination of alcohol and the stress of his diagnosis wearing on him. I want to ask when the last time he slept was. Or ate.

He'd landed back in Belmont only a few hours before me. I doubt he slept much the last few days he spent in California with Nora, knowing it was most likely going to end once he came clean about everything. Couple that with all the alcohol he's had and the jet lag, it doesn't take long before I hear his gentle snores fill the room.

But I don't leave. Instead, I pull him close, pressing a soft kiss to his head, my heart aching for my brother.

When I left Paris this morning, I honestly thought it

would be a quick trip. I'd stay long enough to help him adjust to this new normal, but given how resilient he's always been, I'd probably only need to stay a week. Then I'd return to my life.

Now I fear that may no longer be possible.

CHAPTER FIVE

Creed

"You're home!"

The second I walk into the foyer of my house, I'm assaulted by two small arms wrapping around my torso.

Although, they're not as tiny as they once were.

Adam Jr., or AJ for short, has been growing more and more with every passing day. After only seeing him during our daily FaceTime chats for the past month while I was traveling with Anderson, it feels like he's grown another inch. Like he's starting to resemble his father more and more.

He still has a round face, but his cheeks are becoming more chiseled and angular as he matures. His dark brown hair is a tousled mess, much like his father's was at that age. But what always makes a pang squeeze my heart are his eyes — the same dark irises with flecks of gold as his father.

I have to swallow down the sorrow at the reminder that Adam never got to meet his son. That he wasn't here to watch him take his first steps. Or hear his first word.

But I like to think he's watching over us. That he's seen all the sacrifices I've made and has forgiven me for the things I said to him in his final few hours.

"Hey, little man." I return AJ's hug, inhaling his familiar scent. "Have you been good for your mum?"

"Of course."

"That depends on your definition of good."

I tear my attention from AJ as Rory saunters into the open living area of the house. It's a stark contrast from the formality and order of Anderson's estate. A few cups and dishes are left on the coffee table, AJ's football jersey draped over one of the barstools by the island, his school laptop charging beside it. But it's home. It has been for the past nine years.

After Adam's death, I moved in to help Rory with AJ. It was just supposed to be temporary. Once AJ was a little older, I planned to get my own place.

But even as he got older and became less demanding on Rory's time, I hated the idea of leaving them. It's hard enough to be away from AJ for weeks at a time when I'm traveling with Anderson. Not to mention, I now understand how difficult being a parent is. I may not be AJ's father, but I've tried to be a father figure to him. Tried to instill in him all the values my brother would have. Tried to be a good role model for him.

So instead of moving out, I stayed. I tell myself it's because I want to be here for AJ. But a lot of it has to do with guilt over the way I treated Adam the last time I spoke to him. I may not be able to tell him I'm sorry, but I can make it up to him now. Which is what I've spent the past nine years doing.

"Hey, Rory." I move toward her and bend down to brush a kiss to her cheek.

"How's he doing?" she asks in a hushed voice.

While the news of Anderson's diagnosis hasn't been made public yet, Rory works for the king's private secretary. She has access to more information than I probably do.

"Taking it one day at a time."

She gives my arm a reassuring squeeze. "That's all any of us can do."

I hold her gaze for a beat, then step back, pushing down the emotions over the reminder of the uphill battle Anderson faces in the coming weeks. I may be his chief protection officer, but I'm also his friend. When Anderson told me he'd been diagnosed with MS, it was like a punch to the gut, especially since he's the same age his mother was when she died as a result of complications from the same disease.

"And why would your mum imply you may not have been all that good?" I cross my arms in front of my chest, arching a brow in AJ's direction.

"I have been," he protests but averts his gaze, a telltale sign he's not being completely honest.

"He got into a little…altercation at school."

"Because that tosser was making fun of me for not having a dad."

"Language, AJ," I reprimand.

"Last week was the Breakfast with Dad at his school," Rory explains.

"I'm sorry, buddy." I squeeze my eyes shut as regret weighs down my stomach.

I remember how it felt when my dad didn't show up for those types of things because he was working. I swore I'd never put my kids through that. Granted, AJ isn't technically my child, but I've always acted as if he is.

"I completely forgot."

AJ shrugs, but I can tell it still bothers him. "It's okay."

Then a slow smile crawls on his lips. "Pretty sure he regretted it after I was finished with him."

"Is that right?"

"I did some of the moves you taught me. Took out his pressure points first, then disabled him with a kick in the groin."

I throw my head back and laugh, pulling him against me. "That's my boy."

"Well, your *boy* earned himself a week of detention," Rory interjects. "Not to mention has made my life more difficult, since this kid's mother is the PTA president and has started a campaign to remove me from the Holiday Fair Planning Committee."

"So? I thought you hated doing that."

"I do, but I'm trying to help at AJ's school as much as I can. It's not as easy for me. Not when all the other mothers have husbands at home to help."

"I'm here," I offer, although it's not the same. We may share parenting responsibilities. May share a house. May even share a bed on occasion when the grief hits her particularly hard.

But we don't share a life.

Part of me wonders if I'm keeping her locked in the past by staying here.

If I'm keeping myself locked in the past, too.

"I know you are." She offers me a grateful smile. "Sometimes I just wish…" She looks to the ceiling, blinking back the tears welling in her blue eyes.

She hates crying in front of AJ. He may be a tough kid, but he's also sensitive, as evidenced by the fact he kneed a kid in the junk when he poked fun at him for not having a dad. He picks up on his mum's emotions easily. Hates to see her upset.

I do, too.

Especially when she's upset over something that's out of our control.

And this past decade I've learned that grief isn't something anyone can control.

In the beginning, I thought I'd wake up one day and be over the loss. I soon had to face the hard truth that it doesn't work that way. Some days, even years later, the grief is so profound I feel like I'm suffocating under the weight. Other times, it's barely noticeable.

Regardless, that grief is always with me. It never goes away. It's just something I've learned to carry with me. As has Rory, although most days it seems she struggles with the weight of her grief, regardless of the passing of years.

Clearing my throat, I turn toward AJ. "Why don't you get your football gear? I'll take you to the pitch and we'll kick the ball around for a while. Give your mum a break."

AJ's eyes light up. Like his dad, he loves being out on the pitch and playing football. "Be right back."

He dashes up the stairs, his heavy footfalls making it sound like a herd of elephants instead of a nine-year-old boy.

"Thanks," Rory says, meeting my gaze. "I'm not sure what came over me. I just… This time of year is always hard. Even more so since you weren't around for the anniversary of his death."

I hang my head, pushing out a sigh. "I'm sorry. I should have been here for you."

She places her hand on my chest. "It's okay. Prince Gabriel needed you more."

"I know."

After Anderson collapsed during a public event in the States, I knew I needed to stay with him, even though he claimed it was just due to exhaustion and the heat. While I trust my team and know they wouldn't let anything happen to him, I could tell he was going through something. And it's a good thing I chose to stay, considering everything that transpired over the past several weeks. From him buying a Jeep Wrangler on a whim. To his decision to drive across America. To him meeting a woman and falling in love.

To him finally coming clean about his MS diagnosis.

To everything going up in flames.

"I still wish I could have been here for you."

"Well, you're here now." She forces a smile. "I understand the Princess Royal is also back. I saw footage of her on the tele with that actor boyfriend of hers."

I furrow my brows, unsure why Rory's bringing up Esme. It seems out of the blue. Or maybe it's just my guilty conscience rearing its head, even though I don't have anything to be guilty about. I saw Esme. Spoke to her briefly. Fantasized about cutting off Tristan Hughes' hands because he gets to touch her. Other than that, it was an uneventful interaction. Awkward, stilted, and painful. But uneventful all the same.

"Did you see her?" she asks when I don't immediately respond.

"I was at Wintervale when they arrived."

"How is she?"

I shrug noncommittally. "Fine, I suppose. Worried about her brother."

"Did she mention if she was planning to stay indefinitely?"

"We didn't talk for long. I imagine she wants to get back to her life as soon as possible."

She opens her mouth, hesitating before snapping her lips closed.

"Why? Did you hear something?"

Granted, anything Rory may have overheard should be taken with a grain of salt. Or an entire shaker. The gossip she hears at the office sometimes is just that…gossip.

But sometimes she does have reliable information.

"It could be nothing," she says quickly. "But His Majesty called an emergency meeting of the privy council this morning. Afterwards, his Head of Household met with Princess Esme's former private secretary, Lieutenant Hawkins, seemingly to discuss him resuming his previous duties. Which he would only do if Princess Esme were to resume *her* duties, as well."

I blink, a heaviness settling on my chest.

It was one thing for Esme to visit Anderson after he received his diagnosis. It's another to think she might stay.

Truthfully, the thought never crossed my mind. Based on the things Anderson's mentioned in passing, she's never had any intention of resuming her role as a senior member of the royal family. Not with the freedom she discovered once she left, no longer needing to worry about whether her actions are on "message" for the royal family. She's spearheaded women's rights marches in support of reproductive rights. Protested against gun violence. Has been vocal about conservation issues.

She won't be able to be such a staunch advocate for these causes anymore if she stays.

Not to mention, it'll mean seeing her on a regular basis.

At one point, I would have welcomed that. Would have jumped at any opportunity to see her, even if for only a moment.

Now, I'm not sure if I'm strong enough to see her every day. Not sure if I can bear the reminder of one of the best and worst times of my life.

"I'm ready!"

I snap out of my thoughts as AJ rushes down the stairs and into the living room.

"Great," I reply, my voice not sounding like my own, high-pitched and uneasy.

I can feel Rory's eyes on me, studying me.

But if she senses my nerves over the prospect of Esme being back in my life, she doesn't say anything. Just hugs AJ and tells him to have fun before I pat his shoulder, leading him from the house, trying to focus on him and only him.

It's a lost cause, though, my thoughts constantly floating to the one woman I shouldn't be thinking about.

The one woman I swore to leave in my past.

The one woman I swore to forget.

The one woman I still love, despite wishing I didn't.

CHAPTER SIX

Esme

"What are we doing here?" I ask Archie as he pulls up to the imposing gates of Lamberside Palace.

"I'm sorry, ma'am." My chief protection officer meets my eyes through the rearview mirror. "Call just came in. His Majesty has requested to see you before I take you to your apartment."

"Of course he did." I pinch the bridge of my nose, fighting off a headache I feel coming on from the mere idea of dealing with my father's bullshit tonight.

"My apologies."

"Don't worry about it. You're just doing your job."

He smiles sadly before refocusing his attention forward, navigating the car along the familiar driveway toward the palace. But instead of pulling up to the administrative entrance, he continues toward the residential wing, stopping underneath the port cochère. Oliver, the head butler, opens my door almost instantly, offering me his hand to help me out. Once I have my footing, he releases his hold on me and bows.

"Your Highness."

I greet him with a tight smile. "Good evening, Oliver."

"This way, please."

I follow him into the foyer and up the elaborate staircase toward my father's private quarters. It's been a few years since I've walked these hallowed halls. Despite the passing of time, not much has changed. Portraits of past rulers adorn the walls. Crystal chandeliers hang overhead. Floral arrangements decorate the occasional side table. Everything is pristine, not so much as a speck of dust to be found, marring the façade of perfection. But that's all it is. A façade. Nothing about it is real. It never has been.

I doubt it ever will be.

When we reach the king's residence, Oliver raps on the door. It opens within seconds, my father's personal butler, Gerald, standing there to receive me.

"Your Highness," he bows.

"Gerald."

"His Majesty is in the study. You may go ahead."

With an appreciative smile, I continue through the residence and down a corridor. I'm not quite sure what to expect when I see my father, why he called me here with little notice. I pray my grandmother's not also here, along with the rest of the privy council and PR team. I can only imagine what kind of spin they're planning regarding Anderson's diagnosis. I'd like to think she'd be sympathetic toward him, considering she's his grandmother, but that would require her to see us as people. As family.

I doubt she ever has.

Finding the door slightly ajar, I peek my head inside, expelling a relieved breath when my father's alone.

The study is relatively dark, the only source of light coming from a small lamp on the mahogany desk. I scan my father's frame as he stands in front of the built-in shelves, a framed photo in his hand. He looks...devastated. I can't remember the last time I've seen him display emotion like this. It was probably when my mother died. Even then, I can't be sure. I was too young.

I push the door the rest of the way open and step into the study. "Dad?"

He snaps his head up.

Apart from the occasional photo or video posted online, I haven't seen him much over the past several year. He looks like he's aged ten years in the past two. His hair is all gray, the wrinkles around his eyes and mouth even more prominent. His eyes are bloodshot, as if he's been crying or having trouble sleeping.

Maybe both.

It's odd to see him like this. For him to look so...human.

All my life, he's had a commanding persona. He had to, considering the weight he carries on his shoulders. There's a reason for the saying, "Heavy is the head that wears the crown."

Right now, my father looks absolutely crushed by the weight he's been carrying. Not from leading this country, but due to Anderson's unexpected diagnosis.

"Esme," he exhales as he strides toward me, not even hesitating in wrapping his arms around me.

At one time, his hugs felt forced, more for show than anything else. Not this one. This time, he squeezes me tightly, holding me longer than he has in years.

"How are you?" he asks once he pulls back. But he doesn't let go, his hands still gripping my biceps as if my presence is the only thing offering him even a modicum of comfort.

"Hanging in there," I answer honestly. "You?"

He blows out a laugh. "Hanging in there." He takes a moment to compose himself before releasing me, gesturing to the chair in front of his desk. "Won't you sit down?"

I go to the chair and lower myself into it, crossing my legs at the ankles and angling my knees down. It's been ages since I've been required to sit like this, but old habits are hard to break, especially in this place. I don't even have to think about it, just do it out of custom, something in my brain signaling my body how to act.

I face forward, expecting my father to sit behind the desk. He doesn't, though, assuming the chair next to mine.

"I had Captain Walsh drive you here so I could ask something of you. Something I have no right to ask, but I'm going to do it all the same."

I moisten my lips, smoothing my clammy hands down my dress. "What's that?"

"I'd like for you to consider staying in Belmont a while. Your brother's going through something extremely difficult."

I draw my shoulders back, forcing myself to stay calm, despite how unsettling his request is. "I'm aware."

"He needs all the support he can get right now." He runs a hand over his face, tracing the creases of worry and regret, his eyes hollowed-out pools of sorrow. "I won't sit here and pretend I've been a good father to either of you. I know I haven't."

"You've been better."

I'm not sure if it's what I said to him after I finally stood up for myself and ended things with Jameson, but during my time in Paris, he's reached out to me. Told me how proud he was of everything I've been trying to accomplish, not just in culinary school, but also in founding a community initiative that teaches trafficking victims necessary skills to obtain gainful employment.

While I may not be able to open my own restaurant, not with who I am, I *can* share my love of cooking and the culinary arts in other ways, teaching these women everything I learned in culinary school, giving them the basic skills they need to survive, preventing them from returning to the life they fought to escape from. To my surprise, my father supported this venture since day one.

"I'm still a work in progress."

The corners of his mouth turn up, but his smile doesn't reach his eyes, sadness clinging to his face.

"But you and Gabriel—Anderson," he corrects, using the name I call my brother instead of his given first name. "You've always shared a special bond. He shouldn't be alone. Not right now. Your mother…" His voice quivers, tears welling in his eyes. "She pushed us all away. I figured she just needed time to come to terms with everything. I'm not making excuses for my actions," he adds quickly. "But I was trying to figure out how to run the country, in addition to dealing with all the bullshit the royal household loves to conjure up, usually out of pure boredom."

Covering my mouth, I stifle a laugh.

It's refreshing to hear my father has a similar opinion of the royal household as I do. I doubt he would have said this sort of thing to me ten years ago.

"Now I have the benefit of age and experience on my side, something I didn't possess when your mother isolated herself. I'll be damned if I'm going to stand by and allow your brother to follow the path she did." He grabs my hand and squeezes.

"After your mother passed away, I failed you," he says

quietly but firmly. "Failed your brother. I refuse to fail you now. Being in this position as long as I have has taught me a lot. One of the biggest lessons I've learned is that when adversity strikes, people need someone to look up to. Someone to rely on. Someone who will be there no matter what life throws their way. I'm begging you to be that person for Anderson. He needs you right now, even if he's too stubborn to admit it."

I peer past him at the frames lining the bookshelves of his study. Unlike his office in the administrative wing, this place is filled with personal photos of us before my mother passed. Before our lives changed. When we were still happy.

I fixate on one of Anderson and me. I couldn't have been more than four or five, but even then, you can see how much he loved me, his arms wrapped tightly around me as we stood on the beach, the ocean waves crashing behind us.

"I love him," my voice cracks as I look back at my father. "I'll be here as long as Anderson needs me."

My father slumps in his chair, so much weight released from his body I can almost hear the cushion below him sigh.

"That doesn't mean I'm going to undertake my official duties again." I pull my hand from his, voice determined. "I'm here for my brother. Not the royal household."

The last thing I want is for Anderson to think I have any intention of taking his place.

"Being here for him may require that, Esme," my father states evenly. "Unfortunately, his schedule over the next month is quite hectic, particularly with the referendum. He doesn't need any added stress right now. I want him to focus on starting a course of treatment in the hopes of countering any relapses in the future. Not on wearing himself out."

I squeeze my eyes shut, unable to deny the truth in my

father's words, especially after spending the past several hours with Anderson.

There's no doubt in my mind he needs me. Not only to relieve some of the pressure, but to show him he's not alone. That he has my support. That he'll *always* have my support. Maybe once he sees that, he'll realize there's no need to remove himself from the line of succession.

I slowly return my eyes to my father, promising the one thing I thought I never would. "I'll do whatever you need."

"Thank you, Esme." He squeezes my hand again. "This means a lot."

"*Anderson* means a lot to me," I respond, driving home the point that he's the only person I'm doing this for. No one else. "But under no circumstances is Gianna or anyone else in the royal household to control or manipulate my personal life in any way. Or Tristan's. I may be a royal, but I'm a human being first."

"Gianna?" My dad straightens, giving me a quizzical look.

"Yeah. Gianna. You know. The woman with all the answers. The palace fixer, more or less."

His confusion increases by the second, his brow wrinkling. "Gianna's dead, Esme."

I blink repeatedly, his statement taking me by complete surprise. "What? How? When?"

"I thought you'd have heard. She was the victim of a mugging. Her body was found in an area of town notorious for drugs and prostitution. Stab wound to the stomach."

"When was this?"

He taps at his chin, eyes scrunched in concentration. Obviously, it wasn't all that recent if he has to think this hard.

"If memory serves, it wasn't long after you left for Paris.

Maybe a month? Your brother had already left on deployment. That might be why you never found out. It's not like you stayed up to date with things around here, particularly in the beginning."

"I know. I just…" I trail off, an unsettled feeling forming in my gut, given everything that transpired in the weeks leading up to my departure.

Hayes Barlow accusing Jameson Gates of murder. Learning of Jameson's relationship with Callie Sloane. Adam theorizing that Callie may have gone missing because she was seen as an obstacle to a potential wedding between Jameson and me. Then the attack on the SUV that resulted in Adam's death, and almost mine, too. Throw in Gianna's death, and it all seems suspicious. Not to mention the strange looks I noticed Jameson and Gianna exchange toward the end.

"You don't find that…odd, considering everything else that happened around that time?"

"The Chief of Royal Police handled this case himself. They arrested a homeless man with a history of mental illness. Gianna's purse, wallet, and several of her other belongings were found among his meager possessions. His clothing also had traces of her blood."

"But—"

He holds up his hand, cutting me off. "I understand your concern, but I assure you Gianna's death was just an unfortunate coincidence completely unrelated to…everything else."

"And Hayes Barlow? Has he ever been found?"

I don't know why I bother to ask. I know the answer. I may have avoided paying attention to the news in the first several years after I left, choosing to focus on honing my craft. But there was no escaping the news of Hayes Barlow's death.

Or the *appearance* of death, I should say.

"Hayes Barlow is dead. A boat registered to him washed up on the shores of Norway. Based on the copious amount of blood found, along with the evidence of bullet holes, it's presumed he was attacked by traffickers who frequent those waters."

"And Callie Sloane?" I press, becoming more irritable with every second.

"Her whereabouts are still unknown."

I open my mouth to argue how suspicious all of this is. He cuts me off before I can.

"Unlike with Hayes Barlow, there's not a single shred of evidence that foul play was involved with her disappearance. She could have wanted a fresh start. Go somewhere different. Where no one knows who she is. I'm sure you can understand." He gives me a knowing look.

"Of course I can. That still—"

"I had the same concerns you did when I first learned of Gianna's death, then heard about Barlow's boat washing up on shore riddled with bullet holes. I assure you. It's all just a coincidence. Unfortunate, but a coincidence all the same."

He stands from his chair, and I reluctantly do the same. He grips my arms, running his hands up and down them in a reassuring manner.

"Please don't worry yourself about this. It's in the past. Justice has been served. If Hayes Barlow turns out to *not* be dead and shows his face in public again, he'll get the justice he deserves for what he did to Adam. What he *almost* did to you."

"Unless someone took matters into their own hands and silenced him before he could defend himself."

He pushes out a long breath. "I've always appreciated the sympathy you have for all people, despite the crimes they've committed."

"Alleged crimes."

"Alleged crimes," he corrects, but I can hear his skepticism in every syllable. "Regardless, Hayes Barlow is none of your concern. Like I said, it's all in the past. Right now, I want you to focus on your brother. On being here for him. Okay?"

"Okay," I say, unable to ignore my mounting unease.

From the beginning, something about Hayes' alleged involvement in the accident that took Adam's life never sat right with me. He didn't seem like a violent person. More like a man desperate to find his employee. A man frustrated that nothing was being done to bring her home.

I understand what the evidence says. A man with impeccable driving skills was able to outmaneuver a trained protection officer and former special teams member. Clothing with traces of smoke and accelerant was found in Hayes Barlow's trash bins. A car registered to him was seen on surveillance video following Adam and me. And empty cans of white gas were found in Hayes' trunk.

But what was his motive? Because he lost his sponsorships? That didn't seem to matter to him. All he seemed to care about was finding Callie Sloane. Nothing else.

I didn't raise my doubts in the aftermath of everything, too numb from shattering Creed's heart and nearly dying to think clearly.

But now I can't ignore the nagging voice in my head.

I don't think Hayes Barlow is responsible for Adam's death.

But who was?

And why?

CHAPTER SEVEN

Esme

Exhaustion consumes me as I make my way up the front steps and into my apartment at Gladwell Palace, the historic complex that's comprised of apartments belonging to various members of the royal family, myself included. All I want to do is put on my pajamas, crawl into bed, and sleep for the next week.

And this is only my first day back.

I'm not sure if I'm built for this life anymore. But I can't abandon Anderson. I've never seen him in such a dark place. Never heard such despair in his voice. Once he sees his doctors tomorrow and settles back into his routine, hopefully he'll realize his diagnosis isn't as dire as he believes. He's one of the strongest, most stubborn people I know. I have no doubt he's strong enough to get through this, too.

I *need* him to get through this.

"There you are."

When I hear Tristan's voice, I glance toward the couch in the formal living room.

But there's nothing formal about his attire or the way he's spread a bunch of papers over the surface of a coffee table that's easily several centuries old.

And I love everything about it. Love the loose-fit jeans he wears. Love the untucked button-down shirt that's slightly wrinkled. Love his rumpled dark hair. Everything about him is so…relaxed. After today, it's exactly what I need. A reminder that all this strict tradition and protocol isn't my life anymore. *Tristan* is.

"How are you, darling?" He stands and pulls my body against his, tipping my head back and treating me to a tender kiss that melts me from the inside out.

"Mentally and physically drained," I admit.

Because I *can* admit these things around him. He loves me. Loves the good, bad, and ugly parts of me.

Except he doesn't know *all* the parts of me. Not like he should.

"I'm sorry I didn't stay. It looked like—"

"Don't apologize. Not to sound rude, but I'm glad you left. It gave me a chance to spend time with Anderson. Then meet with my father."

He straightens, concerned eyes raking over me. "And how did that go?"

"It—"

"Actually, hold that thought." He touches his lips to my forehead. "Go put on some pajamas. When you're comfortable, come to the kitchen and I'll feed you. I made you dinner."

"You cooked?"

He nods. "Chicken soup with salad and fresh bread, in

case that earns me any points." His expression grows serene. "Like we had on our first date."

"Not so sure I'd call you picking me up for what was supposed to be an incredible dinner at a Michelin-starred restaurant, only for you to learn I had the flu, a first date."

"That may be true..." He pushes a wayward strand of hair behind my ear. "But it *was* our first meal together, despite the fact your nose was red and your eyes were puffy."

"And I'm pretty sure a bird's nest had grown in my hair from how ratty it was. Not to mention it had easily been three days since I'd showered."

"I still thought you were beautiful. And there was no way I was going to waste an opportunity to take care of you. So I ran out and got all the fixings for some chicken soup, which you said was one of your favorite comfort foods." He runs his hands down my arms before hooking them at the small of my back. "Since I can only imagine how trying today's been for you, not only with the news of your brother but also being back here, I figured some comfort food was in order."

I close my eyes, heart swelling from how thoughtful Tristan is. He didn't have to go through the trouble of planning dinner tonight. Could have gone along with whatever my chef had already prepared. Instead, he went out of his way to treat me to something that would bring me comfort.

"You're too good to me," I murmur against his lips.

"No. I'm just right for you," he replies, as he always does whenever I say something similar. Then he kisses me sweetly before releasing me. "Go get changed. I'll have dinner waiting for you."

Smiling, I turn from him and make my way down the hallway. When I walk into my private suite, I pause in surprise. It doesn't look like I remember. The décor and furniture are the same, but Tristan's presence is overwhelming. His laptop sits on the coffee table, his messenger bag open on the sofa. A notepad rests beside it, his barely legible scrawl etched on the page. His shoes are thrown to the side, his suit jacket hanging over the back of the reading chair. It looks…lived in.

I head toward my dressing room, not surprised to find my things have been unpacked for me, and quickly strip out of my dress and heels, exchanging them for a pair of pajama pants and a loose t-shirt. Exhaling as I unhook my bra, I toss it to the side, then pile my hair on top of my head. To complete the transformation, I walk into the bathroom and scrub the makeup off my face.

When I enter the kitchen minutes later, Tristan doesn't seem to care about my changed appearance. He still looks at me as if I'm the most beautiful woman he's ever seen. He always has.

Swiping a wine glass off the massive marble island, he hands it to me, grabbing another one and raising it.

"Cheers, darling."

"Cheers." I clink my glass with his and bring it to my lips, savoring in the bold red wine, rich and warm with a hint of spice and earth.

"Come sit." He pulls out one of the barstools for me, a napkin and silverware already in front of me.

"You've made yourself quite at home," I remark as he helps me onto the hightop chair.

"It's a talent. Traveling as much as I do, you learn to make yourself at home wherever you are."

With a wink, he heads to the six-burner stainless steel range and spoons out two bowls of soup. After dishing out the salad and slicing the bread, he returns to the island, placing the food onto the surface.

The instant I smell the comforting aroma of garlic and chicken, my stomach growls.

"Hungry?" he jokes as he assumes the chair beside me.

"Famished."

"Then eat."

I dig into the soup, moaning at the flavor. "Delicious."

"I'm glad you think so." Tristan remarks around a mouthful of food. "Although it's not nearly as good as your cooking. *Nothing* is as good as your cooking."

"You're just saying that because you have to."

"I don't have to do anything. I say it because it's true. You're extremely talented."

I lean toward him, touching my mouth to his. "Thank you."

"You're welcome." He briefly deepens the kiss before straightening, dipping a chunk of bread into the broth and taking a bite. "So how did things go with your father?"

"Oh, right." I dab at my mouth, having momentarily forgotten the conversation we started earlier. "He wanted to talk to me about Anderson. His prognosis and whatnot."

"How was your brother once I left? Get any better?"

I smile sadly. "Worse. He's in the depression stage of grief and I'm not sure he'll ever get to acceptance. My father's concerned, and rightfully so. Not just about the physical implications of his diagnosis, but also the mental."

Tristan nods, expression awash with sympathy. "That's understandable."

"Because of that, he requested I be there for Anderson as much as possible."

"Pretty sure you've always been there for your brother."

"Not just emotionally." I bring my eyes to his. "Physically, too. He... He asked me to stay. And to temporarily resume my duties as a royal in order to take some of the pressure off

Anderson so he can focus on his wellbeing — physical *and* mental."

"I see." A contemplative expression crosses his brow. "What do you want?"

On a long sigh, I look forward as I wrack my brain for an answer.

Tristan was one of the first people in my life to always ask me what I wanted. Back then, it was a breath of fresh air to have a say in my future. To make my own decisions.

Now it's a reminder of everything I'll have to give up.

"I want my brother to not have MS. Want him to be happy. Want him to go to sleep every night without the crippling fear that he'll never be able to live a full life."

I pause, sucking in a deep breath to settle my emotions. Something about being back in this place has me wanting to keep them locked up tight yet again.

"But right now, it doesn't matter what I want. All that does is what my brother needs."

"And he needs you," Tristan states very matter-of-factly.

I give him a sad smile. "He does. He needs time to adjust to what will become his new normal. He shouldn't have to do that while attending to his official duties as Crown Prince. This will obviously interfere with my plan to come to California with you for your next film shoot."

"I don't care about that." He waves me off. "While it'll suck to be thousands of miles away, I don't want you to feel like you're letting me down by putting your family first. This is your life. Your decision. You have to do what's best for you." He narrows his gaze, his voice dropping. "Will undertaking your official duties again be what's best for you?"

I've never gone into detail about what led me to essentially cut off all communication with my father and everything to do with the monarchy. The establishment had released a statement that I was taking some time out of the spotlight after my "breakup" with Jameson Gates and nearly dying in the attack on the SUV that took Adam's life. I more or less let Tristan believe that to be the case. It wasn't *that* far from the truth. I *did* need some time out of the spotlight.

It's not the entire reason, though.

I didn't think it mattered. Didn't think I'd return to this place. Or maybe I didn't think Tristan and I would ever be as serious as we are.

"Will *you* be okay being back here?" He places his hand on my leg, giving it a gentle squeeze. "Falling back into your old life? Potentially being surrounded by memories of…everything?"

"I don't know," I answer with a shake of my head. "I need to be here for my brother. Need to do everything I can to make his life easier. And I do believe taking the pressure off him by resuming my duties will help immensely to that end."

"Then you're staying." It's not a question. More a statement.

"I think I have to."

He nods, shifting his gaze forward as he processes this.

"I know it's probably not what you want to hear. Or what you signed up for. But—"

"Hey." He cups my cheek, cutting me off. "I offered to come and support you. The same goes for this, too. Plus, you said it yourself. It's just temporary while your brother adjusts. Before you know it, we'll be back in Paris, spending our days off in bed." He flashes me a devilish smile. "Clothing optional."

"I like the way you think," I murmur as I inch my lips toward his.

"And I like the way you taste, princess."

I suck in a sharp breath, breaking into a coughing fit, his term of endearment a shock to my system. Normally, he calls me darling or beautiful. Not princess.

Never princess.

There's only one man who's ever called me that.

There's only one man who I *want* to call me that.

"You okay?"

I lift my glass to my mouth. "Yeah. I've just always hated that nickname."

He studies me as I guzzle my wine.

If he finds my answer suspicious, he doesn't say anything. Instead, he offers a quick apology before changing the subject to the latest script his agent sent him for a project he's not too sure about yet.

But I don't hear a word he says.

All I can think about is Creed Lawson and the way my body buzzed to live whenever he called me his princess.

CHAPTER EIGHT

Esme

"So how is he with…everything?" Harriet asks as we sit at my favorite sidewalk café in the heart of Montrose, the capital city of Belmont.

It feels like it was just yesterday I sat in this same café and told my best friends about my grandmother's plan for me to marry Jameson Gates, after which they encouraged me to ask Creed to take my virginity. I never would have imagined that seemingly innocent conversation would change the trajectory of my life.

Sometimes I wonder what would have happened if I hadn't met with Harriet and Marius that day. Would I have eventually found my way into Creed's arms? Or would I have gone along with the royal household's plan? Would I be married to Jameson Gates right now and already have two children, as is required?

It's strange to think that an inconsequential afternoon with my friends would have such a drastic impact on my life.

Despite how difficult it's been to see Creed again, I can't say I regret our past. Not when our time together helped me become the person I am now.

I pull my attention away from the trees lining the canals, the leaves painted a mixture of red, orange, and yellow now that autumn has arrived. As much as I love summer, this is my favorite time of year. The beautiful colors. The brisk temperatures. The smell of burning leaves that clings to the air.

"He's doing as good as can be expected, all things considered." I lift my teacup to my lips and take a sip.

While Anderson's keeping his diagnosis quiet for now, he gave me permission to tell Harriet and Marius. He knew they'd become suspicious if I suddenly returned to Belmont for more than a quick visit after avoiding this place for the past nine years, not to mention resume my duties as a senior royal.

"We've spent the week meeting with his neurologist and physical therapist, as well as hired a nutritionist for him. Thankfully, there are a lot more treatment options than when my mum was diagnosed all those years ago. I'm not saying he doesn't have to take his condition seriously. He does. But there are more resources available to him."

Harriet and Marius nod, a solemn atmosphere settling over the table.

While I hate to be the bearer of bad news, especially when it's been a while since I've seen them, they don't mind. That's the type of friends they are. We can go weeks or months without talking and pick up right where we left off. Although, I doubt we've ever gone a day without at least sending an inappropriate meme in our group message.

"And you?" Marius asks after a beat. "What's your plan going forward?"

I sigh, watching as a group of tourists pose for a selfie on a stone bridge spanning the short width of one of the many canals that snake through the city, cyclists zooming by on the dedicated bike paths our country is known for.

"My father asked me to temporarily resume my official duties as a royal to help take the pressure off Anderson while he adjusts to this new normal."

"What did you tell him?" Harriet asks.

"As much as I hate the thought, it's the least I can do, considering everything Anderson's done for me since I left."

I'd hoped as he went to his various doctor's appointments, he'd be in a better head space, see this isn't the death sentence he thought it was. While he hasn't seemed as morose as he was that first day, he's still not the same Anderson. Has still brought up removing himself from the line of succession.

Which is exactly why I have no choice but to stay. Not to take his place, but to show him he has my support. That he can still be an amazing leader, despite his diagnosis. That I'll support him every step of the way, even if that support eventually comes from Paris instead of here.

"You're a good sister." Marius squeezes my hand, his blue eyes awash with sincerity and appreciation.

"He'd do the same for me," I say without a moment's hesitation. "Hell, he *did* the same for me, more or less."

"How does Tristan feel about all of this?" Harriet asks after a long pause, smoothing a hand down her straight, dark hair.

"Supportive to a fault." I pull back. "He's agreed to stay with me as long as he can, but he does need to leave soon to start shooting his next film. It's not the first time we've been away from each other for a long period of time. We've gotten through it before. We'll get through this, too. Hopefully, in a few months, Anderson will be in a better place and I can return to Paris."

"And Creed?" Harriet asks, almost hesitantly.

"What about him?" I sip on my tea, acting as nonchalant as possible, praying they don't notice the way my cheeks heat from the mention of his name.

"I assume you've seen him since you've been here."

I nod, keeping my shoulders square. "I have."

"How did that go?" Marius arches a brow.

"Fine." I wave them off, not looking directly at either of them. "It's been nine years. It's all water under the bridge."

I'm not sure if I'm saying that for their benefit or mine. It *should* be water under the bridge. Especially after this long.

But if it's water under the bridge, why does my heart skip a beat every time my eyes lock with his? Why does my body hum with electricity every time I hear his deep voice?

Why did I picture Creed's eyes when Tristan made love to me last night? And every night since I've been back here?

"Exactly." Marius glances at Harriet. "I told you it wouldn't be a big deal. She's moved on and is with someone else. They both are."

His words steal my breath, his statement a punch to the gut. "What do you mean?"

"You and Tristan. Creed and Rory," he replies, looking at me like I'm crazy.

I blink repeatedly, the air whooshing from my lungs as a boulder lodges in my throat.

"Marius," Harriet mutters under her breath.

"What?" He furrows his brows at her. "You can't tell me she didn't know. Granted, I never mentioned it because we've had a firm 'No Creed talk' rule, but..." He trails off when he floats his gaze toward me. His eyes instantly widen as realization sinks in. "You really didn't know? I figured your brother would have mentioned something since Creed's been his CPO for, like, over five years."

I blink back the tears threatening to fall, my eyes burning.

Why does this news hurt so much? I'm with Tristan. I *love* Tristan. But I can't fool myself into thinking what I have with Tristan is even remotely close to what I shared with Creed.

"How long have they been together?" I ask, doing my best to keep my voice as even as possible.

Harriet and Marius share a look before facing me.

"I'm not sure of the exact details," Harriet begins. "And saying they're together might not be *entirely* accurate."

"How so?"

She leans across the table, throwing out all her etiquette training. "You know how Creed moved in with Rory after Adam died, right?"

Again, this is news to me. "I do now."

Harriet straightens, sharing another look with Marius.

"Will you two stop looking at each other and tell me what you know?" I exclaim, getting more and more irritated with every passing second.

"Why do you care?" Marius presses. "You're happy, aren't you? We've seen how you are with Tristan. He loves you. And you're obviously quite enamored with him. Why rehash the past?"

"I just…" I blow out a breath. "I just want to know. That's all."

Marius sighs, then glances at Harriet, the two of them having an unspoken conversation. After several seconds of brow raises and head tilts, Harriet finally faces me.

"Well, after Adam's death, Creed moved in with Rory to help with AJ." She pauses. "You *do* know who AJ is, right?"

"Of course." I roll my eyes. "Adam Junior."

"Okay. Good. Apparently, he was only supposed to live

there for that first year. Then a year turned into two. Then three."

"And they're still living together?"

Harriet nods.

"In the same house Rory once shared with Adam?"

"If you ask me, it's just a bad situation for all involved," Marius states. "She's probably only sleeping with him because he reminds her so much of Adam, at least in looks. And he's probably only sleeping with her because of some misplaced obligation he feels toward his brother after his death. Rumor is, they got into a pretty big fight the last time they spoke."

"It was about me," I say, not even having to question it. I know it was. Adam implied as much when he told me his brother punched some sense into him the night he died. He even had the bruise on his jaw to prove it.

"It was?" Harriet scrunches her brows. "Why?"

I chew on my bottom lip. I never told them everything that went down those last few weeks between Creed, Adam, and me. While they knew I'd ended things with Creed, I claimed it was getting too risky, as they saw for themselves. While that was certainly true, it wasn't the sole reason. They didn't know Adam essentially begged me to do so.

After his death, I considered telling them the truth but decided against it. Not like it would have changed things. Nor will it change things now, but it might help them understand better.

"Because Creed realized that Adam forced me to break things off."

"He did?" Harriet exclaims, eyes wide, jaw dropped.

"And you never told us?" Marius adds, his expression mirroring Harriet's.

"It was painful enough to essentially rip Creed's heart out

of his chest and stomp on it, destroying any hope he had of a future with me. I didn't want to relive that by telling you what I'd done. Hell, I called him the hired help."

"But he eventually figured it out," Harriet states.

"He did. Or so Adam implied the night of the King's Day gala. Claimed Creed even punched him. Then…" I pause, drawing in a deep breath before confessing my next secret. If the memory of calling Creed the hired help is still painful to admit, this next one is even more so. "Then Adam gave me a choice. He'd take me to the palace where Jameson Gates would propose. Or to Creed's so we could set things right."

I study my friends' reactions, expecting to see their shock increase. Instead, all I see is sympathy.

"You chose Creed," Marius exhales. "You weren't on your way to your mother's grave, like the royal household claimed. You were on your way to Creed's."

I slowly nod.

"He doesn't know, does he?" Harriet remarks after a short silence.

"No," I say through the lump in my throat. "I never told him. It sounds stupid now, but after narrowly escaping with my life and Adam's death, I just went along with the royal household's version of events. By the time I finally stood up for myself, it didn't matter anymore. I just wanted to leave it all behind me. Just wanted to move on."

"Don't you think he deserves to know?" Harriet presses.

"Why? So he'll add even more blame onto his shoulders? If he knew the reason we were on that road was because Adam was taking me to see him—"

"If he knew the truth, then maybe you two could—"

"We could what, Harri?" I exclaim, my voice incredulous. "Be together?"

I place my hands on the table as I draw in a steadying breath. When I address my friends again, my voice is low, preventing anyone from overhearing me.

"We can't be together. He destroyed any possibility of that the second he swore that oath and became a member of the royal guard."

Marius narrows his gaze on me. "I think we all know that if Creed knew the truth, he most likely would never have sworn that oath. He would have chosen you."

"But he didn't. And I don't blame him for it. It doesn't matter now anyway. It was nearly a decade ago now. He's moved on."

I bring my teacup back to my lips, keeping my eyes forward in an attempt to avoid their analytical stares that are always able to weed out the truth from the lies.

"As have I. So let's leave the past where it belongs." I pin them with a determined glare. "In the past."

CHAPTER NINE

Esme

I draw in several deep breaths as I watch the familiar streets of Belmont's capital city pass by. The knots in my stomach are so tight and heavy that no amount of counting or breathing exercises can calm the anxiety filling me.

I remind myself this is just a regular night at the opera, something Tristan and I enjoyed quite often while in Paris.

But we're not in Paris anymore.

And the second I step out of this SUV and walk the carpeted stairs up to the Royal Opera House on opening night, I'll confirm all the speculation in the gossip columns and on social media that I'm back and will be undertaking my official duties as a senior member of the royal family once more.

I can't help but be reminded of that summer all those years ago. How I sat in the back seat of an SUV just like this one, Jameson Gates beside me, queasy over the prospect of stepping out of the car on his arm and announcing to the world we were a couple.

Little did I know that night would change my life. Not because of anything to do with Jameson Gates, though.

Because that was the night Creed showed up at my apartment and agreed to take my virginity.

The night he made me feel things I didn't think possible.

The night I gave him a piece of my heart, even if I didn't realize it at the time.

"It's not too late to back out."

When I hear Tristan's deep voice, I snap my gaze toward his, pretending I hadn't just been thinking about another man.

He curls his fingers around my hand from across the seat and squeezes. "Say the word and I'll have Archie whisk us back to your apartment." A wicked smile lights up his face, and I shiver as he leans closer, his breath tickling my neck. "Where I'll spend the night making you sing like an opera star."

If Archie's embarrassed by Tristan's insinuation, he doesn't show it. After all, he's been with me for over a decade now, first as a member of my protection team, then as my chief protection officer when he was promoted upon Adam's death.

While he hasn't been in Paris constantly, rotating the team so no one was away from home for more than a few weeks at a time, he's grown used to Tristan's somewhat perverse sense of humor. They all have. I'd like to think they appreciate it as a break from the stiff formality they find in this place whenever they return.

"As tempting as that sounds…" I push out a breath, my expression falling, "I have to do this."

He nods in understanding, brushing a soft kiss against my hand. His lips linger, his breath warming my skin. "You're a good sister."

"Anderson's always been there for me, no matter what. Supported my decision to walk away from my duties, despite the added burden it would impose on him." I swallow hard. "It's time I repay the favor."

"I get it." His compassionate smile soon turns mischievous. "Even so, I fully intend on making you sing later on." He dips his head into the crook of my neck. "And scream."

A wave of pleasure spreads through me, my skin awakening with desire. It sends a craving deep within me to crawl on top of him, to feel his hands exploring every inch of my body. But before that can become a possibility, the SUV comes to a stop.

Normally, Archie's quick to jump out and open my door. Tonight, he pauses, glancing my way.

"Are you ready, ma'am?"

I hear the underlying meaning in his question. He's not just asking if I'm ready for tonight, but for everything that will follow. The public engagements. My life being put back under a microscope. The royal household.

But like I've reminded myself repeatedly over the past week. Anderson needs me. As much as being thrust back into this life makes my stomach churn, I have to do it for him.

I'm not the same woman I once was. I've matured. Grown stronger. Found my voice. Learned how to stand up for myself and what I want. I won't allow the royal household to use me as a pawn. Not anymore.

Squaring my shoulders, I give him a determined nod. "Thank you, Archie. I am."

"Of course, ma'am." He jumps out and walks around

the SUV. It only takes him a matter of seconds, but with the nerves swimming in my stomach, it feels like each step lasts a year.

Finally, my door swings opens and Archie extends a hand toward me. I take it, using his support to stand, the lights of the cameras making it difficult to see. I remind myself this is no different from the award shows or movie premiers I've attended with Tristan.

But it *is* different. They're not here for him, although they certainly don't mind the ability to capture shots of him, too. They're here for me.

"Just picture them all naked," Tristan murmurs as he places a hand on the small of my back. "That's what I do."

I meet his gaze, the flashes becoming more incessant as he guides me up the stairs, careful to leave enough room so he doesn't step on the hem of my green silk gown.

"You do not," I shoot back, purposefully ignoring the reporters' questions about whether I'm here to resume my duties as Princess Royal.

"I picture *you* naked." He bites his lower lip, the look he's giving me causing my skin to heat.

His sinful stare, combined with how delicious he looks in his tuxedo, has me teetering on the brink of dragging him to the nearest dark corner to have my way with him, if only for a minute to help me forget everything.

Which is exactly what Tristan's helped me do from the beginning.

He's helped me forget.

And right now, I'd love nothing more than to forget.

"In fact, I'm doing it right now."

"You're horrible."

"That may be so." He pulls me to a stop. "But it worked."

I furrow my brow. "What did?"

"My devious plan to distract you. See." He gestures to our surroundings.

When he does, I realize I'm no longer walking through the throngs of reporters but standing in the lobby of the historic opera house. While it's obvious some of the other patrons are intrigued by seeing me here, they're nowhere near as demanding as the vultures outside.

Without a single care for the rules regarding public displays of affection, I drape my arms over his shoulders and hoist myself onto my toes.

"Thank you." I touch my lips to his.

"Anything for you, beautiful." He draws me close and deepens the kiss, but still keeps it respectful. When he pulls away and flashes a smile, I feel surprisingly at ease.

"This way, ma'am."

I turn my attention to Archie and follow him through the lobby, people bowing and curtsying as I pass. Archie leads us up the grand staircase, more members of my protection team flanking us. It's been a while since I've had this much security. It wasn't necessary when I was in Paris. While I was required to have twenty-four-hour security, even if I just wanted to go for a run or out for a cup of coffee, it wasn't like this.

Yet another thing I'll have to get used to.

We continue past the mezzanine area and toward a guarded door on the far side of the second floor lobby.

A man in a tuxedo, who I recognize as being on my father's protection team, greets us with a bow.

"Your Highness. Master Hughes."

I return his smile as he opens the door, granting us entry to the private corridor before closing it behind us, standing watch once more.

Now that we're away from the crowds, it's silent, barely a sound to be heard, apart from the swooshing of my gown, the lush red carpet cushioning my feet. When we reach a pair of double doors, two more guards standing outside bow toward me, then open the doors for us.

As soon as we enter the foyer of the royal box, my nerves flare up, dozens of eyes turning in our direction.

Including my grandmother's piercing stare.

I've purposefully avoided her the past nine years. Maybe it was childish, but I refused to talk to her until she apologized for the role she played in trying to marry me off, then blaming me for Adam's death. My father may not be perfect, but at least he's tried to make amends.

My grandmother never has.

Never saw anything wrong in her actions.

Sensing my unease, Tristan takes control, bowing toward my father as he approaches, despite the fact I've never reviewed royal protocol with him. He just seems to know.

Then again, he *did* grow up in the White House. His childhood was filled with meeting foreign dignitaries. I have no doubt he's more than aware of protocol.

Or perhaps he asked one of my staff members to review it with him. It certainly wouldn't surprise me. That's just the type of person he is.

"Your Majesty."

A soft smile tugs on my father's lips as he extends his hand toward Tristan. "Mr. Hughes. I'd say it's nice to meet you, but we already have, although you probably don't remember since you were a small lad."

"Of course, sir. It's an honor to be here and see you again."

I study Tristan, brows scrunched slightly, this man

bearing little resemblance to the person he was minutes ago when he told me he couldn't wait to make me scream.

I shouldn't be upset over it. After all, I act differently in public than I do in private. I didn't think Tristan was like me, though. Thought he was different.

"Esme," my father says, snapping me out of my thoughts.

"Your Majesty." I curtsy.

"Allow me to introduce you to Esme's grandmother," my father directs at Tristan. "Queen Veronica. The Queen Mother." He steps aside, allowing my grandmother to join us.

"Your Majesty." Tristan bows, not even needing me to tell him how to address her.

Most people aren't sure, since she's technically a dowager queen and the requirement to bow and address her as such died along with my grandfather. Regardless, we continue to give her the respect she deserves after years of service to the monarchy. Although lately I've questioned whether she does, in fact, deserve it.

"Mr. Hughes." My grandmother extends her hand, allowing Tristan to shake it gently. Then she turns her cold eyes on me, expectation within.

I drop into a small curtsy. "Your Majesty."

"Esme."

She rakes her gaze over me, as if making a mental note of everything about my appearance that displeases her. I'm sure the list is quite long, considering the dress I chose is somewhat revealing, the front dipping low, displaying my ample cleavage.

"So glad you could spare the time to be here tonight."

I grit a smile, pushing down all the aggravation bubbling

to the surface. There's so much I'd love to say in response, but before I have the opportunity, Anderson steps in and wraps me in his arms.

"Hey, Ezzy."

I close my eyes and bask in his embrace, reminding myself why I'm here. Who I'm doing this for. I can't allow my brother to go through this alone.

When Anderson releases me, he looks to Tristan, extending his hand.

"Your Highness." He bows, to which Anderson rolls his eyes.

"Good to see you, mate."

Tristan takes Anderson's hand, and he pulls him in for a quick hug.

"Sorry about the other day," my brother whispers. "I, uh… I wasn't in the best headspace."

"No apologies necessary. How are you now?"

"Up and down," he answers honestly.

"Well, we're here for you."

"Thanks." Anderson turns his eyes toward me. "For everything. I know this isn't what you planned."

"Nothing in life ever is." I grab his hand and squeeze. "But like with everything else life has thrown our way, we've gotten through it. Together. And we'll get through this together, too."

He gives me an appreciative smile as another impeccably dressed man in a tuxedo approaches, probably one of the members of my father's privy council, since he often extends invites to them.

But when I turn toward him, I inhale a sharp breath, my heart plummeting to the pit of my stomach as I stare at a living reminder of exactly what I fought to escape.

"Your Highness." He bows, but his eyes never leave mine, expectation swirling within.

Sensing everyone's attention on us, I snap out of my shock and offer him my hand. "Mr. Gates."

He gives me a sly smile. "I told you. Call me Jameson."

CHAPTER TEN

Esme

"How have you been?" Jameson leans toward me, his familiar leather and citrus scent kicking up around me, transporting me back in time.

As if I haven't been reliving the past enough this week.

I expected that, though. Expected to see my grandmother. My father. Even Creed.

But I never anticipated seeing Jameson Gates again. At least not as a guest of the royal family at the opera.

Did Anderson know he'd be here? Why didn't he tell me?

I glance at my brother, a flicker of an apology in his eyes. Even if he did know Jameson would be here, I get the feeling he'd forgotten. I can't blame him. He has enough on his plate right now. The last thing he needs to concern himself with is who's been invited to attend the opera in the royal box on opening night.

"I heard about your work with trafficking survivors," Jameson continues when I remain mute, still processing this turn of events. "As you may recall, I do quite a bit of work fighting human trafficking myself, so I know how difficult it is for many victims to move on. Teaching them marketable skills and giving them the confidence to make their way in the world, well, it's a remarkable undertaking."

"It's been quite a rewarding experience," I respond evenly as Tristan splays his hand on my back, his touch borderline possessive in nature.

Normally, I hate this kind of gesture. Hell, I hated when Jameson did this precise thing during our fake relationship, especially in front of Creed.

But right now, I welcome it.

I float my gaze toward Tristan, giving him a smile before looking back at Jameson, shoulders squared, head held high.

"Jameson Gates, may I introduce Tristan Hughes. Tristan, this is Jameson Gates. His father is the head of Gates Enter—"

"I know who he is," Tristan interjects gruffly with a hint of animosity.

It strikes me as odd. Granted, Tristan's aware of my history with Jameson. At least he's aware of the lie we told the world.

Still, I can't shake the feeling there's more to Tristan's icy tone.

"And I also know his father is no longer running the company," Tristan adds.

"That's correct." Jameson beams. "Considering he's over seventy, he decided to step back and enjoy retirement. Or as much of a retirement as a lifelong workaholic will allow." He winks, acting as charming as ever.

Which only causes Tristan's muscles to tighten even more, his hand caressing my back, reminding me he's here.

"I have to admit, I'm quite surprised to see you here," I state.

The edges of Jameson's mouth curve up into a sly smirk. "I could say the same for you. I heard you might be taking on some of your royal responsibilities again. Is it true?"

"I didn't take you for someone to follow the gossip rags." I smile, remaining as evasive as possible. "If I recall correctly, you once avoided them like a cat tries to flee from a bath."

"Don't worry. I still do." He winks.

"Then—"

"Your father mentioned something during our last meeting."

Confusion creases my brow, lips parting as I slowly shake my head. "My father? I don't—"

"I'm on his privy council. He found the expertise I amassed during the years I've spent in the Middle East and Africa invaluable, especially these days." He gives me a quizzical look. "I'd thought you'd have heard."

I blink repeatedly, caught off guard by his revelation. That would explain why he's here. But this news still does nothing to diminish my shock over the knowledge that Jameson Gates, the man the royal household once hoped I'd marry, has somehow become one of my father's most trusted advisors. One of the people yielding a great deal of power and influence in the monarchy.

One of the people yielding a great deal of power and influence over me now.

My father may be the king, but he often looks to his privy council for advice and guidance on everything from issues facing the inner workings of the monarchy to the country as a whole.

The idea of Jameson Gates being one of those people doesn't sit well with me.

I have no basis for why I feel this way. During our brief fake courtship, he always treated me with respect. Offered me comfort during those trying weeks after Adam's death. Was glued to my side as I recovered from my own injuries. Not because the royal household ordered him to be there in the hopes of getting photos of my doting boyfriend taking care of me.

He was there because it was the right thing to do. Because he cared about me.

But I still can't shake the strange feeling I get when I recall his behavior during that last meeting, even after all these years. How he kept glancing at Gianna, as if looking for direction or approval. Now she's dead.

Is it all just a coincidence, as my father insisted was the case?

Or is there something more?

The lights begin to dim, snapping me back to the present.

"Looks like the performance is about to start," Jameson says brightly. "It's good to see you again. I'm sure we'll be seeing much more of each other in the weeks to come." He flashes a smile, then looks toward Tristan. "Mr. Hughes."

Tristan simply nods, displaying no warmth.

If it bothers Jameson, he doesn't show it. Much like was the case all those years ago whenever Creed gave Jameson the cold shoulder.

"Ma'am." Jameson bows slightly toward me once more, then turns, making his way from the foyer and into the royal box, sitting in the row directly behind my grandmother and father, beside none other than Silas Archer.

The hairs on my nape stand on end when I notice Silas' gaze directed on me with a peculiar intensity. I try to brush it off, reassure myself it's being back in this life that's stirring up old emotions inside me. Still, something about all of this seems off.

"This way, Your Highness," one of the ushers assigned to the royal box says.

I force a smile, Tristan's hand never leaving my back as the usher shows us to our seats. Just my luck, we're in the front, across the short aisle from my grandmother and father. I have no doubt it was intentional. A way to guarantee everyone sees me.

Normally, this is where my brother sits. Where he *should* be sitting right now.

I glance behind me, meeting Anderson's gaze.

"It's fine, Ezzy," he answers my question before I can ask it. Then he leans closer. "It'll be easier for me to nod off and no one notice."

I laugh, about to turn back around, when a movement catches my eye. A tall, muscular man slips inside the box, his tuxedo clinging to his body, emphasizing his physique in all the right places. If it fit him any more perfectly, it would be illegal.

Sure, Tristan fills out his tux quite nicely. But it's nothing compared to the way Creed Lawson looks right now.

His dark hair is slightly more overgrown than it was all those years ago, but he still keeps it neatly groomed. A dark stubble grazes his jawline, bringing forward memories of the pleasure I experienced as he explored every inch of my body with his lips. But what sets my heart racing is the way his eyes pierce my soul.

I know for a fact he's not supposed to look at me. His role is to keep his attention trained everywhere else, spot potential threats before they can cause harm. But that doesn't stop him from staring at me with a hint of something. Hunger, perhaps?

Or maybe I just wish he'd peer at me the way he once did.

"You okay?"

I quickly tear my eyes from Creed and turn around, meeting Tristan's concerned gaze.

"Of course." I flash him a nervous smile.

"You can talk to me." He takes my hand in his, running his thumb over my knuckles, reminding me how under-standing he is. How compassionate he is. "I can only imagine how difficult it is to be around him again. All the memories it must bring back."

My lips part, but no response comes.

Did he pick up on something the other day when I briefly introduced him to Creed? I didn't think we were that obvi-ous, especially Creed. He was…aloof. Unnervingly so. Still, if anyone's able to notice even the slightest change in my mood, it's Tristan. Five years together will do that.

"You don't have to hide your feelings around me," Tristan assures me with more sympathy than I probably deserve. "I can handle it. I understand how…trying it may be to run into an ex again."

"He's not an ex. He—"

"Not an ex? Most people might be able to make that argument, but your relationship with Jameson Gates was front-page news for several months."

I briefly close my eyes, shoulders falling out of relief that he wasn't talking about Creed. Of course he wasn't. But my mind instantly went to him.

It always does, even all these years later.

"I guess it felt more like we were putting on a spectacle than anything else, especially with all the cameras and reporters following our every move." I look forward just as the curtain rises, revealing the elaborate set of *Aida*.

"Just promise that won't become us."

"What do you mean?"

He stares at our joined hands for a beat before lifting his eyes.

"Promise you won't let this world tear us apart like it did you and Jameson. You two were together for nearly a year before you finally went public with your relationship. Once you did, it ended mere weeks later." He moves his free hand to my cheek, urging my mouth toward his. "I don't want that to be us. Don't want to lose you to all of this."

A lump lodges in my throat at the despair in his voice. It feels like an utter betrayal to not tell him the truth. That the story he saw on the news was a complete fabrication. But living this lie is better than admitting the truth.

"You won't." I force my lips into a smile. "I promise. What we have is infinitely better than what I shared with him."

I can physically feel the relief wash over him as he touches his mouth to mine in a sweet kiss.

Normally, I find comfort in the feel of Tristan's lips. Crave the sensation of bliss I experience whenever we're together. Welcome the escape being with him has always provided me.

Not anymore.

Now, nothing seems powerful enough to distract me from Creed's presence looming nearby.

CHAPTER ELEVEN

Creed

This is bloody torture. It doesn't matter how much I'd prepared for tonight. How much I convinced myself it wouldn't be that big of a deal. It all went out the window the second I saw Tristan kiss Esme.

It shouldn't bother me like it does.

I shouldn't care that she's moved on.

I have, too… Sort of.

It still doesn't make it any easier to watch them together, the picture of the perfect couple. Much like she and Jameson were all those years ago.

But what makes this hurt worse is that she actually likes Tristan.

Maybe even loves him.

She chose him.

She didn't choose me. Not when it mattered.

Throughout the first part of the performance, I do my best to keep my attention focused on everything that's going on outside of the royal box. Taking note of anyone who seems suspicious. Anything that appears out of ordinary. Anything to distract myself from the awareness prickling my skin every time Esme pretends to look at the far end of the stage, only for her eyes to steal a glimpse at me.

When I don't think I can endure another second of this, the theater lights come back on for the first intermission. I slip into the hallway and make my way toward an exterior door, pushing it open and stepping onto a stone balcony. It's doubtful anyone would attempt to scale the wall in the hopes of gaining access to the royal family, but it's still an entry point. When the king and first two people in the line of succession are here, every entry point has to be covered, no matter what.

"Everything okay?" Archie asks. "I didn't hear anything over the com."

"It's fine. I was hoping we could switch for the next act."

If he finds my request odd, he doesn't say anything. I doubt he has to. He's been Esme's chief protection officer since Adam died. He probably knows her better than anyone, her boyfriend included.

No doubt he's more than aware of our history, too. Senses I'd rather walk across a rickety bridge over a river filled with alligators and venomous snakes than have to suffer through another second of watching Tristan touch Esme.

"You got it."

"Thanks, mate."

He gives me a smile before walking past me and opening the door. Just before he's about to disappear, he looks my way. "Hey, Lawson?"

"Yeah?"

He opens his mouth then snaps it shut, seeming to toil over his words. "It's hard on her, too."

He allows his statement to sink in for a beat before continuing into the building, leaving me outside on a chilly late October night. But the cold is a welcome distraction from the emotions warring inside me.

The sound of laughter and boisterous conversation cuts through, and I step toward the ledge of the balcony, eyes scanning the patio below as women in gowns and men in tuxedos mingle, sipping on champagne and other beverages.

"Why did she leave in the first place?" a woman snips, her high-pitch voice echoing against the stone. "I get her bodyguard died, and she almost did, too, but come on. She couldn't have been that shaken up. He was just the help. Would you be that distraught if your nanny or housekeeper kicked it?"

"Of course, I would be," one of her equally catty friends replies, feigning sincerity. "I mean, do you know how hard it is to find reliable help these days? I'm not about to clean my house. And changing nappies? Absolutely not."

Jaw ticking, I close my eyes, resisting the urge to remind them that their housekeeper and nanny are people, too. I've forgotten how much I hate this part of the job. At larger scale events where Anderson's slated to make a speech, I don't typically have to deal with people from high society. Not to mention, he spent all of September and the first half of October in the States.

Now that we're back, I'm reminded why I avoid these events as much as possible, often assigning them to other members of my team. But I wanted to be here tonight. If for no other reason than to observe Anderson for any signs of distress. Granted, I'm not actually in a position to watch him at the moment, but if there's anyone I trust to keep an eye on him and intervene quickly, it's Archie.

"I can't believe Tristan Hughes is *still* with her. Like, what does he even see in her? Other than the fact she's a princess, or whatever. But he's Hollywood royalty. Pretty sure that gives him more clout than *her*. I don't get it. She's not even that pretty."

I grip the ledge, fighting the urge to shout that they should show her more respect. That Tristan's with her because the Princess Royal is one of the most amazing, compassionate, thoughtful, and beautiful people I've ever met. That the world is a better place for having her in it. That *my* life is better for having her in it, regardless of how excruciating it is to watch another man touch her.

Touch what once was mine.

Thankfully, the lights flicker before I do something that would get me fired, signaling the opera's about to resume.

Over the next few minutes, everyone files back inside, the world becoming quiet once more. Until I hear the door to the balcony open and close.

I whirl around, sucking in a sharp inhale when Esme emerges outside.

"Sorry," she says nervously, stopping abruptly in her tracks. "I didn't… I didn't realize you were out here."

"Are you okay?" I step toward her.

"Just… Needed some air." She pauses, chewing on her bottom lip as she shifts from foot to foot.

I expect her to turn around and head back inside without another word. Instead, she keeps coming closer until she's standing less than a foot away.

"You?"

"Same."

I stare at her for what feels like an eternity, unable to look away. She's just so damn beautiful. And what makes her even more so is that she probably doesn't even realize how stunning she is, especially in that sleek green silk gown. It's classic yet still incredibly sensual, a deep V leaving her back exposed.

No wonder I couldn't stop staring at her all night.

"It's hard, ya know? Being here after so long. Some things have changed, but others…" She shakes her head, heading toward the ledge. "Others are the same."

I join her, watching as she draws in several deep breaths.

Like Esme said. Some things have changed. But others have stayed the same.

There's no doubt in my mind she still occasionally suffers from anxiety. How could she not after everything she's been through? Being ripped from the life she once had to become third, then second in line to the crown. Being the one to discover her mother's unconscious body. Then all the years of having every decision made for her.

It's no wonder she struggles being back here.

I doubt this tension between us makes things any easier.

"Five things you can see," I say after several long moments.

She whips her gaze toward me, a wrinkle on her forehead. "What?"

"I know how much that used to help you whenever you were feeling unusually anxious about something. And considering you've been stuck in the royal box with your father, grandmother, Silas Archer, as well as Jameson Gates for the past hour, I'd wager your anxiety is through the roof right now."

"You remember that?"

Nodding slowly, I inch toward her, despite the nagging voice urging me to keep my distance. But the pull of the past is too strong.

"I remember everything about you."

She parts her lips as she searches my eyes, my confession lingering in the space between us.

A confession I should have kept to myself.

"So tell me five things you can see," I repeat, clearing my throat.

She scrutinizes me for several more protracted seconds, her hesitation palpable. Each moment that passes makes it more likely she'll tell me it's not a good idea and retreat back inside.

Which is what she *should* do. What I should tell her to do.

Instead, she straightens her spine as she surveys her surroundings. A slight breeze ripples through the air, causing her to shiver, goosebumps rising on her flesh.

Without a second thought, I shrug out of my tuxedo jacket and drape it along her shoulders, my fingers brushing her skin. Electricity jolts inside me at the same time as she inhales a sharp breath.

I quickly drop my hold on her, increasing the distance once more, a strained silence passing between us.

"The lights strung over the patio below us," she finally states. "The steeple of the National Cathedral. A squirrel in that tree down there, probably stocking up for the winter." She points to a tree a few feet away, the branches rustling. Then she looks at the sky. "A plane taking off from the airport in the distance." She pinches her lips together, searching for one more thing. "And the stars."

"Which star?"

"That one." She points to one of the brighter stars in the sky.

"That's part of Pegasus."

She wrinkles her nose. "Pegasus?"

"Yeah. Right there." I move toward her, tracing the familiar outline of the winged horse in the night sky.

"I don't see it. I mean, I see the stars, but I don't see how a lopsided square and a few lines look like a horse with wings."

"Constellations don't give you the details. Just the bare bits. You're supposed to use your imagination to fill in the rest."

"What are you?" Her mouth curves into a smile I feel deep in my soul, the same one she once reserved for me. "Some sort of astronomy expert?"

"No." I chuckle, a lightness in my chest. "During my military days, I spent a lot of time looking at the sky. I got to know the constellations pretty well. Got good at drawing the rest with my imagination. Like Pegasus here..."

Without thinking, I move behind her and link my fingers with hers. My thumb brushes against her knuckles as I lift our joined hands and point toward the horizon. If this makes her uneasy, she doesn't show it, making no move to step away. If anything, her body relaxes into mine, as if it were just yesterday this sort of contact between us was normal.

At least in private.

"That bright star there, the one you pointed to, that's Enif. It's the nose. Around that, we can draw his head, his mane." I show her, using her hand to outline part of Pegasus. "We go into the lopsided box, as you call it, and that's his body." I inch closer, the sweet scent of her perfume intoxicating me, pulling me forward when I should be retreating.

"What else?" she asks, her voice becoming breathy.

I adjust my stance, placing my free hand on her hip, inching toward the crook of her neck and inhaling deeply.

"These other lines are the front feet." I trace along the two angled lines near his head, my motions slow, prolonging each movement as long as possible.

"What else?" she asks again, in no rush for me to put any distance between us.

"The rest is up to your imagination. Different people see different things."

She cranes her head. "What do *you* see?"

"I see…" I lick my lips, my breathing growing ragged.

"Yes?" She exhales, her chest rising and falling in a quicker pattern, her skin flushing.

"I see…" I lean down, the promise of her kiss warming my mouth.

"Yes," she prods again. This time, it doesn't come out as a request for a response.

More as a confirmation.

My gaze traces over her face, taking in every detail. Vibrant green eyes. Slender nose. Full lips I've had the pleasure of feeling on nearly every inch of my body.

What I wouldn't give to erase the last bit of space separating us and feel them again. Mark her again. Claim her as mine, for once and for all.

But she's not mine. She can't be. Not anymore.

The full weight of what I'm on the brink of doing slams into me, and I hastily back away, refusing to repeat the same mistake I made all those years ago. When I was too selfish to put my family first.

"You should go back inside," I bark, my words coming out harsher than I intended. "Everyone's probably wondering where you are. Including your boyfriend."

She stares at me, her mouth opened slightly, gaze wide and searching. She blinks a few times before squeezing her eyes shut, as if being hit by the same realization I just had.

"I… I'm sorry. I just…"

"Forgot," I finish for her.

She laughs nervously. "Yeah. I mean, I didn't forget. But—"

"No need to explain. Or apologize." I bow slightly. "Enjoy the rest of the opera, ma'am."

She doesn't immediately move. Just studies me, as if deciding what to do. But what choice is there? She made hers. I made mine. There's nothing either one of us can do to change that now.

On a long sigh, she nods, shrugging my jacket off her shoulders.

"Here." She extends it toward me. "I probably shouldn't walk in wearing this."

"Probably not." I take it from her and slide it on, re-securing the buttons.

She meets my gaze once more, then continues toward the door. Just before she's about to turn the knob, she glances over her shoulder, her eyes locking with mine. She opens her mouth, as if about to say something. But instead, she shakes her head, disappearing inside without another word.

CHAPTER TWELVE

Creed

"Y ou okay, mate?" Anderson asks from the back seat of the SUV as I drive him to his estate later that evening.

"Shouldn't I be asking you that? How are you feeling after tonight?"

"We're not talking about me. We're talking about you. How are *you* feeling after tonight?"

"I'm fine," I reply dismissively, ignoring his insinuation.

"Come off it, Creed. You may be my CPO, but I all but demanded you be assigned to me because of how well you know me. How much I *trust* you. You may think we're not supposed to be friends, or whatever bullshit your father force-fed you throughout your life, but I still consider you a friend. My best friend. And I'd like to think you still consider me a friend, too."

"I do." I briefly meet his eyes through the rearview

mirror before returning my attention to the road, the streets of the city still filled with activity, even after midnight.

"Right. Then tell me what's really going on."

"I don't—"

"I noticed you changed positions with Archie halfway through the night."

"Just needed a break from being inside. A change of scenery."

"I noticed Esme also disappeared for a good ten minutes during the second half."

I grip the steering wheel tighter. "She just needed a break from being inside, too. A change of scenery."

Thankfully, he can't see my face. Can't hear my pulse kick up from the mere mention of her name. It takes all of my willpower to keep my breathing steady. But it's no use. Every thought leads me back to Esme and the desire still filling me from the memory of being so close to her.

"She's happy," Anderson comments after several long moments, the strain in the car increasing.

"She appears to be."

Although she didn't seem too happy when she walked onto the balcony tonight. If anything, she was troubled. Anxious.

"No, Creed," Anderson retorts, voice much more forceful than his usual tone. "She *is* happy. With Tristan."

"Okay."

"It took her a long time to get to this point. Even after I'd gotten back from deployment and visited her in Paris, she wasn't the Esme I remembered. Sure, she put on a good act. If there's anything the two of us have mastered, it's pretending to be happy. But I've always been able to see through the façade. Saw that, despite the half-assed smile, despite her telling me how much she enjoyed her life in Paris, something was missing."

I want to ask him what exactly was missing, but bite my tongue. Deep down, I already know the answer.

"Then Tristan came into the picture. For the first time in years, I saw my sister smile. Heard her laugh." He pushes out a sigh. "I love you like a brother, Creed. And it goes without saying I adore Esme. Not just because she's my sister, but because she's always been there for me. I don't want to lose either of you. I don't want to have to *choose* between either of you."

"Why would you have to? We're—"

"I saw the way you were looking at her tonight, Creed."

I snap my mouth shut.

"I also saw the way she was looking at you. And I get it. You haven't seen each other in years. Now that you're in the same place again, it's bringing back all those memories, good and bad. I'm not going to sit here and claim your feelings for her aren't real. Or hers for you. That's not what this is about. I just…" He pauses, drawing in a deep breath.

"I never want to see my sister as broken as she was those first few years in Paris. If that means you need to keep your interactions to a minimum, I'm begging you to do that. Don't seek her out. Don't become overly friendly. You won't be able to avoid her altogether, not with her resuming her official duties, but I request that your interactions be limited to what's required for you to do your job. And I'm not asking as your boss or anything, but as your friend. As someone who cares about both of you. Because despite what you may think, despite what you may want to believe, there's no doubt she'd throw it all away for you, Creed. Are you willing to do the same?"

I lick my lips, chest squeezing. I want to tell him I am.

That I'd happily walk away from everything if it means I could have Esme all to myself.

"At one point I was," I answer.

"What about now?"

I sigh, hanging my head. "I…can't."

"Exactly. So please let her go, Creed. Let her live her life and be happy without getting in the way. She deserves it after everything she's been through."

My throat tightens, the ache in my chest swelling at the thought of never feeling Esme's soft skin against mine. Never inhaling her delicious scent. Never being the one to make her smile. But I made my decision. No matter how much it hurts, Esme deserves to be happy, even if I refuse to afford myself the same thing.

"I'll keep any of our interactions strictly professional."

"Thanks."

"You're a good brother."

He relaxes into the back seat, pinching the bridge of his nose. "I feel like a shite one right now, asking you to essentially be an arse to her."

"You're just trying to protect her," I tell him, able to speak from experience.

My brother had tried to talk to me before I jumped off the deep end. I refused to listen. I've often wondered what would have happened if I'd heeded his warnings. Would Esme and I have found our way to each other anyway? Or would I have kept my distance?

Would Adam still be alive?

"Not just her, Creed. You, too."

"Thanks, mate." I meet his eyes through the mirror and give him an appreciative smile. Then the car falls silent for the remainder of the short drive to Wintervale Manor.

Once I've ensured Anderson is safely inside, I return to

the SUV, my thoughts consumed by Esme as I drive away from his estate, my mood shifting from regret to nostalgia to desire and back again.

Finally, I find myself turning down the familiar tree-lined roads of a suburban neighborhood, all the lawns neatly trimmed, some with toys strewn on them.

I once swore I'd never live in the suburbs, preferring the excitement and pace of life in the city.

But priorities change.

My priorities have changed.

It doesn't matter what I want anymore. All that does is what Rory and AJ need. Nothing else.

I park in the driveway and take a deep breath before stepping out of the car, gazing up at the two-story Queen Anne-style house that's nearly identical to every other one in this development, the only difference being the exterior design.

Mindful of the late hour, I keep my steps light as I slip inside the house. The space is mostly dark, apart from the light over the sink in the kitchen.

"Hey."

Hearing Rory's voice, I look toward the living room as she stands from the couch, closing the cover on her e-reader. She's dressed in a pair of pajama bottoms, t-shirt, and a gray jumper partly zipped.

"What are you still doing up?" I whisper.

"I wanted to make sure you got home okay." She smiles sheepishly as she smooths a strand of red hair behind her ear.

"Sorry. I forgot."

Since I moved in, she made a habit out of waiting up for me to get home before going to bed. At first, it was mainly due to the fact she had a newborn and sleep was more or less non-existent, especially those first few months. But even once AJ started sleeping through the night, she couldn't make herself get into bed without knowing I made it home in one piece. Not after losing Adam.

"Well, I'm home now." I walk toward her, leaning down to place a kiss on her cheek. "No need to worry."

She smiles, but it doesn't reach her eyes. Nothing really makes her face light up anymore. Except AJ. Since the day he was born, he's been the only bright spot in her life.

"How did tonight go?"

"It was fine," I reply, although I know she's not asking about tonight in general, but about seeing Esme again. Rory and I have spent the past nine years lying to each other and ourselves. Why stop now? "Just another opening night at the opera."

"And the Princess Royal? How is she?"

"She seems to be doing well," I say on a hard swallow, hoping she doesn't pick up on my unease.

"Good." Rory forces a small smile, then clears her throat. "Well, now that you're home, I'm going to head to bed."

I give a slight nod, my gaze following her as she walks toward staircase. About halfway up, she pauses, glancing over her shoulder.

"Creed?"

"Yes?" I arch a brow.

"If you don't want to be alone tonight, my door's open."

I don't immediately respond, just stare at her as she continues up the stairs, disappearing into the darkness.

I'm more than aware this arrangement between us is incredibly fucked up. Not to mention bad for her mental health. But we've gotten in the habit of using each other like this.

Every time, I tell myself it won't happen again. That I won't keep doing this to her. Or myself.

Just like I'm sure she tells herself the same thing.

But as I close my eyes, all I see is Tristan kissing Esme. All I hear is her laughter. All I feel is her body against mine as we traced the stars together.

I thought I'd moved on. Thought I was stronger. Thought I'd buried all these feelings.

All it took was mere seconds in Esme's presence to bring them all back to the surface.

So instead of doing the right thing and putting an end to this unhealthy arrangement, I pad lightly up the stairs and slip into Rory's room.

This won't solve anything. It never does.

But for a few minutes, I can forget.

And right now, I want nothing more than to forget that Esme can never be mine.

CHAPTER THIRTEEN

Esme

I stare at the textured ceiling of my bedroom, Tristan's even breathing mixing with the white noise app on my phone. I thought the sound of rain would help me fall asleep, but nothing seems to quiet my mind. Not after tonight.

Seeing Creed again.

Feeling Creed again.

Almost kissing Creed again.

I have no idea what came over me. It was like no time had passed. Like we were back in that bubble where we could shut out everything else and just be us. When I felt his body against mine, I'd forgotten things weren't the same as they once were.

Forgotten that Tristan was mere feet away, waiting for me.

I've never felt as guilty as I did when I walked back into the royal box and sat down beside Tristan, the soft kiss he left on my cheek making the guilt fester even more.

Creed and I didn't do anything.

But I wanted to.

Which is why I immediately resolved to keep my distance from him as much as possible going forward. No more thinking about Creed. Fantasizing about Creed. Hungering for Creed. Instead, the only man who I'll allow into my thoughts is the one sleeping beside me.

But it's easier said than done, especially as I lie in the bed Creed and I shared for mere hours one night all those years ago. Is he thinking about me? Did he use Rory to try to erase me from his mind and body like I used Tristan earlier?

I shouldn't care. Should be happy he has someone, regardless of how fucked up the situation may be. I should be happy *I* have someone.

But every time I think of anyone else being able to kiss Creed, touch Creed, *love* Creed, hot jealousy bubbles inside me, the walls of this place closing in and suffocating me.

Needing to do something to distract myself from these thoughts, I throw the duvet off me and slide out of bed, padding on light feet from my suite and into the kitchen. I ignite the gas on the stove, then place the kettle on it, staring into space as I wait for it to whistle. Once it does, I scoop some of my favorite tea leaves into the infuser and pour the boiling water over it, allowing it to steep.

Teacup in hand, I head toward the den, one of the few informal and relaxing areas of my entire apartment.

One of the few areas of my apartment Creed and I were never intimate.

But as I turn, I glance down the hallway toward the administrative wing where I once spent all my working hours when not at a public engagement.

Where Creed and I routinely met under the guise of

planning Rory's baby shower as a cover for our summer-long tryst.

It's the last place I should want to be right now. If my bedroom contains strong memories of Creed Lawson, my office will be even worse. I wouldn't be surprised to learn his scent still clings in the air.

Regardless, my legs have a mind of their own, carrying me down the corridor and toward the double doors of my office.

Placing my hand on the knob, the metal cool under my touch, I pause, summoning the strength to face the ghosts of my past. I need to do this. Need to confront my memories head on, regardless of how painful.

Tristan has to get on a plane tomorrow and leave for Los Angeles. I'll no longer be able to use him to chase away the memories. I need to be able to do it myself.

Straightening my spine, I turn the knob and open the door, stepping into the familiar space.

Like the rest of my apartment, it's as if I never left. Book-shelves still line the far wall, filled with some of my favorite novels. A few magazines and newspapers are placed on the coffee table in the sitting area, seeming to have been replaced every day despite my absence. My official communications box sits on my desk, the royal family crest embossed in gold foil on the outside of the emerald green leather.

I make my way toward my desk and run my fingers along the cool surface, trying to push down the memories of all the times Creed bent me over it. Or sat me on it and spread my thighs, burying his face between my legs. Or any of the other things this piece of furniture bore witness to.

I lower myself into my chair, the cushions still molded to my frame. Bringing my teacup to my mouth, I take a long sip and stare at the communications box, wondering what's waiting inside. Wondering if my father sent it so I'd be caught up on important matters concerning the monarchy.

Figuring I may as well get started, I open the box, lifting a stack of recent memoranda, running the gamut from updates to the child care policy for palace employees to talking points when questioned about the constitutional referendum on the ballot for next year.

I slide open the top drawer to grab a pen, pausing when I see another memorandum within.

But unlike all the other ones contained in my communications box, this one isn't recent. It's dated over nine years ago.

The day of Adam's death, to be precise.

It's not the date that steals my breath, though.

Instead, it's the name at the top of the cream-colored paper, followed by a draft announcement of my engagement to Jameson Gates written by Gianna.

My thoughts drift back to the conversation I had with my father when I first arrived back in Belmont. How Gianna had allegedly been killed in a mugging mere weeks after Adam died. He assured me it was all just a coincidence, and perhaps it is.

But Adam always encouraged me to trust my intuition. Claimed people often overlook their instincts, and if they tuned into them more closely, they'd probably avoid quite a few dangerous predicaments.

So that's what I do. I trust my intuition.

Returning the memo to my drawer, I stand, tiptoeing down the hall and into my bedroom. Tristan doesn't stir as I grab my laptop from my bag and carry it back to my office.

I sit behind my desk and sip on my tea as the laptop boots up. Then I type Gianna's name into the search engine. It takes no time at all to return dozens of articles about the circumstances surrounding her death, all of them essentially reiterating the same story my father told me.

A few weeks after I left for Paris, a BMW registered to Gianna Vale was seen driving in an area of the city notorious for criminal activity — drugs, prostitution, gangs. I may have lived a relatively sheltered life but even I know not to venture into the four-block area of "The Hive", as it's referred to by locals. Not unless you're looking for trouble.

While I'm more than aware Gianna wasn't exactly a saint, I didn't take her for someone who got her hands dirty. Why would she, when doing so would put her position with the palace at risk? If something needed to be done, she probably had a long list of people she could call.

So why was she in "The Hive"?

Unfortunately, not a single article offers any explanation. They all claim it was a case of wrong place, wrong time. That a homeless man saw her expensive car and figured he could get a big payday. Like my father told me, Gianna's blood was all over his clothes when he was arrested. In addition, her wallet and a few of her other belongings were found among his meager possessions uncovered at a nearby tent city.

I should be sympathetic toward Gianna and the fact she lost her life. A part of me is.

Another part of me can't help but be curious about the man who took her life. Not out of some morbid fascination with criminals. But out of sympathy.

I scour article after article for the name of this homeless man, coming up empty. I'm on the verge of calling the Royal Police Headquarters myself to get a copy of the police report or arrest record when I finally find it.

Matthew Quinn.

According to this one article, in addition to battling

bipolar disorder, Matthew Quinn had a long history of drug and alcohol abuse, which led to him living on the streets. But there's nothing more. No details about the disposition of the case, which strikes me as odd.

After the arrest, the trail essentially goes cold. No articles about what happened during his trial. Did he accept some sort of plea offer? Even if he did, surely there would have been some mention of that, considering the amount of publicity Gianna's murder generated.

I do some more digging, officially down the proverbial rabbit hole. What I find does nothing to assuage my previous skepticism about the timing. In fact, it only increases it.

Especially after learning Matthew Quinn died when the van that was transporting him to the courthouse for his arraignment was involved in a fatal accident.

I understand accidents happen. Even in a relatively small country like Belmont, there are hundreds per day, dozens of them resulting in a fatality.

But what makes my hair stand on end is the fact that the company that operated the transport van is none other than Gates Enterprises.

I bring up a new tab and navigate to the website for Gates Enterprises. I'm not sure why or what I hope to find. It's not like I expect there to be a giant admission of guilt on the home page. But maybe there's some sort of clue.

"There you are."

Tristan's scratchy voice cuts through the silence. I whip my head up as he leisurely strolls toward me.

"What are you doing up so early? Or so la—" He stops in his tracks, his expression falling.

I furrow my brow, wondering what caused this reaction. When I follow his line of sight to my laptop screen and am met with Jameson Gates' charismatic smile, realization dawns on me.

I quickly close my laptop and stand, grabbing Tristan's hand.

"It's not what you think. I was just…"

I worry my bottom lip, trying to find a way to explain this without sounding absolutely crazy. Or like I should be wearing a tinfoil hat.

"I recently learned the former head of palace PR was killed a few years ago and was looking into her death, only to find out the homeless guy accused of it died when the transport van carrying him crashed."

"And reading about the accident brought forward memories of when you nearly died in a car crash, too. Memories of people who were part of your life back then. Especially after seeing him tonight."

"I—" I begin, about to correct him.

But what am I supposed to say? That Jameson Gates, one of the most philanthropic and generous men alive today, killed Gianna and pinned it on some homeless guy, then had him killed to make sure no one figured out the truth? It's so damn absurd. Even *I* have trouble believing it.

Squeezing my eyes shut, I pinch the bridge of my nose, feeling like I'm losing my mind. Maybe my gut's wrong. Maybe the unease I felt was just from being around all those people again tonight, especially my grandmother and Silas Archer. The more I think about it, the more I believe my father's right. It's all just a coincidence.

Tragic, but a coincidence all the same.

"I'm sorry."

Tristan runs his hands down my arms. "You don't have to apologize. If this is what you need to do for your mental well-being, I get it. Just don't shut me out."

I heave a deep sigh as I sink into his arms, resting my head against his chest, his heart thumping a steady rhythm.

"I may not have grown up a royal, but I know what it's like being held to a different standard than everyone else." He pinches my chin, forcing my gaze to his. "Know how isolating growing up in the spotlight can be. I don't want you to feel like you can't share your true feelings with me. You can. And I won't judge you for any of it. I love you, Esme."

My heart squeezes at how easily his declaration falls from his lips. As if it's as innate as breathing, this love he has for me. That it's not something he's ever had to question, just something he knows to be true. Something that just is.

"I love you, too." I touch my lips to his, if for no other reason than to forget everything for a minute.

Forget Jameson.

Forget Gianna.

And especially forget Creed.

Threading my fingers through Tristan's hair, I deepen the exchange, moaning when he swipes his tongue against mine. He grips me tighter, circling his hips, his need for me obvious through the thin material of his pajama pants.

"Come on, beautiful. Let's go back to bed so I can have you at least two more times before I have to leave you for two months."

I pull away, smirking as I lift my t-shirt off my body. "Why not have me here?"

Pushing my shorts down my legs, I step out of them, then walk to the front of the desk, spreading my thighs and toying with myself, spreading my slickness around.

That's all the invitation Tristan needs.

In a heartbeat, he shoves his pajama bottoms down his legs and covers my mouth with his.

As he eases inside of me, all the tension evaporates from

my body. I close my eyes, pulling him closer, meeting his motions thrust for thrust.

A part of me feels like I'm using him.

In a way, I suppose I am.

But I need to rid my home of all memories of Creed Lawson.

And this desk holds too many memories.

They need to go.

PART II

Instinct

*"The very essence of instinct is
that it's followed independently of reason.*

~ Charles Darwin

CHAPTER FOURTEEN

Creed

"Are you sure you're okay?" I ask Anderson as I pull the SUV up to the football stadium at the end of what I imagine has been an exhausting day for him.

It started early this morning with a tour of a new state-of-the-art medical facility, followed by a speech at a local university, a luncheon with scholarship winners from a charity he founded for at-risk youths, then a visit to an equine therapy program for vets suffering from PTSD.

"I'm fine, Creed. Just a little tired."

I narrow my gaze at him through the rearview mirror.

While he seems okay, I still worry he's pushing himself too hard. That he's doing this for all the wrong reasons, either to distract him from Nora or to prove to the royal household and himself that he's healthy.

"Do you know how difficult it is to give up coffee cold turkey? It's bloody awful. Sure, it's been over a month now, but there are still days I could use the caffeine."

"I can take you home. Let your sister handle this one on her own."

Over the past several weeks, Anderson and Esme haven't had many engagements together, apart from the obligatory state dinner or gala. The only times I've seen her have been during the myriad of doctor appointments Anderson's squeezed into his hectic schedule.

But she'll be here tonight for the coin toss at the home-town football team's big game. After that, they plan to watch from the royal suite.

The only thing that will make spending hours in her presence bearable is the knowledge that Tristan won't be with her. He left several weeks ago to start shooting his next film.

"And miss the match? I've been looking forward to this all day. Hell, all week."

I put the SUV in park and turn around, meeting his eyes. "I heard what the doctors said at your last appointment. You need to be careful. It could take a few more months before your treatment becomes effective. Until then, you're at a higher risk of experiencing relapse symptoms."

"I'm fine. I promise."

There's nothing about his demeanor that suggests he's not being completely honest with me, but I still can't shake the uneasiness in my gut.

Then again, it could be due to the prospect of spending the next several hours in close proximity to Esme.

"Okay." I push out a breath. "If you say you're fine, I believe you."

"Thanks, Creed. For caring."

"Of course." I give him a smile, then turn around and open my door.

The instant I step outside, I transition from Anderson's

friend and confidante to his chief protection officer. My eyes sweep the area in front of the players' entrance, assessing the vicinity for any potential threats. Finding none, I open the door for Anderson, gaze fixated on him as he climbs out.

The clicking of heels on pavement draws my attention, and I glance behind me as Esme slides out of another SUV. I ignore the fluttering in my chest as she approaches, purposefully avoiding looking directly at her when I bow. She gives me a curt nod. Facing Anderson, she kisses his cheek before turning toward a man in a tailored suit, who introduces himself as the director of operations for our local football team.

As they exchange pleasantries and the director runs down what to expect, I continue surveying my surroundings. But despite my best efforts, I can't help but steal the occasional glance Esme's way.

While I find her stunning whenever she's in a dress or ball gown, I can't ignore the stirring in my pants when I take in her long legs clad in a pair of tight-fitting jeans, sporting the jersey for the hometown team, her blonde and copper waves flowing to her mid back.

It's a stark contrast to Anderson's crisp suit, proof that, even though Esme's resumed her royal duties, she still refuses to follow all the rules, considering the royal household strongly disapproves of members of the royal family wearing team jerseys.

When the director leads them toward the stadium, I follow close behind, a handful of additional guards joining us, as well. For smaller events, we typically don't have a huge security presence, limiting it to one or two guards.

But during a public sporting event like this, there are too many unknown variables, which is why I always insist on having as many eyes and ears as possible.

After navigating the maze of corridors, we emerge onto the field to stands overflowing with excited spectators, many of them wearing the familiar purple and yellow colors of our home team.

Most of the security team stays on the sidelines, but Archie and I follow Esme and Anderson, remaining several feet behind them as they're led to the center of the field, the announcer introducing them to cheers and applause.

I take my position off to the side and scan the crowds, remaining alert for anything out of place. Anderson stands in the center, his hand outstretched as he greets each team captain.

As he does, he wavers slightly, brow creasing in worry. I rarely watch him when I'm at one of his public engagements, keeping my focus everywhere else instead.

But it's my job to keep him safe from any potential danger. Unfortunately, that now includes keeping him safe from his own body. So instead of scanning the crowd, I fix my attention on Anderson.

Something's wrong. I can feel it. He's smiling, putting on a show for everyone, but he doesn't look like himself. The referee hands him the coin, and I notice him pinch his lips together, as if he's straining. I look at his hand, his fingers seeming unable to close over the coin.

"Why don't you do the honors?" he says to Esme, his voice bright.

But I can hear the worry within.

"You were always a better throw than me."

She beams, happily taking the coin from him to prevent making a scene, but it doesn't escape my notice that she touches her free hand to his elbow, gripping it. Most would probably see it as a sign of affection between two siblings who've always been known to share a close bond.

I see it as confirmation that something isn't right.

That *Anderson* isn't right.

The seconds seem to stretch as Esme tosses the coin, allowing it to fall onto the ground. The referee leans down, announcing it landed on heads, meaning the visiting team won the coin toss.

I don't wait another second, jogging behind Anderson and Esme as they wave at the crowd, the cameras following them every step of the way. They're trying to put on a good show, pretend as if nothing's wrong, but I see the confusion in Anderson's face, eyes blinking repeatedly, as if having trouble focusing.

"You okay, mate?" I ask in a low voice. I touch my hand to his back, doing my best not to draw too much attention to us.

"I'm fine," he grits out, still blinking more frequently and harder than necessary.

It could be due to all the cameras flashing, but I doubt that's the case. Esme and Anderson grew up having their photos taken at every opportunity. At this point, they're immune to the blinding effects of a camera flash.

"No, you're not, Anders," Esme whispers, forcing a smile as she continues waving to the thousands of people in the stands. Then she glances at me. "He couldn't hold the coin." She does her best to keep her mouth from moving. "Couldn't work the muscles in his hand. He also—"

Suddenly, Anderson's legs give out beneath him. If it weren't for Esme and me being here, he would have lost his balance. Instead, I'm able to keep him relatively upright.

But people still notice, the camera flashes becoming even more numerous as reporters descend on us, shouting questions, asking if Anderson feels okay. If this is related to the last time he collapsed a few months ago.

Thankfully, my team's swift to react, forming a barrier as we rush to get Anderson out of here.

"I can't see, Creed," he chokes out, his voice distressed. Panicked. "I can't—"

"It's okay, Anders." Esme swallows hard, pushing down the tears welling in her eyes. There's no mistaking how shaken up she is right now, despite maintaining a collected demeanor.

She's been back a month, but hasn't witnessed the side effects of his diagnosis like this. Sure, she's picked up on the fact her brother gets tired a bit more often. Has even seen him stumble here and there, but nothing too extreme. This is the first time she's seen the reality of her brother's condition with her own eyes.

I can only imagine the memories it brings forward, especially after going through the same thing in her mother.

"I'm here, Anders." She squeezes his hand as we escort them through the back hallways of the stadium and out to the idling SUVs. "I've got you."

CHAPTER FIFTEEN

Esme

I pace the length of the waiting room, my stomach churning with worry. The sound of my measured steps against the tile floor cuts through the silence, most of the typical noises of a hospital absent here in the private wing reserved for members of the royal family.

Every few minutes, Archie glances my way, his concern matching mine as we wait for my brother's doctor to come out and tell us he's okay.

After what I saw tonight, I question whether he'll ever truly be okay again. Not like he once was.

Admittedly, I've held onto a tiny glimmer of hope that the doctors misdiagnosed him. After all, they claim multiple sclerosis isn't hereditary. What are the chances both my mother *and* brother would suffer from the same ailment?

I can no longer deny it. Not anymore. Not after watching his body give out beneath him.

Just like my mum.

Not after seeing him blink desperately in an attempt to focus on something, anything.

Just like my mum.

Not after hearing the fear in his voice.

Just like my mum.

I've been through a lot of shit in my life. I've never been so damn scared before. I don't know what I'd do if I lost my brother. I've never known a world without him in it. I don't *want* to know a world without him in it.

"Your Highness."

I stop in my tracks, whirling around to see an older man in blue scrubs and a white doctor's coat standing in the doorway.

"Dr. Mills..."

Crossing the room, I extend my hand toward my brother's neurologist and we shake briefly. "How is he?"

"Doing better now."

"And his vision?"

"It's back."

I exhale deeply. The tight muscles in my back and shoulders finally release as I close my eyes, the tension that's been plaguing me the past few hours slowly evaporating.

"He's not out of the woods yet," he adds quickly. "As I'm sure you're aware, the treatment plan we devised for him could take some time to become effective. Three months to slow his progression. Six months to reduce the size of his brain lesions."

"Brain lesions?" I choke out, shaking my head. Anderson never mentioned having brain lesions before. My fear returns, welling up in my throat.

"It's fairly common for those with relapsing-remitting MS, like your brother. It's what causes some of his relapse symptoms. Dizziness. Blurred vision. Slurred speech. Muscle weakness. Even though it can be worrying, we must remember that treating MS is a process. While we wait for his treatment to become effective, there's a higher risk of more of these kinds of episodes."

"But I thought he was taking steroids to help control them."

"He is. Unfortunately, it hasn't been as effective as we hoped, so he's agreed to start a more aggressive treatment involving daily steroid infusions at a high dose. He'll need to remain in the hospital for the next five days so he can be monitored. Afterwards, I recommend he cancel all public engagements for the next two weeks, at a minimum. This will allow him the rest he needs. He's working himself too hard. He needs to realize he can't do everything he once did. His body needs time to heal. So does his brain. All this added stress he's putting on himself isn't helping. If anything, it's hurting."

"I read that stress can cause relapses."

"There's nothing conclusive, since everyone handles stress differently, but I can tell you it's certainly not helping. Anything you can do to encourage him to rest and take care of himself would be extremely helpful."

I nod. "Of course. Can I see him now?"

"He's undergoing his first steroid treatment, but I'll take you to him."

"Thank you."

I follow Dr. Mills out of my private waiting room, Archie stepping in line behind me as we walk the quiet corridors, my heels clicking against the linoleum floor. The smell of bleach and coffee fills the air, the pale walls and florescent lighting making everything seem brighter than necessary.

"I'll give you some privacy," Dr. Mills tells me when we reach my brother's room, Creed standing guard outside. "If you'd like to discuss anything further, you can reach out at any time. Your brother's given me permission to discuss everything with you."

I find a certain level of relief in this.

Since I first arrived home, Anderson refused to slow down, keeping the same schedule he always did, despite the fact I'd agreed to stay to relieve some of the burden off him. I get the feeling it was his way of proving to the royal household he can still do this job.

Maybe this is the wake-up call he needs to slow down before it's too late.

"Thank you, Dr. Mills."

"Ma'am." He bows, then turns, disappearing down the hallway.

I lift my eyes toward Creed, taking in the strong line of his jaw as I search for a hint of emotion in his rugged features. His eyebrows are slightly furrowed, his expression a mask of indifference. It hasn't bothered me before. In fact, I welcomed it. It made my decision to keep him at arm's length easier to swallow.

But right now, I'd give anything to see even a touch of compassion in his distant stare. To have him wrap me in his arms and assure me everything will be okay.

Instead, there's nothing but stiff formality, the air thick and oppressive.

Without a single glance my way, he opens the door. I hesitate for a beat, then sigh, slipping inside Anderson's room.

"Oh, Anders…" I exhale at the sight of him in a hospital bed, wires and IVs attached to him.

I hate it. Hate everything about this. Wish this didn't happen to him. Wish it could be me in that bed right now instead of him. If I could trade places with him, I happily would. He doesn't deserve this.

"Hey, Ezzy," he says with a lopsided smile that doesn't reach his eyes.

I rush over to him and wrap my arms around him tightly as relief floods through me. "Thank god you're okay. You bloody scared me back there. So fucking much."

"I didn't mean to. I just… I thought I could handle it all." He laughs under his breath. "I guess there was a part of me that didn't want to admit I'm sick."

"You're not sick, Anders."

I sit on the edge of the bed as I take in his appearance — pale skin, sweat-dampened hair, deep circles under his piercing blue eyes.

"You have to give yourself time and grace to adjust, instead of trying to prove to everyone you're invincible. Trying to pretend you're okay when you're not. You can't ignore this. Not when doing so could cause more harm than good."

"I know. I see that now."

I squeeze his hand, grateful when he's able to return the gesture. It's not as strong as is typically the case, but after the feeling of absolute helplessness I experienced tonight when he couldn't move his fingers, I'll take it.

"Have you…" I chew on my bottom lip, hesitating.

"What?"

"Have you considered going public with your diagnosis?"

"I don't know." He sighs, briefly glancing out the window. The night sky is dark, the lights from the stadium in the distance a heavy reminder of everything that's happened tonight. "Don't know what it'll accomplish, other than angering the royal household, since they're hoping to keep it quiet while they determine what the 'optics' of something like this might be."

"Sounds like something they'd say." I roll my eyes. "Only in this world do we have to run polls to see if and when we can share a life-changing medical diagnosis."

"I can understand where they're coming from, though, especially with everything on the line in the next election."

"But what about what's on the line for you? Shouldn't that matter more?"

He furrows his brow. "What do you mean?"

"Maybe going public with it is what you need to finally come to terms with it. To *accept* this."

He parts his lips, but I cut him off before he can say anything.

"Like I told you all those weeks ago, I don't think anyone will see it as a weakness, despite what the establishment wants you to believe. I didn't press the issue because I figured you needed some time to adjust. Not just to this, but also everything…else," I say, not wanting to bring up Nora right now. "But you've been back for over a month now, Anders. You've been *pretending* for over a month. It's got to be exhausting."

"You have no bloody idea," he exhales, his entire body sinking into the mattress.

"Don't carry it all. Mum did that, too. She pushed everyone away, made it her burden to bear. I don't want that to be you. I don't want to lose you, too," I choke out, the tears I've kept at bay all night streaming down my cheeks. "You're the only family I have left."

He swallows hard, his own eyes glistening with emotion. "You won't lose me, Esme. I promise."

I exhale deeply, finding comfort in his reassurance.

"Then stop being so goddamn stubborn and just admit

you can't do it all on your own." I playfully punch his arm. "For fuck's sake. I'm convinced the men in this country were born with extra-thick skulls. You're all bloody stubborn."

A raspy chuckle falls from his throat, and I've never been so happy to hear my brother laugh. "I'll be sure to take that under advisement."

"You do that." I flash him a smile before my expression falls. "But I'm serious, Anders. You don't have to carry this alone. Not anymore. I'm here to help you relieve some of the burden. So let me do that."

"What about your life in Paris?"

I narrow my gaze on him. "Please don't tell me you've been pushing yourself like this so I'd be able to go back to Paris."

He simply shrugs.

"Anders," I sigh, grabbing his hand in mine. "I agreed to stay for you. To *help* you. As long as you need me here, I'll be here."

He closes his eyes, the weight visibly lifting off his shoulders. When he returns his gaze to me, emotion swirls within his blue orbs, allowing me to see the vulnerability he hides from everyone else.

"I need you, Ezzy."

His confession hangs heavy in the air, and I squeeze his hand.

"Then I'm here. No matter what."

CHAPTER SIXTEEN

Esme

I look around my father's conference room, the walls dark with gold leaf, our family crest displayed prominently on the wall as a reminder of who we are. I remain as composed as possible, pretending being here doesn't bring back memories of all those years ago when the royal household attempted to marry me off to a man I didn't choose, planning my future without giving me a voice in the matter.

It doesn't help that many of the same people are present at this privy council meeting, including Jameson Gates.

I haven't seen him since the night of the opera.

The night I looked into Gianna's death and learned the man accused of her murder died in an accident while being transported to his arraignment, and the company that owned and operated that prison transport van was none other than Gates Enterprises.

I'd convinced myself it was all a coincidence.

That any unease I felt was just because I was around all these people again.

But I still can't help but feel like I'm missing something.

I don't have time to dwell on it too much, though. Not when Pippa, the new head of public relations, shifts gears from discussing preparations for the traditional midnight service on Christmas Eve to the upcoming goodwill trip.

"As noted previously, we believe it's in the monarchy's best interests for Prince Gabriel to go this year. Not only will you be retiring in less than two years…" She looks from my father, addressing the rest of the council, "but with the referendum on the ballot next year, it's imperative we remind people who they're voting for. Prince Gabriel is extremely popular, especially with the younger demographic, who make up the majority of those in favor of turning the monarch into a ceremonial role. We can use that popularity to our advantage."

"I'm sorry to be the bearer of bad news," I interject without a care for the typical rules of procedure. "Prince Gabriel won't be able to make the trip."

Pippa blinks repeatedly, looking toward my grandmother, then my father, obviously surprised by my announcement.

"Why's that?" my grandmother asks finally, her cold eyes turned on me. Her shoulders are squared, a slight smile curving her thin lips. Despite nearing her nineties, she's still the picture of poise and grace.

"His relapses have gotten worse over the past month, so much so that he momentarily lost his vision during the coin toss the other night. His doctor recommended a course of daily intravenous steroids to diminish the severity of these relapses."

"It's my understanding he's been taking oral corticosteroids since the incident in the States," she replies with an air of authority.

"And they're not working as well as Dr. Mills hoped. Anderson agreed to undergo a more aggressive steroid treatment. He'll receive daily IVs for five days, after which the doctor recommends he rest to allow his body time to adjust."

"There must be a better option," my grandmother snips out, obviously frustrated. "The timing couldn't be worse."

"Oh, I'm sorry." My voice oozes with sarcasm. "Should we have consulted you first to see when he should be allowed to have a relapse? In fact, we probably should have gotten your approval for him to be diagnosed in the first place."

"Don't be ridiculous, Esme," she scoffs.

"I'm not being ridiculous. What *is* ridiculous is everyone in this room. My brother has been pushing and pushing himself, pretending he's okay because of all of you."

With every word I speak, my irritation with the situation increases, chest tightening, the beginning of a headache forming behind my eyes.

"He's so damn scared of losing everything he's worked hard for because you'll see his diagnosis as a weakness."

"We're simply preparing ourselves," she replies evenly. "In situations like these, it's wise to consider all options. Make sure we have contingency plans in place in the event—"

"Contingency plans?" I exclaim before she can finish her thought.

Not wanting her to finish her thought.

Refusing to even entertain the notion of something horrible happening to my brother.

"You'd do that to your own grandson?" A sour taste forms in my mouth, my throat burning. "Of course you would," I sneer, not even trying to hide my disgust. "Not like you've ever seen us as people."

"This is neither the time nor the place to discuss your opinion on how I run things." She folds her hands on the table in front of her, holding her head high. "The privy council is a place to discuss matters impacting the monarchy. And your brother's…condition certainly does just that." She looks at Pippa. "What did your first round of polling suggest regarding how Prince Gabriel's diagnosis might affect public opinion and the referendum?"

Pippa focuses her attention on her laptop, hurriedly typing away at it.

"It appears—"

"No."

At the sound of my father's commanding voice, all eyes shift to him. His normally analytical expression is intense, jaw clenched.

"Gabriel is my son," he says gruffly, a subtle waver in his tone.

"I'm aware of who the heir apparent is," my grandmother retorts dismissively.

"No," he repeats, this time louder. "Not the heir apparent." He stands, his tall frame formidable as he towers over all of us.

Including my grandmother.

I don't think I've ever seen her flinch or back down. Yet right now, she sinks a little in her chair.

"My *son*," Dad continues. "Not a what. A who."

He glares at my grandmother for what feels like an eternity, his stare icy. Then he turns, all eyes on him as he walks toward the window, looking out over the famous Lamberside Palace gardens. The vibrant flowers that line them during the spring and summer have since died, the grass and hedges coated white from a fresh dusting of snow.

My mother may not have lived at the palace long, but she loved the gardens. Would often bundle Anderson and me up in our winter coats and drag us outside to build a snowman, to hell with how the royal household thought we should behave.

Every time I see snow, I think of building a snowman with my mother. I wonder if that's what my father's thinking about, too.

"I didn't stand up for Grace when she was diagnosed," he begins softly. "Not like I should have." He glances over his shoulder, his blue eyes finding mine. "It's the greatest regret of my life. And you can be damn sure I won't make the same mistake again." He strides back to the table, nothing but raw determination in his expression.

"My son is, and will remain, the Crown Prince of this great nation. When I step down in two years, he will become king. *Your* king." His voice thunders in the room, everything about him powerful and in control, not allowing anyone to question his authority.

"Anyone who so much as implies otherwise will be swiftly removed from this council, regardless of their length of service to the monarchy." He pins Silas Archer with a stare before looking at my grandmother. "Or family ties."

His statement rings in the air for several long moments before he addresses the entire council once more. "I won't allow anyone to consider his diagnosis a weakness. Is that understood?" He looks around the table, everyone nodding and murmuring their acquiescence.

Including my grandmother and Silas Archer.

"Good."

He lowers himself into his chair, the tension in the room thick.

And I couldn't be happier. For the first time in years, I'm proud to call this man my father. He actually *feels* like a dad.

"That still doesn't solve the issue of the goodwill trip," my grandmother pipes up.

"We could delay it," Dad suggests.

"With all due respect, sir," Dalton Peele, my father's head of household, begins. "I don't believe a delay is in our best interests."

When most people hear the term head of household, they typically think of a head butler or something like that. In our world, the head of household is my father's right-hand man, even over his private secretary. He essentially makes sure the monarchy continues working like a well-oiled machine. He's often compared to that of the chief of staff in the States.

"The goodwill trip is an annual event," he continues. "An opportunity to meet with community leaders and the people of this country. It's no coincidence it's planned for the holiday season every year. While we try to promote our charitable endeavors year round, it's of particular importance during the holiday season. When those in need…need more."

"I'm not going to put Gabriel at risk by—"

"I'm not suggesting that. Just that perhaps you might want to clear *your* schedule and go in his stead. It's traditionally a trip the monarch takes anyway. We suggested to have the Crown Prince go as the new face of the monarchy."

"Which I still believe is important," my grandmother interjects. "We've all seen the numbers. The majority of support for the referendum comes from people in their thirties, particularly females. We—"

"Why doesn't Her Highness go?" a deep voice suggests.

I instantly dart my eyes to the opposite end of the table, meeting Jameson's gaze. His posture is relaxed, a smirk crawling on his lips.

I expect everyone to tell him it's a horrible idea, especially since I've only been back a month. The royal household has been quite particular about the public events I've attended, making sure it wasn't something that required me to speak on the monarchy's behalf.

There's no way anyone will agree.

"That might actually be better." Pippa's the first to break the silence.

"What?" I whip my attention toward her.

"Solely based on numbers," she clarifies. "You're extremely likable. Out of the entire royal family, people think you're the most relatable. Not to mention, you're dating one of the most popular actors right now."

"I'm not involving Tristan in this," I interject quickly. "I made it quite clear when I agreed to undertake my duties again that my personal life was not to be trifled with. And Tristan is part of that."

"And we won't involve him," my father states with authority before softening his expression. "But this could actually be good for you, Esme. A way for you to…reconnect. Remember where you came from before you decide where you want to go."

His statement catches me off guard. But there's no denying it makes me think.

When I first came back here, I had absolutely no intention of staying. Figured I'd help Anderson through this initial difficulty, then return to my old life.

Return to Tristan.

Lately, I've felt lost, for lack of a better word. Have felt unsure of my place. Have questioned what I really want. It could simply be because Tristan's thousands of miles away, and he's the only thing anchoring me to what once was my life.

But maybe my father's right.

Maybe this is exactly what I need to figure out my next step.

At the very least, it'll be nice to have a break from the constant memories of Creed Lawson surrounding me everywhere in this city. That alone will make the trip well worthwhile.

"Okay." I give my father a small smile. "I'll do it."

CHAPTER SEVENTEEN

Esme

"Can you spare a minute?" I ask Dad once he dismisses the meeting.

"For you, of course. Come on." He leads me into his office and closes the door behind us.

My gaze scans the room, everything almost exactly as it was the last time I was here. Same built-in bookshelves, rows of books carefully arranged by size. Same elaborate mahogany desk that's centuries old. Same intricate detail carved into the ceiling.

Despite it all, this place *feels* different.

My father's different.

I like this version of him much better.

I may even *love* this version, something I didn't think possible in our family. Not when I was raised to believe there's no place for love in a monarchy.

Maybe there is.

And maybe it's not too late for my father to have

love, too.

"Drink?" he asks as he heads toward the wet bar in the far corner, taking the top off a crystal bottle containing a dark liquid.

I can't recall if I've ever had a drink with my father.

I've sipped on champagne at a gala or state dinner when he was in the same room, sometimes at the same table. But I don't think we've ever had a drink together.

"Sure."

"Scotch okay? I can call down and have some wine or champagne brought up, if you'd prefer."

"Scotch is more than acceptable."

He nods, pouring a couple fingers into two glasses. "Any water or ice?"

I shake my head. "Neat."

He blows out a low whistle as he adds a few cubes of ice to one of the glasses. "You're made of tougher stuff than I am." He approaches, handing me the glass. "Your mother was, too. Took her scotch the same way." He brings his drink to his lips and I do the same, savoring in the woodsy flavor and fiery warmth that spreads through my chest.

A brief silence passes over us before he gestures to the couch. I walk toward it, lowering myself onto it.

"I just wanted to thank you," I tell him as he sits beside me.

"Thank me?" He sets his drink on a coaster. "I'm the one who should be thanking you for agreeing to all of this. Not just the goodwill trip, but undertaking your duties again."

"Truthfully, it's been good to be back. Yes, there are some things I still hate, but I don't feel…trapped like I once did."

He nods. "I can see that. Paris has been good for you."

"I've enjoyed my time there. But that's beside the point." I take another sip of my drink before setting it on the table.

"What you did in there, how you stood up for Anders, I actually saw my dad again. The dad you were before everything changed."

His eyes shine with affection. "I'm just trying to live up to my end of the bargain."

"What do you mean?"

"The day you left, you told me I needed to show you I planned to do better with my actions." He shrugs, the most powerful man in the country nowhere to be seen. In his place is just a dad. *My* dad. "This is me trying to do better."

Without even thinking about it, I fling my arms around him, hugging him tightly. "Thank you." I hold him several moments longer, wanting to savor in this moment.

The moment I feel like I have a father again.

"Those things you said in there…" I pull back. "Have you mentioned any of that to Anders?"

He heaves a sigh, pinching the bridge of his nose. "Not yet. We haven't exactly been on great terms."

I place my hand on his bicep. "This could help, especially since he's suggested formally removing himself from the line of succession."

My dad's eyes widen, jaw dropping. "He has?"

"The first time, I brushed it off. Figured it was just the shock of his diagnosis. But he keeps bringing it up. Thinks he's saving us from having to do it ourselves. But if he knew he had your support, knew you weren't going to push him away like you did Mum—"

"I didn't mean to push her away. I just—"

I grab his hand in mine. "Tell him. Not me. He needs to know you love him, no matter what happens. It'll mean a lot to him. Despite any differences you may have, he still respects you."

He briefly closes his eyes, his shoulders falling. "Okay. I'll talk to him."

"Thanks." I take another drink of my scotch, then stand. "I'll let you get on with your day. Apparently, I have some packing to do. Not to mention, getting up to date on all the issues facing this country."

"Just be yourself, Esme." He rises to his feet. "They'll love you even more for it."

"Even if it's not the perfect, poised princess the royal household thinks I should be?"

He grips my biceps. "*Especially* if it's not the perfect, poised princess the royal household thinks you should be." He presses a kiss to my forehead before dropping his hold on me.

I give him a smile, nothing about this man bearing even a remote resemblance to the person I thought he was. Then I spin, making my way from his office, the noose that once suffocated me whenever I walked these halls practically non-existent.

Until a familiar voice calls out, "Your Highness."

I pause, slowly turning around as Jameson Gates strides toward me. His blond hair is as impeccably groomed as it was all those years ago, the three-piece suit he wears giving him an air of sophistication.

"Mr. Gates," I say evenly.

"I hope you're not upset with me."

"Upset?" I furrow my brow.

"About throwing you to the wolves in there. Suggesting you take this trip instead of your brother."

"Not at all. My father's right. It's time for me to reconnect with the people."

"Good."

He keeps his blue eyes trained on me for several long seconds, something unnerving about it. It reminds me of the way he briefly looked at me after he caught me eavesdropping in on a phone conversation when we were at the beach villa all those summers ago. His voice was so different from the gentle one I'd grown accustomed to. Instead it was full of anger as he demanded someone find a recording.

Was *Gianna* the one on the other line?

I'd forgotten all about that somewhat unnerving encounter until this moment.

Now I wonder if maybe my gut *is* right.

"Do you really think that homeless guy killed Gianna?" I blurt out before I consider the ramifications.

"That's a random question." He laughs nervously, his Adam's apple bobbing up and down.

I shrug, but don't back down. "Being back here has brought up some memories. Adam's death. Hayes being declared dead, but his body never being found."

"The wreckage of his boat washed up on the shore of Norway riddled with bullet holes and covered with blood. *His* blood. There's been no sign or trace of him since."

"Kind of like Callie," I state in an attempt to bait him. To disclose what, I have no idea.

"I guess so." His shoulders slouch as his head drops in defeat. He looks like he did when he first shared their story. Heartbroken. Anguished. Shattered.

"And then there's Gianna, too," I continue, as if adding yet another dead woman to the mix will have him change his tune.

He pushes out a sigh, dragging his fingers through his hair. "What are you getting at?"

"I don't know." I glance up at the ceiling, chewing on my bottom lip. "After being gone for years, all these questions I was too numb to ask before have returned to the forefront of my mind. For instance, why would Hayes target Adam? Or me? I just… I feel like I need to know what really happened because nothing I've been told makes sense anymore. Maybe I just want Adam's death to have meaning," I confess in a surprising moment of honesty. "I need to know there was a reason for it."

"And there was." He runs his hands down my arms, eyes awash with sincerity. "It may not be something big or profound. But the evidence doesn't lie. His car—"

"I'm well aware of what the physical evidence indicates. I just don't understand why. Why did he go after Adam? Or me? Why didn't he target you?"

"I've asked myself that very question every day for the past nine years. I've *blamed* myself every day for the past nine years." His words come out choked. "Unfortunately, the only person who can answer that for certain is gone. All I can think is that maybe Hayes blamed Adam for losing his sponsorships. For a driver like Hayes, that's his entire livelihood. He was already on edge before that. It was most likely the last straw and he took it out on the first person he could. Sadly, it happened to be Adam… And you."

I close my eyes and draw in a deep breath, nodding. "You're probably right."

"I am. Trust me. It's best if you just forget about the past. It doesn't matter anymore. I hate the idea of anything horrible happening to you because you went digging somewhere you shouldn't have." His fingers tighten around my arms, his grip on me borderline painful. Then he steps back and bows. "Your Highness."

It's probably just my overactive imagination at play, the result of watching too many true crime documentaries.

But I can't shake the feeling that Jameson's parting statement wasn't that of a concerned friend. Not when it sounded more like a threat.

CHAPTER EIGHTEEN

Creed

"You wanted to see me, sir?" I ask, stepping into the General of the Royal Guard's office early Monday morning.

When I received an email late last night, ordering me to come here first thing in the morning, I assumed he wanted to discuss plans for delaying Anderson's trip scheduled for this week.

But when I see my father and Archie are also here, I get the feeling this isn't simply a meeting to tell me the trip is off and to make new arrangements for a later date.

"Have a seat, Captain," General Hudson states.

I do as instructed and sit in the middle chair, stealing a discreet glance between my father and Archie. As always, my father gives nothing away, as unmoving and emotionless as a statue. Archie, on the other hand, looks just as confused as me.

"I asked you here to let you know there's been a change

of plans. His Royal Highness will no longer be going on the goodwill trip this week."

Sitting straighter in the simple chair, I meet General Hudson's dark eyes from behind his desk, not a single paper out of place.

"When is it rescheduled for? I'll reach out to his private secretary and start advancing it right away."

General Hudson holds up his hand, cutting me off. "It's not rescheduled."

"They're canceling it?"

This doesn't sound like something the royal household would do, especially with the referendum on the ballot. I can't remember the last time it was canceled. Even during wartime, the monarch always made sure to connect with the people, especially during this time of year.

"It's not canceled," General Hudson assures me. "The royal household has decided that Her Royal Highness will make the trip in his place."

"Very well." I nod, doing my best to push down the heat washing over my face at the mere mention of Esme. "I'll brief you on everything," I tell Archie.

"That won't be necessary," General Hudson interjects. "You'll still be running point."

I jerk my eyes toward him, unsuccessfully hiding my shock. "Excuse me, sir?"

"I debated how to best handle this…situation." General Hudson steals a glance at my father. There's no doubt in my mind his concern isn't about my ability to act as chief protection officer on the week-long trip I've spent the past month advancing.

Instead, it's about me working in such close proximity to Esme, considering our history.

General Hudson may have turned a blind eye to our

indiscretions all those years ago. When Esme and I were together, I hadn't yet been sworn into the guard. I was free to be with her, apart from the fact she was technically with Jameson Gates.

Still, most people seemed to overlook any of my past misjudgments, especially after Adam died. Since then, I haven't strayed once.

I may have *wanted* to stray, especially that night at the opera.

But I haven't.

"As you know, our priority is the protection and safety of the members of the royal family," General Hudson continues.

"Of course, sir."

"Because of that priority, I believe it's best for you to remain on point for this trip. With the trip scheduled to start tomorrow, I don't feel that gives you sufficient time to properly brief Captain Walsh on all the advance work you've done. For the next week, you're officially reassigned as Princess Esme's chief protection officer."

"Yes, sir," I reply in an even tone that hides my unease over the idea of spending the next week with Esme.

And I won't just be seeing her in passing, as has been the case this past month. I'll be her chief protection officer. I'll have no choice but to remain mere inches away every waking hour from the time the plane takes off until it lands.

"Captain Walsh will be your second in command." He glances toward Archie, who agrees with a curt nod. "Everything else remains exactly the same. The only difference is that Princess Esme will be traveling instead. You may need to make slight adjustments, since the potential threats against her are different than those against Prince Gabriel."

"You can be assured that my team is more than capable.

And with Captain Walsh's assistance, we'll be able to keep Her Highness safe from any and all threats."

"Very well. You're all dismissed."

"Sir," we say in unison before standing and filing out of his office.

"Do you have some time to go over things?" I ask Archie as we make our way through the palace halls.

"Esme's schedule has been cleared for the day so she can prepare. Which means *my* schedule is now clear."

"Great. I—"

"Creed."

At the sound of the booming voice, I glance over my shoulder and meet my father's eyes.

"I'd like a word."

It's not a request.

It never is with him.

I look toward Archie.

"I'll meet you in your office," he offers, not needing any explanation.

Archie's more than aware of how my father can be, not just because we're all members of the royal guard and tend to know everything about one another.

But because he saw it all himself when Adam was alive. After all, Archie was on Adam's team. His right-hand man, really.

"Will you be able to handle yourself appropriately?" my father asks once we're alone.

I keep my expression indifferent, ignoring the meaning behind his question. "I always handle myself appropriately, on *and* off the clock."

"That's not what I mean." He steps closer, dropping his voice so no one can overhear. "You'll be spending the next week with the Princess Royal in very close quarters. I just want to make sure you remember what's important. Your legacy. It won't be like before. You're a member of the royal guard now. As such—"

"I'm aware of the rules. Anything that may have happened between us is in the past. I know my place. Know what's important. Know my duty."

He studies me for a beat, his analytical gaze sweeping over me for any sign I'm not being completely truthful. But he won't find any. I've made sure of it.

"Good," he says finally as he gives me a slight nod of approval, having passed his assessment. "Don't let me down."

With that, he spins, steps precise as he continues down the hallway.

I take a minute, running a hand over my face as I process exactly what this trip will mean.

Seven days of traveling the country.

Seven days of always being within an arm's reach of Esme.

Seven days of hearing her voice. Seeing her smile. Listening to her laugh.

So much for keeping my distance.

I can only hope I make it through this assignment with as little trouble as possible.

CHAPTER NINETEEN

Esme

The SUV crawls through the airport gates and onto the tarmac, driving past all the reporters and photographers assembled to catch a shot of me leaving on the annual goodwill trip.

Bringing the car to a stop, Archie steps onto the asphalt, strides purposeful as he walks to my door and opens it for me. The instant I emerge, a barrage of flashes and questions assault me. But I don't offer a response, especially when the reporters ask if my last-minute substitution on this trip has something to do with Anderson's stumble at the football game the other night. Instead, I simply smile as I walk toward the plane. A pair of guards stand at the bottom of the stairs, bowing toward me as I pass.

When I reach the top, I turn, giving the photographers one last opportunity to snap a photo of me outside the plane.

Then I duck inside.

I've never gone on an official trip like this, not in my role as Princess Royal. Sure, I accompanied my father on these kinds of trips when I was little, but I was too young to truly understand what was going on.

Now that I'm about to embark on a week-long tour of the country in the hopes of reminding people how strong our monarchy is, I feel enormous pressure. No wonder Anderson's been so stressed.

"Your Highness." Lieutenant Hawkins is the first to greet me when I enter the cabin.

"Thomas," I exhale, grateful to see a friendly face.

Having him as my private secretary again has made resuming my official duties much easier. It's like having an old friend or confidante back. He may technically work for the royal household, but he's always been extremely loyal to me. Not to mention, I'm fairly certain he was aware of my fling with Creed, yet kept it to himself, despite the potential ramifications.

"How are you feeling?" he asks as one of the flight attendants approaches, offering to take my coat, which I hand to her.

"Would you think any less of me if I said I'm nervous?" I ask under my breath.

"Just be yourself, and they'll adore you."

I nod, forcing a smile.

Everyone tells me to just be myself. But I'm not sure how to reconcile being who I am with being who the public expects me to be. I've never been myself in public. Always kept who I really am under lock and key, only sharing it with those I trust the most. After being free to do and say whatever I want for the past decade, I'm not sure I can turn it off and mold myself back into nothing more than a puppet.

"Your Highness."

I quickly snap out of my thoughts as a man in a pilot

uniform bows toward me, the bars on his jacket indicating he's the captain.

"I'm Captain Daws. We've been cleared for takeoff."

"Wonderful. Thank you, Captain."

"Right this way." Thomas extends his arm toward the cabin. "There's a conference room in the back we'll use to go over your agenda for the day, as well as any potential security concerns."

I follow him through the large space filled with comfortable chairs and tables, my team of publicists, secretaries, and security personnel bowing as I pass. When we reach the conference room, Thomas opens the door, allowing me to enter in front of him.

The handful of people sitting around the table shoot to their feet, bowing toward me, murmuring greetings of "Your Highness."

I continue into the room, smiling cordially as I say a quick hello to the individuals responsible for planning this trip. But when my eyes land on the final person, I nearly stumble at the sight of Creed Lawson.

The air between us is heavy, as if I'm in a vacuum, his presence paralyzing me. I search my brain for some sort of coherent thought, but no words come.

I knew they'd brought on additional guards for this trip. It's protocol.

Why would they transfer Creed to my detail?

Chief protection officers don't get moved around like this. Their sole job is to be in charge of that one person's protection detail. Nothing else.

"Shall we begin?" Thomas suggests, cutting through the tension.

"What are you doing here?" I direct at Creed, finally finding my voice.

I probably shouldn't have asked him this in such a harsh tone, everyone's curious stares ping-ponging between us. But if he's irritated by the attention my behavior has placed on him, he doesn't show it. He stands tall, adjusting his posture and squaring his shoulders.

"Due to the fact I did all the advance work for this trip, it was decided that I should accompany you."

I part my lips as I attempt to come up with a reasonable argument why this is a bad idea, but I can't find one that doesn't include our history and the tension that's grown thicker and more awkward between us over the past several weeks.

His presence *does* make sense. I'd agreed to go on this trip in Anderson's place a few days ago. I may not be aware of all the ins and outs of advancing a trip like this, but I imagine it's not something he could adequately brief Archie on in such a short period of time.

"As your chief protection officer," he adds after a brief pause.

"What?" I shoot back, this turn of events removing my ability to bite my tongue.

"Captain Walsh is still here, as you see." He nods toward Archie. "He'll be second in command. Because of the complexities involved, it's not possible for me to properly convey to Captain Walsh everything he'd need to know to effectively run point. I'll be doing that."

Drawing in a deep breath, I turn toward my private secretary. "Can you give us the room please, Lieutenant Hawkins?"

He arches a single brow at me, silently asking if I'm sure about this. When he sees the determination in my expression, he simply nods and heads out of the room, everyone else following suit.

Once my private secretary closes the door, I take a minute to collect my thoughts, all of them a jumbled mess, as always seems to be the case around Creed. Then I level my stare on him, crossing my arms in front of my chest, as if that will protect me from the effect his mere presence has on me.

"Do you really think this is a good idea?"

"Of course not," he snips back harshly. "I'm not happy about this, either. But General Hudson is right. I've spent weeks advancing this trip. Know all the potential security concerns. Know where anyone wishing to do you harm could try to do so. I've driven the motorcade routes. Developed alternate routes. I can show Archie pictures, talk to him about every detail, where each tree, fire hydrant, and possible sniper's nest could be located, but it's no replacement for walking these roads and seeing it for himself. While I can appreciate how awkward this situation may be, it's for your safety. Rest assured, when this week is over, we can go back to being…whatever we are."

I pinch my lips together, a pang squeezing my heart.

How did we get to this point? How did we go from friends, to lovers, to strangers, to this? I understand it's for the best, especially after we nearly kissed on the opera house balcony. There's no denying there's still a spark. Still an unrelenting craving anytime he's near.

But how did we become nothing to each other?

Or maybe we're not nothing to each other, and that's the true problem.

When a knock sounds, I look toward the door as Thomas peeks his head in.

"I apologize for the interruption, ma'am, but we're starting our taxi. We've all been instructed to take our seats."

I grit out a smile. "Of course." I turn from Creed,

making my way toward the head of the table, sitting in what's normally my father's chair.

Everyone files back into the room, re-taking their seats and strapping the belts across their laps. The only one who doesn't sit right away is Creed. He waits, looking at me, as if waiting for my permission.

What am I going to do? Throw him off the plane now? It's not like we'll be sharing a hotel room. He's here to ensure my safety. Nothing else.

I give him a curt nod, but don't look at him any longer than necessary. As if not looking at him will make him disappear. Will make his presence in this room less noticeable.

"Shall we go over the agenda for today?" Thomas suggests as the plane turns toward the runway.

"Certainly."

I open the folder in front of me and attempt to listen as he goes through what's expected of me, Pippa chiming in when it relates to the perception the palace hopes to create.

But I barely hear a word anyone says. How can I when I'm distracted by the heat from Creed's intense stare warming my skin?

CHAPTER TWENTY

Esme

My feet screaming from being on them practically all day, I waste no time in kicking off my heels the instant the door to my hotel suite closes later that evening.

I've never been so damn happy to be alone. And not because I spent my day delivering speeches, posing for photos, and meeting with locals and community leaders.

It's because I finally get a break from Creed Lawson's imposing presence.

There was no escaping him today. As my temporary CPO, he's essentially an extension of me, glued to me at all times. Maybe if he were just another member of my protection team, it wouldn't be that bad.

But where I go, he goes, too.

He was by my side from the second I stepped off the plane to the instant I disappeared into my suite mere moments ago. I've tried to tell myself it would be okay. That we could put aside any of our differences and act professionally. That it might feel awkward at first, but eventually I'd be distracted by all the public engagements, meetings, and luncheons that I'd soon forget he's even here. After all, that's the mark of a great protection officer. To blend in with the background.

But Creed Lawson can never blend in with the background. At least not for me.

Everywhere I turned, he was there. Every time he touched his hand to my elbow as he steered me through a crowd of people, my skin prickled with heat from the sensation. Every time he leaned down to whisper something into my ear, I craved for him to curve a little closer and brush his lips against my flesh. And every time I slid into the back seat of the SUV, I was overwhelmed with his woodsy scent, the aroma bringing me back to that one summer.

Even now, in my private suite, I can feel his presence from the sweep he did earlier.

And it's driving me crazy.

Needing to push Creed as far from my mind as possible, I grab my cell phone and bring up my FaceTime app, hitting Tristan's contact.

As it rings, I move into the bedroom and throw my mobile onto the mattress, stripping out of my dress and stockings before ridding myself of my bra. Opening a drawer to learn all my things have already been unpacked for me, I grab a t-shirt and yank it over my head.

"Hey, darling."

When Tristan's voice fills the room, I dash toward the bed, raising my phone in front of me. The second I see his face, my anxiety disappears.

"Tristan," I exhale.

"Hey." He treats me to one of his panty-dropping smiles. "How did it go today?"

I sigh and collapse onto the mattress, relaxing against the mountain of pillows, the Egyptian cotton sheets cool against my skin.

"Tiring. My feet are killing me. Think the royal household would get mad if I wore a pair of tennis shoes tomorrow?"

He laughs, his smile making his eyes gleam. "I can't be sure, but I have a feeling they might have a few choice words. Although, from what I remember of your grandmother, it's probably preferable to wedge sandals."

"*Anything* is preferable to wedge sandals in her book. Not like I'd wear them this time of year anyway because it's so cold."

"So I shouldn't mention how beautiful the weather is here." He gets up from what looks like the couch in the living area of his trailer and pulls back the curtain, blue skies and sunshine visible for miles.

"I don't mind the winter. Gives me a reason to snuggle by the fire. Especially with you."

He bites his lower lip in that flirtatious way that always causes my pulse to increase. "Tell you what. The second I have a break in my shooting schedule, even if it's just a few days, I'll get on the first flight out to you and we can snuggle by a nice, warm fire. Clothing optional."

"Just snuggle?" I pass him a coy look. "I mean, if it's clothing optional, I can think of more interesting things we can do than just snuggle."

"Oh, yeah?" The background shifts again as he relaxes against the couch.

"Yeah." I nod slowly.

"Like what?" His tone becomes husky, the light expression on his face turning sensual. Wanton.

This is what I need right now. A reminder of how much

Tristan wants me. How much he craves me. How good we are together. We make sense. Creed and I never did. We never will.

"Since clothing's optional, I'd suggest we both choose the no-clothes option, but not before giving you a little show. After all, I know how much you enjoy watching me strip."

When his eyes close, I know he's picturing the last time I did this precise thing.

I once asked why he liked watching me strip so much, figuring most guys would want to get to the good stuff as quickly as possible, namely a naked woman between their sheets. But Tristan told me there was something incredibly intimate about being allowed to watch a beautiful woman take off her clothes. How, with each article she sheds, she's letting you see another piece of her. Letting you *have* another piece of her until you no longer know where one ends and the other begins.

Except I'm not sure I've truly allowed Tristan to have a single piece of me. Not where it matters.

"Do I ever," he groans, pulling me from my unnerving thoughts. "What's next?" His jaw ticks, chest rising and falling in a quicker pattern, his words rough and hungry.

"I'd have you sit on the couch and straddle you. But I wouldn't let you touch me."

"Fuck, Esme. Do you know how much I miss you in my bed? It's been torture."

"I'll stop if it makes you feel better."

"Don't you bloody think about it. Tell me everything you want, and I promise to make it a reality the next time I see you."

I moisten my lips, my body heating as desire spreads through me. An ache settles deep in my core, growing more intense by the second.

"I'll slide my pussy all over your cock, but won't let you inside. I'll get you all worked up. Get you so damn hard until you're ready to explode."

"Then will you let me fuck you?"

Giving him a sly smile, I shake my head. "Not yet. I'll torture you even more. I'll slide off you, then make you watch as I fuck myself with my fingers, knowing how desperate you are to do it yourself."

"God, am I ever. I need you so bad, babe. I—"

Suddenly, a knock sounds in the background, and Tristan looks away from the screen.

"What is it?" he calls out with a gruffness I don't often hear from him.

"You're needed on set in five, Mr. Hughes," comes a muted reply.

He curses under his breath, jaw tight with frustration. "I'll be right there." Drawing in a deep breath, he returns his gaze to mine. "Sorry, darling. I have to go. I was supposed to review the next scene, but someone distracted me." He playfully waggles his brows.

"I'm sorry."

"Don't be," he shoots back. "I'd rather talk to you, especially when you get like this. Can I call you later tonight so we can pick this up again?"

"Tonight for you is morning for me, and I have another busy day."

"Then maybe we try again tomorrow around this time?"

I give him a smile, trying to hide my disappointment. "Of course. Have a good day."

"Good night, Esme. I love you."

"I love you, too," I tell him, but his face has already disappeared.

After today, I really needed more time with Tristan. I

knew the distance wasn't going to be easy. Not only are we on two different continents, but we're in opposite time zones, too. When he's just waking up, I'm winding down for the day. And when he's done with a day of shooting, I'm starting my morning. This isn't the first time he's been this far from me.

But it's the first time I can feel the distance.

I close my eyes, fighting down the frustration bubbling to the surface. Not just about the distance, but from being deprived of the release I desperately need. I didn't FaceTime Tristan with the expectation of getting off, but now that he has me all worked up, it's all I can think of.

Sliding off my bed, I walk toward the marble vanity in the bathroom and pull open the bottom drawer of my makeup case. It's sad I have to keep this hidden, but the last thing I want is for one of my staff members to unpack my suitcase and come across something they shouldn't. They wouldn't say anything. They'd be fired if they did. Still, there are some things I like to keep to myself.

With my vibrator in hand, I return to the bedroom and crawl under the duvet. Lifting my hips, I slide my panties down my legs, tossing them onto the floor before powering on my vibrator.

I bite my lip as the sleek toy brushes against my clit, sending sparks of pleasure through me. I let out a shuddering sigh, relaxing for the first time all day. And that feeling only increases as I ease it inch by deep inch inside me, already slick from my conversation with Tristan.

As I work it in and out of my body, everything else fades away. I'm no longer worried whether Tristan and I are going to survive this distance. No longer consumed by the uneasy tension between Creed and me. The only thing on my mind is this feeling of ecstasy growing stronger and more vibrant with every thrust, every pulse, every tease.

"Yes," I hiss, rocking my hips against the toy as I use my free hand to lift my shirt and squeeze a nipple.

Pleasure curls through me, and I close my eyes, savoring in it. I'm gentle at first, but as my desire increases, I pinch harder, desperate for that mixture of pleasure and pain Creed was so good at giving me.

From our first night together, I craved that strange dichotomy. Craved the darkness and light. The anguish and relief. The misery and bliss.

And that's exactly how my relationship with Creed was. Up one minute. Down the next. There was no in between. No middle ground. No neutral.

No relationship could survive such wild swings.

I grind my hips with more intensity, twisting and contorting my nipple harder, hoping it will erase all memories of Creed Lawson from my mind and body. For a moment, it works. My muscles tighten as I climb higher and higher, chasing that euphoria I haven't experienced in too long now.

Nine years, to be precise.

But I'm not going to think about that.

I *refuse* to think about that.

I'm only going to think about Tristan. Nothing else.

I part my lips on a silent gasp as I plunge the vibrator deeper inside me, imagining Tristan on top of me. His teeth clamping onto my nipple. His hand yanking my hair. His breath hot on my neck as he commands me to look into his eyes.

But when I imagine his eyes, I don't see his chestnut orbs.

I see Creed's dark stare, his hair disheveled, his scruff scratching my skin as he orders me to come.

An explosion of sensation consumes me as I cry out

Creed's name, my vision a blur of kaleidoscopes, pleasure causing my body to convulse and quiver.

I'm in such a state of bliss, I struggle to decipher fantasy from reality. Even in this in-between stage, I swear I hear someone call my name.

The sound of determined footsteps cuts through the fog, snapping me back to the present.

Then the bedroom door bursts open.

CHAPTER TWENTY-ONE

Creed

"What's wrong?" I ask frantically, barely even looking at Esme as I scan her bedroom for a sign of what had her screaming for me.

I stopped by to deliver her dinner, but when I knocked on the door to her suite, she didn't answer. Figuring she might be in the shower or taking a bath, I left her food on the coffee table in the living area and was about to head back to my room.

Until she screamed my name.

Panic raced through me, my mind going through all the possible holes in security at this hotel. We chose this place because it has the least potential weaknesses.

Did someone get a hold of my security reports and exploit that weakness for his own gain? It's always my biggest fear on one of these junkets.

"Is someone here?" I press when Esme doesn't immediately answer. "What happened? Why did you scream?"

Adrenaline heats my veins as I continue assessing my surroundings. The enormous bed with mountains of pillows. The ornate wooden dresser. The crystal chandelier hanging overhead. The lush carpeting at my feet.

As I step closer to the bed, my pulse throbs in my ears. And that's not all. There's a low buzz of electricity coming from somewhere. Like I'm standing next to a live wire.

"Creed…" Esme takes several deep breaths. "There's no one here."

I shift my gaze to her and study her appearance. Her hair and makeup are exactly as they were when we arrived at the hotel earlier, but she's wearing a t-shirt.

Her mobile is tossed onto the mattress beside her, her heels, dress, and bra thrown in a pile by a chair. I try not to focus on her lace bra. Try not to wonder if she has a matching set of knickers. I don't have to wonder for long, though, glimpsing a matching pair beside the bed.

I quickly look away. "Are you okay? Why were you calling for me?"

"Creed," she begins again, attempting to get her breathing under control.

Her chest heaves, her face and neck slightly flushed. Her pupils are dilated, and there's a subtle tremble to her motions. It almost reminds me of how she looked after I got her off. The glow on her skin. The trouble catching her breath. The tingles that continued to affect her long after my touch was gone.

And that's when it hits me. She wasn't screaming my name because she was in trouble. She was screaming my name because she was fantasizing about me while getting herself off. And that buzzing filling the room isn't a live wire. Not in the traditional sense.

Blinking, I glance at the foot of the bed where the muffled sound is coming from. She moves her leg under the duvet, as if reaching for something with her foot.

Suddenly, a thud echoes in the stillness, the hum growing louder. In the grand scheme of things, it's probably no louder than the subtle whirring of the heating unit. But as I snap my eyes toward the floor and see a bright pink vibrator on the carpet, the buzzing seems more deafening than a jet engine.

I should look away. Excuse myself and pretend I never saw this.

I can't, though. Not with the knowledge that Esme screamed my name as she fucked herself with this vibrator. All I can do is stare, my heart caught in my throat.

A part of me wants to ask if she was finished. If she wants me to use it on her. If she wants me to make her scream again, but this time even louder.

God, I'd give anything to do that. To feel her body shake beneath mine. To taste her need for me.

But I made an oath to serve the royal family. I can't break that oath.

Can't disappoint my father.

Can't betray Adam.

"Creed, I—"

"I brought your dinner," I interject curtly, my demeanor stiff and disinterested once more.

Then I spin on my heels and continue out of her suite, not even stopping to check in with the guard stationed outside as I make a beeline for my room.

Which is right next to Esme's.

I pace the length of my room, clenching and unclenching my fists. If there were ever a time for a drink, now would be it. While I may not be on duty right now, as Esme's CPO,

I'm essentially on call twenty-four seven. I won't touch a single drop of alcohol until I'm back home.

I don't know what I thought I'd find when I burst into her bedroom. I was convinced something was wrong. That, despite all my hours of planning and closing any potential security loopholes I found in my analysis, someone still managed to sneak into Esme's suite undetected.

I should have known better.

Should have known those weren't screams of fear.

After all, I know exactly what she sounds like when in the throes of passion. When she's so overcome with pleasure she can barely contain herself and releases all her desperation in a lust-filled scream. When she fights it for as long as possible until her body loses all control, her cries echoing in the air.

It's the last thing I should be thinking about right now. But every time I close my eyes, all I see is her flushed complexion. All I hear are those tiny whimpers that once drove me wild. All I taste is her essence on my tongue.

It's been nine years, but the memory of how she felt, how she moved, how she tasted is so fresh it's as if no time has passed.

I do everything to push it to the recesses of my brain, but the harder I try to focus on something else, the more she invades those thoughts. I shouldn't be surprised. I learned years ago that there's no erasing Esme from my mind or my heart. But I need to do something to silence this unmatched hunger slowly building inside me.

Storming toward the bathroom, I strip out of my clothes and turn on the shower. I should make the water as cold as possible in the hopes of shocking this increasing desire from my system. I doubt even a cold shower will work right now, though.

Instead, I step under the scalding hot water and succumb to my urges, feverishly working my erection. The entire time, I imagine Esme on her knees in front of me, her bright red lips sucking me off.

CHAPTER TWENTY-TWO

Esme

I've never wanted to disappear as badly as I did last night when Creed walked into my room. As if it wasn't bad enough he heard me calling out to him, I kicked my bloody vibrator onto the floor as I attempted to turn it off with my foot, making it obvious what I'd been doing that made me scream his name.

When I should have been screaming Tristan's name.

If the tension between Creed and me was strained before, it's even worse now. He's barely looked at me today. Granted, I'm more than aware he's not supposed to be watching me, keeping his gaze trained elsewhere as to remain hyper alert to any potential threat to my safety.

It feels like he's consciously doing everything he can *not* to look at me.

A part of me wants to pull him aside, bring up the giant elephant in the room.

Or, more appropriately, the giant vibrator.

But what do I say?

Sorry I screamed your name while I got myself off. I was pretending you were biting my nipples like you once did, making me feel that combination of pleasure and pain I've been desperate to experience for too long now.

I doubt that would go over well, especially with the stoic and borderline icy demeanor he's treated me to all day. I just need to get through this week, then Creed and I can go back to whatever we are to each other, which these days seems more like sworn enemies than even strangers.

I hate everything about it. Hate how awkward I feel in his presence when it was once the only thing that brought me comfort.

I remind myself it's for the best. We've proven time and again we don't know how to be friends without crossing that line.

"While I endeavor to help those in need throughout the year, it's most important during this season," I say into the microphone as I stand on a makeshift stage set up in front of a local soup kitchen. "Unfortunately, many soup kitchens, like the one behind me, are only able to open their doors a few times a week due to a lack of donations and volunteers to serve those in need. In the past year, charitable organizations have reported a sixty percent decrease in the number of volunteers. This holiday season, I urge everyone to find some time to give back to those in need. Even a few hours can go a long way. Thank you."

I press my lips together, a practiced smile on my face as cameras flash around me. Then I turn from the podium and make my way down the stage, Creed casting his ever-present shadow behind me.

"Thank you so much, Your Highness," a woman says as

she approaches. "It means a lot that you took the time out of your busy schedule to be here today."

I offer her a sympathetic smile, a complete change from the forced one I allowed the reporters to see seconds ago.

"I wish I could do more, Ms. Stewart," I tell the director of the charity that operates several shelters and soup kitchens in the area.

"You've already done a great deal by bringing attention to the issues we're facing."

"Sorry to interrupt, ma'am," Thomas says politely, "but you're scheduled for a luncheon at the Belmont Horse Society. We should be going."

"Of course." I return my gaze to Ms. Stewart. "Best of luck."

She curtsies. "Thank you, Your Highness."

I turn from her, walking with my team toward the waiting SUVs, reporters calling out questions. As I've grown accustomed to on this trip, most of them are about the referendum, with a few still regarding my brother and why I replaced him at the last minute.

Like I did all day yesterday, I ignore them.

But I can't ignore the line of people snaking around the soup kitchen as I pass, making me feel like a complete fraud.

I arrive with an entourage — private secretaries, public relations reps, protection officers. I give a speech, bringing attention to an issue the royal household believes needs to be addressed, if for no other reason than doing so makes the royal family look sympathetic. Then I'm whisked away to my next engagement.

I encourage people to take a certain action, but I don't take that action myself. Nor does anyone else in the royal family. How is that helping? Wouldn't it seem much more genuine if the people saw me, as a representative of the monarchy, getting involved? Not making some speech before moving on to what's next?

I stop in my tracks, causing Creed to nearly slam into me.

"Ma'am?" He narrows his gaze, meeting my eyes for the first time all day. "Is everything okay?"

I pinch my lips into a thin line and shake my head, my mind spinning with possibilities. Then, in one swift motion, I push past him, determination in my stride.

"Ms. Stewart," I call out, making my way back toward her.

"Yes, Your Highness?"

"Are you short volunteers today?"

"Today and every day this month. I only have four people, including myself. As you can see, there's a line around the block."

She gestures behind her to the men and women lining the sidewalk in front of the soup kitchen, some with children in tow.

My heart aches when I see the blank expressions on some of the little faces. I've never known what it's like to be without any of life's basic necessities. To not know when the next time I'll be able to eat will be. I'll be damned if I walk away from this place without making sure each and every person who wants a warm meal gets one.

"Not to mention, no one with any experience in a kitchen to prepare the food, apart from me."

"Then today's your lucky day. I've got a small army of people at your disposal. And I went to culinary school, so I can run the kitchen."

"I'm not sure I understand." She blinks, confused and surprised.

Truth be told, I'm a bit surprised, too. No doubt I'll get an earful from the royal household about this. But I don't care. This is supposed to be a goodwill trip. What's the point if I don't do any goodwill myself?

"I'll help. We all will."

"Your Highness," a voice growls behind me.

I ignore the shiver it causes down my spine, remembering all the times he growled my name as he had me bent over my desk and pounded into me.

With steely resolve, I lift my eyes to Creed's. "Yes?"

"While I'm sure Ms. Stewart appreciates the gesture, there are security concerns."

"Like what?" I cross my arms in front of my chest. "Because you haven't been able to run the requisite background checks?"

"Yes."

"I'm allowed to greet people and pose for photos at other events. None of them had been screened."

He leans down, eyes intense. "That's because you're not a sitting target like you would be in there."

"Those people aren't a threat to me, Creed," I tell him, not backing down. Not from this. "They're *hungry*. They just want a warm meal." I look back at Ms. Stewart. "These people who come to your center, how often do they come?"

"Some every day." Her expression falls. "Unfortunately, some days we have to turn them away because we don't have anything left to give them."

I turn toward Thomas and take his tablet, opening a notes app. I type feverishly for several moments before handing it back to my private secretary. "I want you to arrange for everything on this list."

He looks between Creed and me, unsure who to listen to. When I give him a heated glare, holding my head higher, he finally nods.

"Certainly, ma'am." With a slight bow, he spins, striding toward a few of my other staff members and issuing orders.

"We're going to stay and make sure every single person who needs a hot meal gets one," I assure Ms. Stewart. "Even if it means canceling the rest of my engagements scheduled for the day." I glower at Creed, waiting for him to fight me on this.

He wants to. At least the royal guard part of him does.

But that's at odds with the part of him that knows this is the right thing to do.

After what feels like an eternity, he pushes out a sigh. "Fine." He pins Ms. Stewart with a harsh stare. "But I'll need to have agents posted at every door."

"Of course."

He looks back at me. "And you do not leave my side for even a second. This is non-negotiable."

I smirk. "I'd expect nothing less."

CHAPTER TWENTY-THREE

Esme

I can't remember the last time I've felt so fulfilled. So content. Like my life has purpose again.

Within twenty minutes of announcing my decision to stay, food started to arrive, which is a good thing, because the refrigerator and store room didn't have much. I put a few of the members of my team to work peeling potatoes, then cutting them so we could boil them for mashed potatoes. I had others chop up a bunch of different vegetables to be sautéed. And I set about seasoning the dozens of roast chickens that had arrived, getting them in the oven as quickly as possible.

It's been hectic and exhausting, but over the past three hours, hundreds of people have filed through the doors, each one grateful to receive a hot meal.

And, as I instructed my team, not a single reporter was allowed inside. I'm not here as a publicity stunt. I'm here to help. To put my words into action.

Through it all, Creed hasn't left my side, as he promised.

Or, more accurately, threatened.

At first, I wasn't sure how it would go, considering the constant strain between us. While we haven't spent the hours laughing and making jokes like we once did, it hasn't been too awkward, our sole focus on the importance of what we're doing.

"Do you miss it?" Creed asks as I work beside him, mashing a fresh batch of potatoes.

"What's that?" I glance his way.

After I showed him the proper way to carve a roast chicken to get the most meat off the bone, that became his job. Truth be told, it looks like he's actually having fun for once. It looks like *everyone's* having fun.

Especially me.

"This." He waves his hand at the frenzied atmosphere in the kitchen where nearly a dozen people are stationed throughout, each charged with a different assignment. "Cooking."

I shrug. "I started a program in France where we teach trafficking survivors basic life skills, including cooking."

"I'm more than aware of that. But I doubt that's the same as getting your hands dirty, so to speak."

"It's a wonderful program." I force a smile, ignoring his remark. "Through it, hundreds of survivors have moved on from the trauma they endured. Some even loved cooking so much that they went to culinary school."

"And I find it quite remarkable." He pauses. "But is that enough?"

"In the few short years since I began the initiative, we've helped hundreds of women."

"I'm not asking if the program's doing enough for the

women you're trying to help." He narrows his gaze on me. "I'm asking if it's enough for you."

I part my lips, a response on the tip of my tongue. But I quickly snap my mouth shut, not wanting to lie to him. To anyone else, I'd insist it's a great program that helps hundreds of women and leave it at that. But Creed's always been able to strip away the façade and see my true feelings.

Even all these years later.

I add some milk to the potatoes and continue mashing, a heavy silence settling between us as his remark echoes in my mind.

Is it enough for me? Something in his tone makes me think he's not just asking about my charity work, but my life in general.

"I wanted to open up a community restaurant," I say after several protracted moments.

"A community restaurant?" He scrunches his brows.

"It's like a combination soup kitchen and restaurant. Anyone can eat there. If you can't afford to pay, you can do so by volunteering at the restaurant. All the food would be healthy, locally sourced gourmet meals."

"Why didn't you pursue it?"

"That requires money." I smile sadly. "Anytime I want to do something that costs a substantial amount of capital, I need approval before the royal household agrees to open the privy purse, as I call it."

"And they told you no."

I taste the potatoes, content with the rich flavor. "They believed it wasn't the right project for someone of my... status. But I'd bet all the money in the privy purse it was my grandmother's doing. She may not have been able to stop me from attending culinary school, not once my father stood up for me. But she could certainly use the so-called powers of the purse to prevent me from continuing to pursue this passion. Essentially tie my hands in the hopes I'd give up and come home."

While I don't know for certain that's why the royal household refused to support my initiative, based on my grandmother's past actions, I can all but guarantee that's precisely what happened.

"But they're okay with you helping trafficking victims? You're still using your culinary background to teach them those skills. Are you not?"

"I sold it as an education program. Some of these girls were taken from their homes when they were barely teenagers. They've been completely reconditioned to believe their only value is in selling their bodies. My organization tries to remove that idea from them. Give them a safe place to learn everything they missed when held prisoner. And one of the necessary survival skills just happens to be cooking." I wink, giving him a mischievous smile, but it doesn't reach my eyes.

"It sounds like a great program, and much needed, since we all know how prevalent human trafficking is here in Europe."

"Precisely."

"But why settle?"

"What do you mean?"

He refocuses his attention on carving the chicken, his strong hand working the knife into the breast bone.

"If you're going to put your time and effort into something, shouldn't it be something you truly love? That you're passionate about? It sounds like you're much more passionate about the idea of starting a community kitchen. I could be wrong, but teaching young women how to cook isn't the same as running a kitchen like you have been today."

He lifts his eyes to mine, and I have to push down the butterflies erupting in my stomach from the sincerity within his dark, penetrating orbs.

"I've watched you all day. You're a natural. And you seem genuinely…happy."

"I *am* happy."

"What about Tristan?" He licks his lips, obviously not too keen on mentioning him. "He's wealthy. Why not ask him?"

"We don't have that kind of relationship." I grip my masher tighter as I work on the next batch of potatoes that Archie just placed in front of me. "Plus, I never told him about it."

Creed darts his gaze toward mine. "Why not?"

"I never told anyone about it. Not after the royal household told me no. Figured it didn't matter."

"But you're telling me?"

I stop mashing and meet his eyes. "I am."

"Why?"

I shake my head, searching my brain for a valid reason, coming up empty. "It just feels…right."

A slight smile curves on his lips as he traces his stare over my features.

For the briefest of moments, I'm transported back nine years. To the night of my twenty-fifth birthday. The last time we worked in a kitchen together.

To this day, it's one of my favorite memories, one I continue to return to when life gets hard. It was one of the few times I felt truly happy.

Even after all the years I've spent with Tristan, not a single moment with him has amounted to what I felt that night with Creed.

Clearing his throat, he quickly shifts his gaze forward, a strained silence falling between us once more. I want to tell him it doesn't need to be this way. That it doesn't have to be so goddamn uncomfortable. That he doesn't have to be hot, then turn this frigid with the flip of a switch.

I'm about to do just that when Thomas approaches.

"I apologize, ma'am, but it's five o'clock. While I happily canceled your public appearances this afternoon, it won't look good if you blow off the premier's invitation to attend the ballet tonight, as noble and charitable as this is. There are other people here to help now."

He waves around the industrial kitchen that's now filled with more volunteers than this place has seen in years, at least according to Ms. Stewart.

Once word got out that I canceled my afternoon engagements to volunteer in the kitchen, in heels no less, heaps of people started to show up. And not just at this soup kitchen, but around the country, as well. I'm still not sure how the royal household has responded to my break in protocol, especially knowing I'm currently working in a kitchen. Even if they berate me for blowing off a bunch of aristocrats and wealthy business owners, it'll be worth it to know there are enough volunteers to ensure people in need don't go hungry.

Isn't that the point of this trip?

"Of course." I wipe my hands on a dishtowel and remove my apron, then allow Thomas to help me into my coat.

"Thank you so much for all you've done," Ms. Stewart says as she walks up to me, assigning a few volunteers to take over for Creed and me. "It means so much."

"It felt good to be in the kitchen again. To feel…useful."

"You're more than welcome to come back any time. We'd love to have you."

"I'll definitely be taking you up on that." I give her a genuine smile, the idea of doing something like this again filling me with a strange feeling of hope. Something I haven't felt in too long now.

"Please do."

I shake her hand, then turn toward Creed, who escorts me through the kitchen.

Just as he's about to open the back door, he pauses, affectionate eyes locking with mine.

"What you did this afternoon… The people of Belmont are lucky to have you back."

Warmth blooms in my chest, especially when I see the pride in Creed's gaze.

I've never been one to care much about people's approval. Not when I grew up in a world where approval is rarely given, if ever. I'm not sure it's Creed's approval that makes my skin heat. Maybe it's simply that he understood what I was trying to accomplish and didn't stop me, which he easily could have.

Instead, he supported this crazy idea, regardless of how much more difficult it made his job.

In a life where I feel like I never have anyone's support for what *I* want, it meant the world to me.

It meant that he actually listened instead of simply brushing off my idea as ridiculous.

"Thank you."

"Ma'am." He nods, turning back into my chief protection officer.

Facing forward, he talks into his com unit to let the other members of his team know we're coming out. Then he opens the door.

But despite the sudden shift in his demeanor, I still feel a hint of affection coming from him, especially as he touches his hand to my elbow, steering me from the back of the building and toward the main road.

Dozens of people line the sidewalk, some of them reporters, shouting questions my way, most notably whether this was all just some publicity stunt to make the monarchy look good now that there's a possibility the people may vote to turn it into a ceremonial position.

I know I'm supposed to bite my tongue and get into the idling SUV, allow my PR team to release a statement on my behalf, but I can't stay quiet about this. It was one thing to avoid answering questions when it pertained to my brother. I won't do it now, too.

Breaking away from Creed, I storm toward the assembled group of reporters, jaw set and eyes blazing.

"You think this was all just some publicity stunt? That the only reason I could possibly want to help people is for some positive press. Is that it?"

I'm met with camera shutters as microphones are shoved in front of me.

"That couldn't be further from the truth. The truth is I felt like a bloody fraud when I was giving that speech earlier today. There I was, encouraging people to give up their precious time, which I know is in short supply these days, when I wasn't willing to do the same. So I put my money where my mouth was. Instead of attending a luncheon at some aristocrat's house, I stayed here. Worked for hours in a dress and heels to ensure people didn't go hungry. What have any of you done to give back?"

With every word I speak, my anger increases, blood boiling in my veins. I can feel Creed looming nearby, but I don't stop. I've always had a somewhat tenuous relationship with the press but kept my feelings to myself. It's how I was trained. It's what was expected of me.

I can't do that anymore. Can't allow them to twist what was supposed to be a selfless act into one for political gain.

"You show up here to get a sound bite, hoping to prove I'm just another spoiled princess who doesn't actually care about the people of this country, when you could have easily spent the hours you waited out here doing something useful. Like volunteering. Like *helping* people."

I lean into them, muscles straining, adrenaline coursing. I have no doubt this will be all over social media within minutes. Hell, it could be right now. But it's not enough of a reason to stop.

"*That's* why I did this. Not for the headlines. But because people are hungry. Being able to enjoy a hot meal isn't a bloody privilege. It's a goddamn right. And if you can't see that, if you can't wrap your privileged mind around that, I feel sorry for you."

I spin, about to hurry into the SUV so Thomas can tell me what a shitstorm I started, when another question is shouted my way.

"How can you claim you care about the people of this country when you've spent the past decade in France?"

Pausing, I slowly turn around, addressing the various reporters and photographers once more. "You're right. I can't claim to care about the people of this country. At least, I *shouldn't* claim to, not when I haven't lived here in years. I'm not perfect. I make mistakes. And now that I'm back, I realize that running away from my problems wasn't the right thing to do."

I blink, my words surprising me as much as they do the press. But I can't deny the veracity within them. Today made me see that.

I left because of the way the royal household treated me. I thought by standing up for myself, I was showing strength. But in doing so, I abandoned the people of this country.

"I guess you can say I lost sight of what was important.

And it's not attending galas, state dinners, or art auctions. *This* is what's important. Making sure the citizens of this country have all their basic needs met. Going forward, you can be damn sure that will be my top priority, no matter where I am."

I give another practiced smile, allowing the photographers one more opportunity to snap my picture, when a face in the crowd catches my attention. His dark eyes burn like embers as he stares at me, something about the flecks of gold in a sea of black making me feel like I've seen them before.

And not simply at a prior event. He looks out-of-place holding that camera, as if my subconscious is telling me he doesn't belong here. But why would I think that?

A few reporters shout more questions, some asking if this means I plan on staying in Belmont indefinitely. Others ask about my thoughts on the referendum. And still others ask about my brother.

While I wouldn't mind answering some of them, especially regarding the referendum, I can't shake the uneasy feeling that steadily increases. All because of that photographer's familiar eyes.

Nothing else about him stands out. He's dressed all in black, bundled up with gloves and a beanie to fight against the chilly temperatures, a scarf obscuring the bottom half of his face. But the coldness in his stare gives me pause. As if I've seen him glower at me with that same malevolence in a former life.

"That's all I have time for today," I tell the reporters, my voice wavering slightly. "Feel free to reach out to my PR team and we'll do our best to get you a statement."

I grit a smile, trying to hide my unease as an icy sensation trickles down my spine. I should retreat, but something has me stealing another glance at the mysterious photographer, as if looking at him one more time will help me place him.

After that, everything happens so quickly. One second, I'm looking at his camera.

The next, I'm staring down the barrel of his gun.

I need to move, run as fast as I can. But all the training I've gone through over the years goes right out the window, leaving me completely frozen, panic rendering my legs useless.

Cries of alarm and desperation echo around me as people scramble in every direction, tripping over each other to get away. But all I see is the man and his gun before a deafening shot rings through the air.

CHAPTER TWENTY-FOUR

Creed

I hate transitions more than anything. It's my least favorite part of this job. Because it's the part I have the least control over. While several of my team members have been doing constant patrols around the five-block perimeter of the soup kitchen all day and haven't found anything suspicious, that still doesn't set my mind at ease. I won't be able to relax until I have Esme safe in the SUV and we're on our way to our next engagement.

Since she pulled up to the airport yesterday, she's played the part she was told to play. Wave at the reporters, but don't answer their questions. Show up at events and give the speech that was written for her. No matter what, don't stray from the plan for a second.

That all went up in flames when I agreed to let her help at the soup kitchen. I have no doubt I'll probably get chewed out for doing so, especially since I'm not sure I would have done the same for Anderson.

But Esme had a point. She's on a goodwill trip, trying to encourage people to give back during this time of year. What better way to accomplish that than by giving back herself? Not to mention, Esme's never exactly been one to play by the rules. She's always been outspoken about causes she believes in, to hell with what the royal household thinks.

Which is why I shouldn't be surprised that she refuses to stay quiet when some of the reporters accuse her of only staying here as part of some publicity stunt. If they knew Esme like I do, they'd realize that thought never even entered her mind. She pushed to do this because she genuinely wanted to help. That's the type of woman Esme is. Always giving to the causes and people she believes in.

After giving the reporters a piece of her mind, she starts to turn back toward me. Then her body tenses, her gaze locking on one of the photographers in the crowd. It's subtle and only lasts a second, if that.

But I know Esme. Can read her reactions, probably better than I care to admit. Something's made her nervous.

The hair on the back of my nape stands on end, every inch of me on high alert for anything suspicious, not taking my eyes off that one photographer.

As he relaxes his grip on the camera hanging around his neck, I move closer. He opens his coat and reaches into the inside pocket. I assume it's probably to retrieve his mobile. Maybe a new memory card.

But I still don't look away, keeping him in my sights.

And when he yanks out a pistol and aims it directly at Esme, I'm glad I listened to my gut, immediately rushing toward her.

The cacophony of screams is deafening as terrified people run in all directions, some of them pushing others aside as they try to escape. Despite the chaos and terror, my sole focus is on Esme and getting her out of the line of fire.

Just as I reach her, a gunshot echoes around me. I quickly tackle her body to the ground, using my frame to shield her from danger while the rest of my team surrounds us, protecting her from the pandemonium erupting on the streets.

Adrenaline surging through me, I roll off Esme and lift her up with me. Her eyes flicker open, her chest heaving in a ragged breath. She may be scared shitless, but at least she's alive.

"I got you," I assure her, keeping her low.

I wrap my arm protectively around her small frame as we sprint toward the idling SUV. The other guards move in unison with us, their bodies creating a barrier between us and the crowd, as we've practiced hundreds of times.

Once we reach the car, I open the back door and push her inside, probably too roughly, but there's no such thing with her life on line. The second I hop in beside her and close the door, Archie peels out, leaving the commotion behind for the police to sort through and hopefully find the bastard responsible.

But even though we're in the SUV, I can't lower my guard. Instead, I turn my attention on Esme, every inch of her visibly shaking.

"Hey." I grab her hand in mine, gently rubbing my thumb along her knuckles. "You're okay."

She searches my eyes, panicked tears falling down her cheeks. "I… I bloody choked, Creed."

I slide across the leather seat, pulling her against my chest. A sharp pain shoots through my bicep and shoulder, making me wince. I glance down at my coat, noticing a small hole with singed edges in the upper arm. Archie meets my gaze through the rearview mirror, concern creasing his brow. I subtly shake my head, telling him I'm fine.

Although, with every second that passes, the pain throbs more and more, especially now that the adrenaline has started to wear off.

"It doesn't matter how much you train for this kind of scenario. Or how many times you're told exactly what you need to do. When you're in the thick of it, all bets are off. There's no way of knowing how your brain will react." I pull back and tilt her chin, forcing her eyes toward mine. "And that's okay. That's not your job. It's mine. It's why I'm here. To protect you and keep you safe."

I rake my gaze over her face, cringing when I see the scrapes on her chin and bruising on her forehead. "Sorry to say I may have been a bit too exuberant. Do you have aches or pains anywhere else?"

"I don't... I don't think so."

I lean close to examine her pupils, not seeing any signs of them being dilated. "Can you take off your coat? We're on our way to the hospital now so a doctor can check you out, but I need to, as well." When I sense her hesitation, I add, "It's protocol."

"Of course." Her fingers tremble as she attempts to remove her coat. I help her, doing my best to keep any discomfort at bay.

In reality, it feels like dozens of knives are constantly slicing away at my skin. There's no doubt in my mind I've been shot. But I don't want Esme to worry about me. That's the last thing she needs right now.

Once her coat's removed, she meets my gaze. I do a visual inspection to make sure she doesn't have any injuries requiring immediate medical attention. Thankfully, she's free from any additional bleeding, apart from some bruises and scrapes on her knees.

I bring my hands toward her torso. "I need to make sure there aren't any internal injuries. Cracked ribs. Something like that. I tackled you pretty hard."

She nods, giving me permission, and I press against her ribs, trying to keep my hands as steady as possible. Focusing on her physical well-being instead of how my body reacts to the simple act of touching her.

"Any discomfort?"

"No," she responds, her voice husky and low.

"Good." I smile, but don't pull back. Not until the SUV slows to a stop in front of the hospital.

Hardening my expression, I look out the window and observe a team of doctors and nurses waiting for us.

But there are also several photographers and reporters.

Vultures.

I've always had a rather strained relationship with the media, especially after they camped outside of Rory's house in the weeks following Adam's death. She'd just lost the man she hoped to share a life with, the father of her unborn child. All they cared about was getting a clear shot of my brother's grieving girlfriend.

What I wouldn't give to ream them all out right now. Tell them Esme was less than a second away from arriving here in a damn body bag and to act like decent humans by allowing her time to process everything. Not shove a micro-phone in her face when she's still obviously shaken up.

Drawing in a deep breath to push down my increasing pain, I open the door and step out of the SUV, then extend my good arm toward Esme, helping her to her feet. The second she emerges, flashes light up the area, reporters shouting questions. Each time a flash goes off, she startles, as if it's a gun and not a camera.

A woman in scrubs pushes a wheelchair toward her, and I fully expect for Esme to claim she can walk just fine. Thankfully, she doesn't, probably because she's so rattled by all the commotion that she just wants to get somewhere peaceful.

The second she's situated in the chair, the nurse pushes her inside. Archie and I remain mere steps behind as the medical staff asks her questions. Some she's able to answer. Others I do for her.

After navigating the maze of corridors, the nurse brings her into a private room. I'm about to follow them and conduct a quick sweep, as is required, but Archie places his hand on my forearm.

"I got it."

Normally, I'd insist on doing it myself, but I'm struggling to remain upright, my head spinning. I lean against the wall outside of Esme's room and watch as Archie checks every inch of it.

When he's done, he steps back into the hallway and closes the door, standing guard in front of it to prevent anyone from going inside without being searched.

"You okay, mate?"

I clench my jaw, then carefully shrug out of my jacket, the sleeve of my black shirt sticky with blood.

"Fuck, Creed." Archie's concerned gaze focuses on my arm as I push my finger through the hole in my shirt.

"The bastard got me, Arch."

CHAPTER TWENTY-FIVE

Esme

"You'll need to change your dressings twice a day and clean them with soap and water," a nurse tells me after she finishes bandaging up the cuts on my face and knees.

It feels like overkill to have been subjected to various tests and scans for the past hour, considering most people wouldn't have the luxury of receiving this level of medical care.

But I'm not most people.

"You may also experience some discomfort, so be sure to keep ibuprofen on hand."

"Thank you."

"My pleasure, Your Highness." With a subtle curtsy, she retreats from the room, Archie stepping inside moments later.

Which surprises me.

While Archie is technically my CPO, that's not his role

on this trip. If anyone should stand guard outside my room it's Creed.

"How are you?" he asks softly, worried eyes scanning my frame.

My attempt at a smile feels unusually fake. "A little sore," I say evasively, not ready to admit that every time I blink, all I see is that damn gun. Every time I hear a door close, I jump, the sound reminding me of the gun going off.

It's probably natural after something like this. Once the shock wears off, I doubt I'll be so skittish. Right now, though, I'm still on high alert.

"That's a relief."

"Where's Cr—Captain Lawson?" I ask as I slide off the bed. "Considering he's been glued to my hip since the plane touched down, I would have thought he'd burst in here the second they told him he could."

Archie's expression instantly falls. "He…uh…"

I step toward him. "What is it, Archie?"

"Creed was… Well, he was shot."

My heart drops to the pit of my stomach, his words stealing my breath. "He *what*?" I place my hand on a nearby table, needing to steady myself against the sudden bout of vertigo consuming me. "Is he okay?"

He runs his fingers through his blond hair. "He's got a bit of a flesh wound."

"Where is he?" My chest squeezes, the shaking in my hands increasing as panic grips every inch of me.

It doesn't matter that Creed was upright when we arrived here an hour ago. He was bloody shot. There's no such thing as a harmless gunshot wound.

Archie opens his mouth to say something, probably tell me he has orders to take me straight back to the hotel while we await the royal household's decision on whether I'm to continue on this trip.

Then he sighs. "Come with me."

Archie places a hand on my elbow as he steers me out of the room, more of my protection team now lining the hallways. I want to ask if they caught the guy who tried to kill me, but I don't care about that right now. All I do care about is making sure Creed's okay. Until I see it with my own eyes, I won't believe it.

After leading me down a few more hallways, Archie brings me to a large room, the only privacy afforded the dozen or so patients a thin curtain between beds. Reaching one of the partitions, he pulls back the curtain and allows me to enter, but stays just outside, giving me some privacy.

The instant I step inside, I stop dead in my tracks. Not because of the gaping wound on Creed's left bicep.

But because he's not wearing a shirt.

And he has tattoos covering his upper chest and arms.

When I arrived back in Belmont and saw Creed for the first time in nine years, I knew he looked bigger. Bulkier.

Sexier.

But seeing just how much more defined his body is leaves me momentarily stunned.

Makes me briefly forget my reason for being here.

Until he looks up from his mobile, his eyes locking with mine.

I snap out of my thoughts and storm the few feet toward him, unsure whether to hug him because he's okay or yell at him for not telling me he was injured.

"You stubborn arse."

I wrap my arms around him, trying to ignore how warm and inviting his skin feels. How much my pulse increases when I inhale his familiar scent.

How much I still ache to feel him on every inch of me.

"Why the bloody hell didn't you tell me?" I quickly drop my hold on him and direct my attention to his wound, bile rising in my throat when I see how deep it is.

"You were my priority. What did the doc say? How are your injuries?"

"You're asking me about a few cuts when you've got a bullet lodged in your arm?"

"It's a flesh wound." He shrugs dismissively, as if he simply skinned his knee or stubbed his toe. "The bullet just grazed me, more or less. The only reason this is taking so long is because they needed to do x-rays to make sure it didn't nick the bone."

I glance at his arm again, the wound much deeper than anything I'd consider a "graze".

"Seriously, Creed." I drop my voice, fighting against the lump forming in my throat. "You should have told me."

"Like I said…"

"I know." I throw my hands up. "I'm your priority."

He nods, expression even. "You are. I will always put your well-being before mine." His stare bores into mine. "Always."

Something about the way he looks at me makes me think he's not simply saying this as a member of the royal guard and my temporary chief protection officer.

Instead, he's saying it as someone who cares about me. As someone who couldn't live with himself if anything happened to me.

I hadn't even stopped to think what Creed must be going through right now. What he's been going through since he noticed that guy aim his weapon at me. He didn't even hesitate in throwing himself on top of me, getting shot in the process. I understand it's his job. Still, I can't imagine the terror that must have gripped him when he saw my life was on the line. Unlike me, he didn't let it consume him. He acted as he was trained, even though he may have died in the process.

I'm not sure I've ever done anything to warrant such a sacrifice, apart from being born.

I clear my throat. "Any word on the shooter?"

"His name is Charles Thacker."

"Is he in custody?"

He adjusts his position on the bed, obviously in pain. I want to storm out of here and demand a doctor come treat him immediately. It seems patently unfair I've already been patched up for my minor scrapes and bruises when Creed's been sitting here, a gaping wound in his bicep, slicing a stunning tattoo of a knight chess piece in half.

"He was observed fleeing the scene on foot. Some of the team saw the car he got into and gave the plate information to the local authorities. His vehicle was located a few kilometers away at a park. When they approached the car, they saw blood staining the window." Creed swallows hard. "He'd taken his own life."

"Who is he? And why did—"

"He founded *The Modern Times*, an online news site that specializes in publishing more…controversial pieces. Ones most mainstream news sources wouldn't. He was also a staunch anti-monarchist. It is believed he'd been planning this. Several additional weapons were found in his car, as well as aerial maps of the various locations you'd be going this week, complete with potential motorcade routes, as well as the best places to attack."

He squeezes his eyes shut, lips pinching into a tight line, the veins in his neck throbbing. "When we changed plans, he used that to his advantage. He used my lack of adequate preparation to his advantage."

"Hey." I cover his hand on mine. "This is *not* your fault."

"The second I agreed to let you stay at that soup kitchen a moment longer than planned, I put your life at risk. So yes, Esme. It *is* my fault."

"Plans change all the time. And you know damn well nothing you said or did could have prevented me from staying."

"I could have refused. *Should* have refused. Should have picked you up and forced you into that SUV kicking and screaming if that's what it took. I promised the General of the Royal Guard I wouldn't allow our past to cloud my judgment. Yet that's precisely what I did. I allowed my feelings for you to—" he stops short, flinging his wide gaze to mine.

"You still have feelings for me?"

I don't know why this matters so much. It shouldn't. I'm with Tristan. But there's this part of me that needs to know I still possess even a sliver of Creed's heart.

Because he still possesses a huge part of mine.

Even if I wish he didn't.

He opens his mouth, his steely determination making me think he's about to tell me he doesn't have feelings for me. Not like I think. Not like I *want*.

Then he sighs, his expression softening with a vulnerability I haven't seen in a while. Perhaps since the night all those years ago when he begged me to stay with him. To run away and start a life.

When he told me he loved me.

My surroundings seem to disappear as I wait for his response. I no longer hear the constant beeping of nearby machines. No longer hear occasional announcements over the intercom. No longer hear nurses discussing various patients' treatment with each other. The only thing I do hear is the thrumming of my heart.

"I think no matter how much time passes, I will always have a weak spot for you. I will always have feelings for you. And that thought fucking terrifies me more than getting shot ever will."

"Why?" I lean closer, tension mounting between us.

But it's no longer strained.

It's fire.

It's electricity.

It's hunger.

He brings a hand to my face, cupping my cheek the way he once did.

I briefly close my eyes, basking in the feel of his skin on mine. His breath dancing on my lips. His nearness as I allow myself to be consumed by him once more.

"Because I don't—"

The sound of curtain rings scraping against the metal rod cuts through. Creed quickly drops his hold on me at the same time as I straighten.

"Okay, Captain Lawson." A petite blonde wearing blue scrubs and a white coat walks in, another woman in scrubs right behind her. "Let's get you all stitched up." She stops abruptly when she sees me, dropping into a curtsy. "Your Highness. I'm sorry. I didn't mean to interrupt. I—"

"Not at all."

I pull myself to my feet, pretending not to be disappointed by her interruption, if for no other reason than I'm desperate to find out what Creed was about to say.

I have a feeling the moment is officially lost. That I'll go the rest of my life not knowing what he was on the verge of confessing.

"I was just about to leave."

I start to turn when Creed darts his hand out, wrapping his fingers around my wrist. Electricity rushes through me, his touch causing an intense fluttering sensation to erupt in my stomach. I snap my gaze to his.

"Stay."

One word. One syllable. But that's all it takes to chip away at the wall I've erected around my heart over the past several years, especially in the last month.

He could just want me to stay because of everything that happened today. Or because he's still my temporary CPO and would feel better having me in his sight. I can only imagine how frustrated he must have been to leave Archie outside my door so he could get treatment for his wound.

The second we leave this hospital, Creed could very well return to the same brooding, aloof man he's been the past several days. Hell, the past several weeks. But he's not that man yet.

Right now, I see a glimpse of the old Creed.

My Creed.

And I really miss the Creed I knew before this life forced us to become the people we are.

So instead of keeping my distance, I lower myself back into the chair beside Creed's bed and link my fingers with his.

CHAPTER TWENTY-SIX

Esme

"Princess Esme! Princess Esme! How are you feeling?"

I do my best to look as composed as possible, offering a small smile to the reporters swarming the front entrance of the hotel. In reality, I'd give anything to tell them to shove off. But I don't. I do what I've been trained to do.

I smile. I wave. I pretend everything's okay, even though my body seizes every time I hear the click of a camera shutter. Every time a flash blinds my irises.

I feel like a sitting duck out here, but the royal household insisted I show my face. That I enter the hotel through the front as a way to demonstrate how resilient the monarchy is. That it can bounce back from any hindrance.

I should have known they'd use my near-death experience for their gain.

"I'm perfectly fine," I tell a group of reporters. "Just a few scrapes and bruises, thanks to the quick reflexes and bravery exhibited by the members of my protection team."

More shutters. More flashes.

And with each one, my balance grows more unsteady. I flinch a little harder. My breathing becomes increasingly labored.

Through it all, I grit a practiced smile, making eye contact with the various reporters, using every ounce of energy I possess to keep myself upright.

As I'm about to disappear into the hotel, I pause in my tracks, my gaze locking with the same man as before. The same man whose familiar eyes sent an icy chill down my spine.

The same man who aimed a gun at me in a crowd of people.

The same man who fired that gun and would have killed me if it weren't for Creed.

The same man who allegedly took his own life mere minutes after attempting to take mine.

Was Creed given bad information? Did they get the wrong guy?

I try to tell my legs to move, to put one in front of the other and run. Like earlier today, they refuse to take direction.

A surprised gasp erupts from the crowd as the man pulls out a gun and aims it at me.

Again.

And like before, I remain immobile until I'm tackled to the ground, a thunderous gunshot ringing through the air.

I don't move for several long moments, expecting to feel Creed's hands on my body as he lifts me to my feet.

But there's nothing.

I peek my head up, confused when the hotel has disappeared, along with Creed and everyone else. Instead, I'm in the back seat of a car, everything dark, apart from the full moon shining in the sky.

Feeling like I'm losing my mind, I take in my surroundings, hoping to figure out what the hell is going on. As I do, I notice a body slumped over the steering wheel, the front of the SUV smashed into a large tree as smoke billows from the engine.

I've been here before. This is eerily similar to the scene I woke up to after the crash that took Adam's life. But it can't be. He's dead. He's been dead for nine years.

Panic sets in and I reach for the handle, but the door won't open, no matter how hard I try.

That's when I hear it. The sound of liquid hitting the metal roof of the car, like a torrential downpour. But it's not rain. Rain doesn't smell like this.

I dart my eyes toward the window to see the same man from earlier watching with amusement. But this time, he's not holding a gun.

He's holding a match.

A smile curves his lips as he tosses it onto the ground, flames surrounding the car. I push against the door, to no avail. Smoke fills the compartment, the flames getting closer and closer. Sweat drips down my face and back, my lungs burning.

I scream for help as I continue kicking and pushing at the door, desperate for someone to hear me.

For anyone to hear me.

For anyone to *help* me.

But no one can.

I'm trapped in a prison of my own doing.

Defeated, I collapse onto the seat, wondering if this is how Adam felt in his final moments. I curl into a ball, staying as low as I can. Suddenly, someone calls my name. It's faint but clear. Not foggy like everything else.

I part my chapped lips to shout for help, but a coughing fit seizes me, making me dizzy and weak.

And tired.

So damn tired.

I try to tell myself to stay awake. To fight the darkness. To fight for myself.

"Esme."

I struggle to open my eyes, but they're glued together. Too heavy. Everything is so damn heavy.

"I'm here, Esme." The voice is panicked. Strained. "I've got you, princess."

I normally hate when people call me princess. But not this voice. I like when *this* voice calls me princess. Miss hearing this voice calling me princess.

"Creed," I croak out his name, reaching in the dark for him.

Is he even here? Or am I imagining it? Why can't I feel him? I want to feel him. Want his arms around me.

"It's just a dream. Try to fight it. Whatever you see isn't real. I swear to you it's not."

A hand brushes my face, pushing my sweat-drenched hair behind my ear, the voice becoming clearer still. Less cloudy. Less muted.

"I've got you. You're okay. You're dreaming. Tell yourself that. Tell yourself it's not real. Just focus on my voice. Because that's real. Nothing else is. Just me. Only me, princess."

With every assurance he gives me, the more the flames licking my skin subside, his words extinguishing the fire. My surroundings slowly disappear. No car. No man with a gun.

My body's no longer too exhausted to move, my eyelids no longer heavy.

I flutter them several times before opening them, Creed's concerned gaze staring back. I'm disoriented at first, wondering if this is a dream, too. I've lost count of the number of times I've dreamt of Creed over the years.

But when he lifts a hand to my face and cups my cheek, I can feel the warmth of his skin. Feel the callouses on his hand.

"Creed…"

"It's okay." He expels a long breath, shoulders falling. "You're okay."

I'm not sure if he says it for my benefit or his.

Maybe both.

"How… How are you here?" I manage to ask through my scratchy voice.

He pulls back, straightening. My eyes float to the bandage on his arm before raking down the rest of his frame. He's shirtless, clad only in a pair of gray sweatpants.

All these years later, and Creed Lawson in a pair of gray sweatpants still makes my pulse increase.

"I heard you calling for help. Thought…" He runs a hand over his face and shakes his head. "Thought someone had gotten to you. Almost didn't barge in after, well…" He smiles sheepishly before his expression sobers once more. "But when I heard you screaming, I knew it wasn't that, so I came in to help coax you out of it."

"You didn't just shake me awake?"

"You never wake up somebody in the middle of a night terror."

"Night terror?" I sit up, the duvet falling off me. I welcome the cool air, especially after my dream.

"It's common to experience them after enduring something traumatic." He pauses. "Do you want to talk about it?"

I lift my gaze to his and part my lips. Then I stand, walking toward my dresser and pulling out a fresh pair of pajama bottoms and t-shirt. Slipping into the bathroom, I run a cool washcloth over my face before changing. When I return to the bedroom, Creed's no longer sitting on the bed, but standing.

Renewed heat washes over me. This time, it's not because of my nightmare. Instead, it's because of how damn incredible he looks. Broad chest, defined muscles, and that delicious little V that disappears into his pants.

I shouldn't be thinking about him this way. Not when I just dreamed about my two near-death experiences, one of which involved his brother. I can't seem to control myself when he's around, though.

"I needed to change," I explain as I make my way back toward the bed, pulling the duvet up and sitting on it. Creed arches a brow, asking for permission to sit. I nod and he lowers himself onto the mattress, keeping his distance.

"So…do you want to talk about your dream?" he asks again. "Sometimes it helps."

Something in his expression and tone makes me think he's talking from experience. I can only imagine some of the shit he's seen during his time in the military. What I experienced today is most likely nothing compared to what he's been through.

I settle further into the bed, curling onto my side. "I was talking to reporters about…today. But he was there again."

"The shooter?"

I nod. "It felt so damn real, Creed. I was convinced it was happening again. That maybe you got wrong information and he didn't kill himself."

"Trust me." He reaches across the bed and grabs my hand in his. "I saw the photos. He's dead. His brain was splattered all over the window of his car. The car that was registered to him. The car dozens of eye witnesses saw him get into and flee the scene. I promise you, Esme. You're safe."

"I know. I just…" I push out a long breath, attempting to make sense of everything. "You know how dreams can be, your subconscious making you second-guess everything."

He gives me an understanding smile as he squeezes my hand. "I do."

I still struggle to wrap my mind around the fact that, mere days ago, I did everything I could to keep my distance from him.

Now, I never want him to leave my side. Want him as close as possible. Need him near just so I can feel safe again.

He clears his throat. "In your dream, did he…?"

I nod. "And you tackled me out of the way again. But when I hit the ground, the reporters and photographers were gone. I was somewhere else."

"Where?"

I worry my bottom lip, then say, "I was in the car. With Adam."

"Oh." He pulls his hand from mine as he looks into the distance, brow furrowed in concentration. "What happened?" His voice is hesitant, muscles taut.

I sit up and take a sip of water from the bottle on my nightstand before facing him. "I was trapped in the back seat. Heard the liquid as it hit the roof of the car. And then…" I pause, trying to steady my trembling voice. "Then I looked out the window and he was there."

"Adam?"

I shake my head. "The man with the gun. Charles

Thacker. But he wasn't holding a gun anymore. He was holding a match. I was fighting to get out of the car but couldn't. That's when I heard your voice."

"It's okay." Creed grabs my hand and runs his thumb over my knuckles. "Although it can feel real when you're in it, it was just a dream. Charles Thacker wasn't responsible for that fire. Hayes Barlow was."

I'm about to raise the same concerns I've been having lately, but hesitate.

What am I supposed to tell him? That, despite the mountains of physical evidence tying Hayes Barlow to the attack that took Adam's life, I'm starting to question whether it was him simply because of some crazy dream I had?

Because of a feeling in my gut?

I doubt that would withstand muster in a court of law. But the compelling physical evidence uncovered in Hayes Barlow's possession all those years ago certainly would.

Why can't I be satisfied with that?

Why am I questioning everything now?

"You're right," I finally say. "It was just a dream."

He studies me for a beat, obviously sensing I'm not being entirely forthcoming. But instead of pressing the issue, he stands. "You should get some sleep."

My heart drops at the idea of being alone. Of him being in another room if the nightmare finds me again. Of him not getting to me in time.

I know it's just a dream. That it's not real.

But during those terrifying minutes, it *feels* real. I don't want to go through that alone. Not right now. Not when I'm feeling more vulnerable than I have in years.

Not when I can't shake the feeling there's more to my dreams than Creed wants me to believe.

Than *I* want to believe, too.

"Can you stay?" I ask with a subtle tremble.

"Esme," he exhales, turmoil swirling in his deep, penetrating eyes. I can physically feel his hesitation. His reluctance. His rejection.

He *should* reject me. Should tell me he'll check in on me but can't stay.

"Please. I just… I don't want to be alone right now, Creed."

He closes his eyes as he heaves a drawn-out sigh. When he returns his gaze to mine, he parts his lips, but his response seems caught in his throat. Finally, he nods.

"Okay."

Treating me to a soft smile, he turns from me and heads toward the living room of my suite. Seconds later, he returns with the extra blanket from the closet and drapes it over me before stepping around to the other side of the bed, the mattress dipping slightly as he lays down.

Reaching for the lamp, he turns it off, shrouding us in darkness, the only light coming from the bathroom. He shifts onto his side, facing me so he's not lying on his wound, then closes his eyes.

Not wanting to fall asleep without something anchoring me to the real world, I extend my arm and grab his hand.

He flings his gaze open, stare fixated on our joined hands. I brace for him to pull away. Remind me of who we are to each other.

He doesn't, though. Instead, he links his fingers with mine, thumb brushing against my knuckles.

"Sweet dreams, princess."

CHAPTER TWENTY-SEVEN

Esme

I flutter my eyes open what feels like only minutes after falling asleep, but based on the bright light streaming into the hotel room, it's been much longer. Hours probably. I don't even remember falling asleep. I didn't want to. Not because I was worried about more nightmares.

But because I didn't want to miss a second of feeling Creed's skin on mine.

Now as I take in my surroundings, there's no sign of him. His side of the bed is empty, the duvet pulled tight, hiding any indentation. He even fluffed the pillow, making it look like he was never here.

Maybe he wasn't. Maybe I dreamt him, too.

I grab my mobile off the nightstand to see it's already after eight. The last thing I want is to leave this bed and face reality, including the media. But I can't hide forever.

I'm about to slide out of bed and head into the shower when my phone buzzes in my hand. Hope flickers inside me that it's Creed. Instead, it's a text from Anders checking to see how I'm doing.

The second he learned what had happened, he was beside himself. I assured him I was fine and would be home today, since the royal household made the decision to cut my trip short. I didn't argue with them. After yesterday, I welcome the opportunity to deal with this out of the public eye.

I type out a quick response, letting him know I'm a little sore, but otherwise doing well. I consider mentioning my dream to him, but don't, not wanting to worry him more than he already is. Just as I click send, the door to the bedroom opens, the unexpected intrusion causing me to startle, my heart ricocheting into my throat.

Am I always going to react this way? Jumping at every sudden movement or loud noise?

"Shit. Sorry." Creed comes to an abrupt stop when he sees my wide, panicked eyes and stiff posture. "I didn't mean to frighten you. I hoped to sneak back in before you woke up."

Drawing in a deep breath to settle my nerves, I stand and pad across the room toward him. He no longer wears a pair of gray sweatpants. Instead, he's dressed in his typical attire when on a protection detail — black suit tailored to his tall frame, his pants perfectly creased. His hair is still damp and nowhere near as disheveled as it was last night.

"Is everything okay?" I ask, refusing to allow my eyes to linger on his body.

"Of course. I ran out to get some coffee. And a few French pastries from the bakery around the corner." He holds up a bag, the aroma of butter and sugar wafting in the air.

My stomach instantly rumbles, begging for food. I can't

remember the last time I ate. Probably yesterday during breakfast. I was too on edge to eat anything substantial for dinner last night.

"Come on, princess," Creed says with a wink, making his way to the living room, lowering himself onto the couch. He sets the coffees and bag of pastries on the table in front of us. "Let's eat."

I should tell him not to call me princess, but I've missed hearing his raspy voice murmur it into my ear.

I join him, purposefully keeping some space between us. Creed places one of the cups in front of me.

"Hope you still take your coffee the same way."

"I do." I bring it to my lips and take a sip. I close my eyes, savoring that first taste. When I open them again, Creed's studying me intently. He quickly looks away, clearing his throat as he digs through the bag to show me the various pastries he selected.

Which makes my stomach growl even more. They all look incredible. Much better than my typical breakfast of fruit and yogurt. After yesterday, I deserve to treat myself. Deserve some comfort food.

And there's nothing more comforting than buttery, flaky pastries.

"How are you feeling today?" Creed asks after I've had a chance to indulge in a few of the pastries, including my favorite guilty pleasure — cream puffs.

"Shouldn't I be the one asking you that?" I glance at his arm.

"I'm not talking about physically, Esme. I'm talking about up here." He taps the side of his head. "In my experience, the physical wounds are the easiest to heal. It's the mental ones that take a bit of time. So... How are you?"

I pull my lips between my teeth, debating what to tell

him. Do I tell him I still can't stop thinking about my nightmare? I know it was just a dream. But it felt so real.

Too real.

It makes me wonder if it *is* real. If my subconscious has been protecting me from the truth of the night Adam died, and seeing that man point a gun at me removed whatever block I've had the past nine years.

"What is it?" Creed presses when I don't immediately respond.

"What do you mean?" I reply dismissively, taking a long sip of my coffee.

He narrows his gaze on me. "I know you, Esme." A shy smile tugs on his lips. "Probably better than I wish at times. I can see the wheels turning in that brain of yours."

"It's just…"

I shake my head and gaze out the window as I attempt to formulate my thoughts. Try to figure out how to bring this up with Creed, considering he lost his brother in the car accident I'm questioning more with every day.

"Do you wonder if they got the right guy?"

"I told you last night. A dozen eyewitnesses saw him getting into a vehicle registered to Charles Thacker. The deceased man found in the vehicle matched the shooter's description."

"I'm not talking about yesterday." I set my coffee cup back on the table and smooth my hands down my pajama pants. "I'm talking about Hayes Barlow."

"Oh." He sinks into the couch, shoulders dropping.

"Have you ever wondered if he's really the one who did it?"

He's quiet, his Adam's apple working in a hard swallow, his expression tightening in deep concentration. I've always loved this look on him. Loved watching his mind work as he debates a course of action. So intense. Determined. Steady.

Finally, he shifts his gaze back to mine. "It's kind of difficult to question heaps of conclusive evidence. His car was seen following the SUV Adam was driving. White gas canisters were found in his trunk. The clothes they found thrown in a trash bin at his house had traces of accelerant and reeked of smoke. Not to mention his car exhibited signs it had recently been involved in a collision. Paint transfer evidence was found on both vehicles — his *and* Adam's."

"I understand that." I pause. "But what if there wasn't any physical evidence? If we were just basing this on motive, means, and opportunity—"

"Did I miss hearing about your degree in criminal justice or forensic psychology?" He flashes a smile, and it takes everything I possess not to melt into the couch.

I love that smile. The slight lifting of the corners of his lips. The sparkle in his eyes. The way he looks at me and makes me think he's smiling for only me.

"I just have a bit of an affinity for true crime documentaries," I tell him with a small shrug. "I've always found it fascinating to learn *why* someone would act a certain way. Like Hayes Barlow. If you look at his background, he had a clean criminal record. Not so much as a parking ticket until Callie Sloane went missing. At that point, he was arrested for a misdemeanor breach of peace when he begged a local cop to investigate her disappearance, but he refused. I don't know. I just…" Shaking my head, I blow out a long breath. "Based on everything I've read about him, he doesn't seem the type."

"You never know what might push someone over the edge. Losing his sponsorships could have been his tipping point."

"But what if it wasn't? What if——"

"Is this because of your dream last night?"

I snap my mouth shut, then nod subtly.

"Esme," he exhales, angling toward me. "I've been where you are. Been through something that completely flipped the balance of my life. For months, I was forced to relive… certain events nightly. And like you, the dreams twisted reality to the point that I wasn't sure what was real and what was simply my imagination playing tricks on me. That's all this is. *Your* mind playing tricks on you." He brings his hands to my face, forcing my eyes to his.

"In the past decade, you've almost died twice. If you ask me, that's two times too many. Still, your subconscious has linked those two traumatic events together when, in reality, they're two isolated events. As much as I try not to think about it, you're an extremely high-profile target. As is your brother. While we try to do everything in our power to dispense with any and all threats to your safety before it becomes a reality, I failed you yesterday."

"You didn't fail me, Creed."

"Yes, I did," he interjects gruffly, determination in his voice. "I'd never be able to live with myself if I lost you." He briefly closes his eyes and shakes his head, as if to ward off the regret flooding his features. "If he were a hair faster on that trigger, he…" His voice catches, emotion clogging his throat.

"But he wasn't." I lean in and the warmth of his breath wafts over my mouth, giving me a taste of the sweet mixture of coffee and sugar. I should retreat, rebuild that wall between us once more.

I don't think I can. Not anymore. Not after yesterday. And last night.

I need Creed in my life. Need to feel safe when I fear I never will again.

Creed's the only person who's ever made me feel that way.

"You made sure of that," I continue. "You kept me safe."

"I'll always keep you safe, Esme," he murmurs. "Always." He moves closer until there's barely any space between us.

Fire heats my veins, anticipation coiling inside me as I brace myself to feel his lips again. To lose myself in everything he's always been to me.

The seconds tick by, neither one of us making a move to cross the last whisper separating us. Our breathing increases, my quickening pulse thundering in my ears. His grip on my face tightens, and I whimper as his mouth skims mine, igniting the flames that have lain dormant for the past decade.

Until a loud chiming cuts through the room, shattering the moment and ripping us back to reality.

Creed jumps to his feet, pulling his mobile from the inside pocket of his jacket. He winces, the quick motion causing some discomfort.

"I have to take this," he says after glancing at his screen, voice lacking any warmth.

I tighten my lips into a forced smile. "Of course."

With purposeful movements, he strides toward the door and opens it.

Before he slips into the hallway, he pauses, eyes meeting mine. I search his expression for even a hint of the desire that flooded his gaze mere moments ago.

But it's gone, making me wonder if I imagined that, too.

"Wheels up is scheduled for ten, so we'll be leaving here in about an hour," he clips out.

"I'll be ready."

He nods curtly, then disappears into the hallway.

The second the door closes, I fall against the couch, exhaling deeply.

I shouldn't be upset the phone rang. If anything, I should be grateful, considering we were about to do something we shouldn't.

Something I'd soon regret.

I have a boyfriend, for crying out loud.

Granted, I haven't heard from Tristan since the other night. I texted him yesterday but didn't go into any details. Just let him know I was okay and to call when he has a chance so I can fill him in on what happened.

But he never called.

That's still no excuse for almost kissing another man.

And not just any other man. But the one man I swore I'd never kiss again.

It's probably just a result of him risking his life to save mine. Some sort of rescue-savior syndrome.

That's all.

I refuse to believe I almost kissed him because of any other reason.

There *is* no other reason.

There can't be.

CHAPTER TWENTY-EIGHT

Creed

The tension's back.

I should be relieved. Should welcome it.

Instead, as I continually glance in Esme's direction during the short flight home, I can't help but long for the way things were between us yesterday.

And last night.

And earlier this morning when I nearly kissed her.

If my mobile didn't ring, there's no doubt in my mind I would have, despite the promise I made Anderson not to do anything that could interfere with the happiness she found with Tristan.

But the more time I spend with Esme, the more I question whether she actually *is* happy.

I think she's just trying to make everyone believe she is, including her brother.

Maybe even herself.

When we finally land back in Montrose, I glance out the

window, dozens of reporters and photographers at the airport to cover Esme's return after nearly being killed.

"What's the plan?" I ask Esme's private secretary, the cabin buzzing with activity now that we're on the ground.

"Get her into the car and home. No bloody publicity stunts."

"Good." I stand, buttoning my suit jacket, and head down the aisle toward Esme. "Ma'am," I begin, pulling her attention away from the window.

"Captain."

I fight the urge to grimace at the formality in her tone. I remind myself it's for the best, though.

"We're going straight from the plane into the SUV. No stopping to entertain the press."

She blows out a small breath, a crack in the armor she's worn all morning. "Good."

I nod, about to retreat, but pause. "Will you be okay?" I drop my voice. "With the camera shutters and flashes? Will it—"

She holds her head high as she rises to her feet, turning into the woman the royal household molded her into years ago.

"I'm perfectly capable of navigating the steps of a plane with the media present, Captain. I've been doing it my entire life."

I'm about to remind her she hasn't done it after nearly being shot, but she pushes past me, stalking toward the open door of the plane before I have a chance to voice my concerns.

I share a look with Archie, the only other person I informed about her nightmare last night.

At least the part where she dreamt about getting shot again. I didn't mention she also dreamt about being in the burning car with Adam. Or that she thought her shooter might be the same person who lit Adam's car on fire. It was just a dream. We caught the guy who killed Adam.

And the man who attempted to kill Esme.

They're two different people.

"She okay?"

"Claims she is," I tell Archie. "But I'm going to stay closer than usual, just in case. You'll sweep the crowd so I can keep her in my sights?"

"Of course."

"Thanks, mate."

"You bet."

I head toward the front of the plane, giving Esme a small nod to go ahead.

She faces the door and steps onto the stairs, bright lights flashing from dozens of cameras. Reporters push forward, shouting her name. Asking about her injuries. If she's healing.

As she glides down the stairs, she maintains her composure, but I make sure to stay only a step or two behind her instead of allowing her to walk down on her own, as is typically the case.

She's halfway down the stairs when I first notice her flinch, her body stiffening, shoulders becoming tense. It's subtle, and lasts less than a second before she continues, but I can tell every second is a hard-fought battle. As the flashes and camera shutters become more incessant, she grips the railing for support, her knuckles turning white.

I move toward her, touching my hand to her elbow. When I do, she whips her eyes to mine, panic swirling within like a stormy ocean.

"Just look at me. I got you."

I can see how much she wants to break down, curl into a

ball and make it all go away. But she can't. Or maybe she won't. Won't admit she's struggling with what she endured yesterday.

Just like I can all but guarantee she refused to admit she struggled in the aftermath of Adam's death.

Not taking my hand off her as we navigate the rest of the stairs, I lead her toward the waiting SUV, doing my best to shield her from any flashes. Once we reach the car, I help her into the back seat before jumping behind the wheel. The second Archie slides into the passenger seat, I peel away, the photographers and reporters now nothing but specks in the distance.

It's silent for several minutes, but I keep looking into my rearview mirror to check on Esme. Her eyes are focused outside, her shoulders rising and falling as she attempts to control her breathing.

It's probably the only thing she feels she *can* control right now.

"Five things you see," I say, cutting through the silence.

She tears her gaze from the window, looking forward. "What?"

"Don't get stuck in your head. That's the worst thing for you right now. Believe me."

While our situations are vastly different, I've been in Esme's shoes more times than I can count. I know how much narrowly escaping death can fuck with your mind. You think of all the *what-if* scenarios. You get stuck in that split second when you stared down that barrel.

Some people never find the strength to move on from that moment, allowing it to torture them for the rest of their lives.

I refuse to let Esme fall victim to that.

"Fine." I adjust my hands on the steering wheel. "I'll start."

I scan my surroundings, unsure if Esme will play this game with Archie in the car. But he's her CPO. I'd be surprised if he didn't already know about her occasional bouts of anxiety. If anything, this will give him a tool he can use when he notices she's having a rough time.

"The snowcapped mountains in the distance. Now you go."

She doesn't say anything right away, but I can feel the heat of her stare on me as she deliberates.

"The steeple of the National Cathedral," Archie states after a few beats.

"Good one, Arch." I flash him an appreciative smile before glancing in the rearview mirror once more, the reluctance slowly waning from her expression.

Finally, she sighs. "A few rays of sun trying to peek through the gray clouds. A couple holding hands as they walk along the canals. My favorite café."

"Now four things you can feel."

She closes her eyes and draws in a deep breath. "My wool coat. The heels on my feet I can't wait to take off the second I'm home."

A low chuckle rumbles from my chest.

While Esme may exude more glamour and class than anyone I've ever met, making it appear as if she can walk effortlessly in her heels, I know how much she hates them. During that summer all those years ago, I lost count of the number of times I walked into her office to find her barefoot, her heels hidden under her desk.

I loved that about her.

Still do.

Love that she prefers to walk around her apartment in

yoga pants and an oversized t-shirt than any of the designer clothes she owns.

"What else?" I press.

She closes her eyes again, covering her chest with her hand. "The beating of my heart, reminding me I'm still alive. And…" She licks her lips.

"Go on," I encourage her.

She opens her eyes, meeting my gaze through the rearview mirror. "Safety."

"You feel safe?"

I pull to a stop outside the gates of Gladwell Palace, waving to the guard, even more photographers and reporters lining the entrance. Thankfully, I prepared for this scenario and had additional guards stationed here to keep them contained.

"With you, I do," she confesses as the gate opens, then quickly adds, "And Archie, of course."

"Of course," I meet her gaze through the mirror, able to sense she only said that as to not raise suspicion.

I have no doubt Archie will always do everything he can to keep her safe. But there's a difference between being around someone who will keep you safe and someone who makes you *feel* safe.

Refocusing my eyes forward, I navigate the short path up to her apartment and come to a stop under the port cochère, her butler hurrying down the steps and toward the SUV.

A part of me doesn't want to get out of this car. Not when it means my obligation to her will be over. I hate the idea of things going back to the way they were before this trip.

When I first boarded the plane, I wanted nothing more than to be released from my duty to her. Now that I am, I'd love nothing more than to return to our bubble from last night.

But as I've reminded myself since we nearly kissed this morning, this is for the best. I need to remember my place.

And it's not here.

Opening the door, I join Esme as her butler helps her out of the SUV. Then we follow him up the short flight of steps to her apartment, stepping into the high-ceilinged foyer, her apartment to the right, Anderson's old apartment to the left, which currently sits vacant now that he's moved to Wintervale.

"I'll check everything out," I tell Archie. "That way, you can review the new security measures."

"New security measures?" Esme asks. "And why do you have to check the apartment when my household staff has been here the entire time I was gone?"

"It's standard procedure," I answer as I cross the threshold, keeping my eyes peeled for anything suspicious. "Especially after—"

"Got it," she interrupts.

I give her a reassuring smile, then head into her apartment, checking every room for any vulnerabilities, trying to push down the memories her apartment brings forward, especially when I walk into her bedroom and am instantly reminded of the night I took her virginity.

It was the only time I ever shared her bed, regardless of the fact she kicked me out immediately after, not wanting any of her staff to find out what we'd done.

Now as I check her bedroom, all I can think about is the fact that Tristan gets to share this space with her. Has made love to her in this very bed.

Not wanting to be here any longer than necessary, I run

through the rest of my checks as quickly as possible, leaving the office for last.

And for good reason.

After all, it was where Esme and I usually met.

When I open the double doors and step inside, it's like no time at all has passed, the familiar scent of fresh linen and lavender invading my senses. I can almost see the ghost of Esme sauntering up to me, wrapping her arms around me and kissing me, murmuring that she's not wearing any knickers.

The things we did in this room, the pleasure and love I felt, it's too much to bear.

Satisfied there's nothing suspicious in her apartment, I make my way back to the living room, finding Esme staring into space as Archie briefs her butler about the necessary changes.

When I approach her, she snaps out of her daze. "You're all clear," I tell her.

"Thank you."

"Just doing my job."

"I don't mean checking my apartment for any potential threats." She steps toward me, dropping her voice to little more than a whisper. "I'm talking about being here for me. It's nice to be able to talk to someone who understands."

"You can always talk to me." I meet her eyes, my expression softening. "Don't try to go through it alone. If things get bad, pick up the phone, no matter the hour. Okay?"

I may regret this decision later, but the only thing that helped me in my darkest moments was being able to talk to someone who understood. I want to give Esme the same thing.

"Thank you."

"If you'd like," I begin, but am interrupted when heavy footfalls sound from the foyer.

We all glance toward the doorway just as Tristan Hughes appears.

His panicked gaze scans the room, his worry turning to relief the instant his eyes land on Esme.

"Tristan?" She increases her distance from me. "What are you…"

He rushes toward her and draws her into his embrace before she can finish her question. "A madman pulls a gun on you and you don't think I'd drop everything to be with you?" He cups her cheeks, his grip on her tight. "My god, Esme. I was fucking worried."

I look to the floor as I take measured breaths, willing myself to stay calm.

"I'm fine," she assures him as she pushes out of his hold, floating her gaze toward mine. "Captain Lawson was hurt worse than me."

Tristan looks my way, as if noticing me for the first time. He strides toward me and places his hand on my arm and squeezes.

Where I was shot.

I wince, backing away.

"Sorry. Forgot you were shot."

I push out an aggravated laugh, rubbing my bicep. "That makes one of us."

"Right. Well, thanks for taking care of my girl. Risking your life for her."

"No thanks required," I tell him. "It's my job."

"I know. I just…" He pulls his lips together, shaking his head. "If you didn't respond as quickly…" He squeezes his eyes shut.

He may be an actor, but it's obvious how distraught he is over the entire situation.

Over the thought of losing Esme.

"I hate to think what could have happened." He wraps an arm around her waist and pulls her close, kissing the top of her head.

When he does, she flinches. Like she doesn't want him to touch her.

Or maybe she just doesn't want him to touch her while I'm here.

"There's no need to worry about her," Archie cuts through the mounting tension. "Her protection team is the best of the best."

"Exactly," I add, then look toward Esme. "If you don't need anything else, I'll head out."

"Of course." She forces a smile. "I'm sure your family will be happy to see you."

I nod, looking toward Tristan. "Mr. Hughes."

He extends his hand and we briefly shake before I bow toward Esme. "Your Highness."

"Captain."

I skirt past them and walk toward the door.

Just as I'm about to step into the foyer, I pause, some outside force urging me to look back at Esme.

When I do, her gaze meets mine, a hint of longing within, before she quickly snaps her attention back to Tristan.

Where it belongs.

CHAPTER TWENTY-NINE

Creed

"Oh, thank God," Rory exhales the second I step into the house, rushing from the kitchen island to greet me.

The plates on the counter are full of cookies, a telltale sign she spent the morning stress-baking, as she's prone to do.

Without hesitation, she wraps her arms around me and presses her lips against mine in an unexpected display of affection.

I momentarily freeze.

Our physical relationship is typically limited to the bedroom. It doesn't bleed into the rest of our lives. It's compartmentalized.

Not today.

"I'm fine," I assure her, pulling out of her embrace. "I told you I was when I called."

"I know." She wipes at her cheeks. "It just… It rekindled some memories. That's all."

I squeeze my eyes shut, silently cursing myself. Of course it would. It brought back memories for Esme. Why didn't I stop to think it would do the same for Rory?

Probably because I barely gave her a moment's thought since I left on this trip.

"I'm sorry, Rory."

"You have nothing to apologize for. This is the job. I knew that when I met your brother." She draws in several shaky breaths before attempting a smile. "Now that you're home safe, I'm going to get out of here. Hit up the gym before picking up AJ from school."

"Do you want me to grab him?"

"It's okay. I'll do it. You need to rest. And heal." She runs her hand along my arm, sucking in her bottom lip to hide the quiver in her chin.

Then she turns from me and slings her gym bag over her shoulder on her way out of the house.

Once I'm alone, I shrug out of my suit jacket and fold it over the back of one of the barstools by the kitchen island. I loosen my tie and unfasten the top button of my shirt, kicking off my shoes as I trudge upstairs to decompress after the last few days.

And take a painkiller now that I'm no longer on the clock.

But as I'm about to slip inside my room, my eyes float to the door to Adam's office. No one's stepped foot inside it in years. Not after Rory had a meltdown when I tried to surprise her by hiring cleaners to help around the house, and she saw them walk into Adam's office. After that, it became an unspoken understanding that the door was to remain closed.

I never questioned it. And we never spoke about it again.

Truthfully, I had no desire to surround myself with memories of how I treated my brother the last time we spoke. All I wanted was to put the past behind me and move forward.

But I can't stop thinking about Esme's dream.

I tell myself it was only a dream. Hayes Barlow is responsible for Adam's death. Charles Thacker attempted to kill Esme. Both traumatic, but completely isolated events.

That doesn't quiet the voice in the back of my mind, though.

So instead of continuing into my room, I approach the door and place my hand on the knob.

When I open it, a strange eeriness washes over me. While the rest of the house has been updated, this room hasn't. It's frozen in time. In the moment of Adam's death.

Dust swirls around me, the sliver of sun coming in through the blinds illuminating it. A mustiness clings to the air from years of neglect, a coffee cup still on the desk with a few stains along the rim.

I push down the lump forming in my throat from all the memories being in here brings forward. Especially when I see the framed photo of the two of us as kids placed prominently on the filing cabinet.

Further proof of the love he had for his family.

For me.

Despite wanting to leave and never step foot in this place again, I continue farther inside, albeit with laden feet, and lower myself into the chair behind his desk. His laptop sits on the surface, sticky notes with his barely legible scrawl beside it. Reminders of Rory's prenatal appointments. A few measurements, probably for the nursery they were in the middle of renovating that I finished. Then a list of dates.

I furrow my brow, trying to figure out the significance of them. Birthdays or anniversaries, perhaps?

But none of them seem familiar.

Could it be related to Hayes Barlow? Adam *was* looking into him in the days before his death.

Or am I hoping to see something that's not there?

I know what the physical evidence says. And every single piece of physical evidence uncovered points emphatically to Hayes Barlow having forced the SUV off the road and setting it on fire, leaving both my brother and Esme to die.

But what if the police got it wrong?

Sighing, I relax into the chair, squeezing the bridge of my nose, a tension headache starting to throb behind my eyes. If there was ever a time I wished Adam were still alive, it's now. He was always practical. Always had a knack for seeing the truth through a mountain of lies.

Hell, he figured out the truth of what was going on between Esme and me. Granted, we were pretty careless toward the end, but he picked up on my attraction to her before we started sleeping together.

"What do you think I should do?" I ask, as if Adam were right next to me. "Do I listen to reason? Or do I follow my gut, regardless of how ridiculous it may be?"

The second the words leave me, I know exactly what he'd say. He'd remind me how easy it is to manipulate physical evidence. But one thing that can't be manipulated is your instinct, your gut. Too many people don't listen to their instincts, often to their own detriment.

And right now, my instinct is telling me there's more to Adam's death than just some race car driver being pissed off about losing his sponsorships. But if Hayes isn't responsible, who is?

I stand and begin pacing Adam's office, rewinding to those few weeks leading up to his death.

And the few weeks following it.

I make a mental list of everything that happened, starting with Hayes Barlow accusing Jameson Gates of murdering Callie Sloan at a public event. Hayes Barlow running Adam off the road and lighting his SUV on fire, killing him. Being sworn into the royal guard earlier than planned. Esme breaking off her fake engagement to Jameson Gates and moving to Paris for culinary school. Learning Gianna, the former head of palace PR, was mugged and killed by a homeless man. Then learning a boat registered to Hayes Barlow washed up on the shores of Norway, the extreme amount of blood evidence coupled with bullet holes indicating he was most likely attacked by traffickers known to use the waterways as transportation routes.

Is there a connection between Adam's and Hayes' deaths, as well as Callie Sloan's disappearance? Maybe even Gianna's death, too? The only thing they have in common is Jameson Gates. But that connection seems tenuous.

As I debate if there's a dark side to Jameson Gates, like Hayes Barlow tried to convince the world, a book on the shelf catches my attention.

Most people wouldn't think twice about it. Would just figure Adam saved a history textbook from his grade school days.

But I know my brother. He used to hide things in this book so Dad wouldn't find them — condoms, cigarettes, and folded up notes from girls with their phone numbers.

My gut says that's not what he's hiding now.

Heading across his office, I place my finger on the thick hardcover binding and pull it from the shelf. It's relatively light, compared to how heavy a textbook like this *should* be. But that's because he hollowed out the inside of the book.

But unlike all those years ago, there are no condoms. No cigarettes. No love letters from whoever his secret admirer of the week was.

There's an envelope.

I step toward the window and peek through the blinds to confirm Rory's still gone. When I see my SUV is the only vehicle in the driveway, I return to Adam's desk, my heart rate slowly increasing as I stare at the envelope.

It could be nothing. Could simply be a rough copy of his vows for when he and Rory were finally married.

I don't think that's what I'll find, though. He hid it in this book for a reason.

A part of me wonders if he did so in the hopes I'd eventually find it, since I was more than aware of what he used this book for when he was a teenager.

With trembling fingers, I open the envelope and pull out a handful of papers, initially confused at what I see.

There are photocopies of various IDs. Passport. Social security card. Driver's license. All with the name Dylan Knox.

But all bearing the photo of Hayes Barlow.

Did he have a different identity? Is this what my brother found that led to his death? Did he uncover something Hayes didn't want him to?

I grab my phone and type Dylan Knox into the search engine. As expected, I get thousands of hits, many with photos. But none bear any resemblance to Hayes Barlow.

What am I thinking? Of course they wouldn't. Hayes Barlow is dead. His body may never have been found, but according to the forensic report, no one could have survived losing the amount of blood found on Hayes' boat when it washed ashore. And it *was* his blood. DNA doesn't lie.

Finding these documents doesn't prove anything. It certainly doesn't prove Hayes' innocence. If anything, it confirms Adam had information Hayes didn't like. Information he was willing to kill over.

Blowing out a breath, I pull myself to my feet and return the envelope to the book.

Just like I need to keep what happened between Esme and me in the past, I need to keep Adam's death in the past. Reopening these old wounds won't help anything.

I need to move on. For Rory. For Adam.

And for me.

CHAPTER THIRTY

Esme

"Excuse me, Your Highness." My butler pops his head into the living area of my private suite later that afternoon as I lounge on the couch with Tristan.

While I'm happy he's here, I'm starting to feel suffocated. Every few seconds, he asks how I'm doing. If I need anything. Tells me how worried he was about me. How agonizing the flight here was.

His heart's in the right place. I have no doubt I'd feel the same way if our roles were reversed. I just want five minutes without being reminded of the fact I was seconds away from death.

I just want life to go back to the way it was before.

I fear that's no longer possible.

"Yes, Frederick?"

"His Highness Prince Gabriel is here to see you."

Closing the book I've been reading, I slowly push to my feet. "Can you prepare tea for us in the garden room?"

"Certainly, ma'am." He bows, then disappears into the hallway.

"I won't be too long," I tell Tristan as he's about to stand.

"You don't want me to come?"

"He just finished up intensive steroid treatment and I want to be able to talk to him about how he's doing. I know you get along with my brother, but I worry—"

"He won't be as forthcoming if there's a third wheel, so to speak."

"I'm sorry." I smile sheepishly, hoping he doesn't pick up on the fact that *I'm* the one who doesn't want a third wheel so I can talk freely with my brother.

"Don't be." Standing, he pulls me into his arms and places a soft kiss on my forehead. "I understand. Just don't be gone too long."

"I won't," I promise, then slip out of my suite, grateful to have a brief reprieve from him.

I've never felt this way. I've always craved his presence.

I tell myself it's natural to be a little off after the past few days. That the fact I haven't been able to stop thinking about Creed since I watched him walk out of my apartment is simply because he saved my life. Because he was there for me when I needed him the most.

When I step into the garden room, Anderson rushes toward me, crushing my body against his.

"I've never been so happy to see you before," he whispers through the audible lump in his throat.

"I'm happy to see you, too," I tell him as I bask in his warmth.

"All I can think is that should have been me."

"I don't think it would have been," I say before I can stop the words from falling from my mouth.

Pulling back, he tilts his head, giving me a quizzical look.

All things considered, he looks pretty good. A lot less rundown than I was expecting, especially since he spent the past several days in the hospital. Maybe that's a good thing, though. Maybe it means he's responding to this course of steroid treatment better.

"What do you mean?"

On a long sigh, I head toward the small table by the floor-to-ceiling windows, Anderson following close behind.

Normally, I'd be able to look outside and see the vibrant colors of the courtyard gardens, the flowers in full bloom. This time of year, everything's gone to sleep for the winter, the shrubs and lawn sporting a fresh dusting of snow.

The second we're seated, my butler re-emerges with a tray. He sets a teapot in the center of the table, along with a platter containing various cakes and cookies. He pours my tea first, preparing it how I like it, then does the same for Anderson.

"Is there anything else I can get you, ma'am?"

"That'll be all."

"Certainly." He bows toward us, then retreats, closing the door behind him.

"You don't think that guy was targeting you specifically, do you?" Anderson presses once we're alone. "The police claim it was political, since the guy was a staunch anti-monarchist."

"I know all that." I take a sip of my tea before returning the cup to its saucer. "But he looked familiar, Anders. Not because he was a photographer. It was something else. And then last night…"

"Yes?" He leans closer, not touching his tea.

I tap my nails against the tablecloth as I attempt to collect my thoughts. "I dreamt of him shooting me."

"Dreaming about a traumatic experience is common. After time, it—"

"And also the fire."

"Oh." His postures slumps.

"Charles Thacker, the shooter, was there, too. He was standing right outside the SUV. He lit a match and set the car on fire."

"Ezzy…"

I hold up my hand. "I know it was just a dream. But what if it wasn't? What if that's why this guy was so familiar to me? What if I saw him outside the car that night, but my brain forgot until I was face-to-face with a reminder?"

"When the car crashed into you, you lost consciousness. You didn't wake up again until the SUV was fully engulfed in flames."

"I know that." I worry my bottom lip, debating whether to finally share the one part of that night I've never told anyone. "But I did steal a glance back at the car. When Adam realized we were being chased. He told me to stay down. I didn't listen." I swallow hard. "I peeked up and looked out the back window seconds before the car hit us."

I don't tell my brother I've replayed that one second over in my mind for the past nine years. Wondered if Adam would still be alive if I'd listened to him and stayed down.

"Are you sure about that?" Anderson asks. "It's not that I don't believe you but—"

"Truth be told, I'm not sure of anything. I haven't thought about any of this stuff in years, but now that I'm back here…"

"It's bringing forward all these memories." He pauses, then narrows his gaze on me, giving me a knowing look. "And feelings."

I part my lips, about to tell him I don't know what he's

talking about. But I respect my brother too much to blatantly lie to his face. I should have known he'd pick up on the fact that my unease isn't solely due to my unsettled dreams but also my confusing feelings toward Creed.

"That doesn't matter," I say flippantly. "It won't change the past."

He sighs as he grabs my hand in his. "If there's anyone who knows how impossible it is to change the past, it's me. All we can do is move forward and hope to learn from our mistakes."

"My dear brother, is that hope I hear in your voice?" I joke in an attempt to cut through the thick tension.

Or my unspoken confession that I still have strong feelings for the one man who can never be mine.

"And if it is?"

"Then I'm bloody relieved." Pulling away, I place one of the *petit-fours* on the small plate beside my teacup and slice into the light cake with a fork. "Does this changed outlook have something to do with Nora? Have you heard from her?"

"Unfortunately, no, but I had a long chat with dad, thanks to someone spilling the beans about me potentially removing myself from the line of succession." He gives me a playful look of admonishment.

"He deserved to know."

"I'm grateful you told him. He helped me realize this isn't the end of the world. I suppose you did too."

"Me?" I straighten. "How?"

"By what you did at that soup kitchen. You saw a problem and did everything you could to fix it, to hell with how the royal household would respond. I saw the old Esme again. It made me realize I'm in a unique position. I can give a face and voice to those living with MS. I've decided to talk publicly about my diagnosis. Already reached out to a journalist and sat down for a phone interview."

My eyes widen. "You did?"

The royal household seemed quite insistent on controlling when he went public with everything, unsure of how this might affect the referendum.

"And it's not anyone in the royal household's pocket, either. In fact, it's not a reporter from this country. That way, I know the story will be free from the royal household's influence."

"Who is it?"

"A friend of Nora's is a public affairs editor at a magazine in New York. I reached out to her for help. After she gave me a strongly worded piece of her mind, she agreed to have a chat with me. The piece will hit newsstands mid-December. Which will coincide with my exhibit."

"Exhibit?"

"Photography."

Most of his life, photography's been one of my brother's true passions. It helped him cope with all the changes in our lives after our uncle's death. Then our mother's. I've always told him he has a true talent for it. Not just in pointing a camera and shooting, but in finding picture-worthy subjects. Because of who he is, he's never shared his talent with the world, despite all the times I've encouraged him to do so.

I'm glad he finally is.

Maybe this will help him cope with all the changes he's currently going through.

"I'm proud of you." My lips lift into a smile. "I just better be on the guest list, or there'll be hell to pay." I wink.

"You know you are."

"Good."

I reach across the table, grabbing his hand in mine. For

what feels like the first time in ages, his grip on me is firm. Confident.

"I'm happy for you, Anders."

"I suppose now you're off the hook and can go back to Paris." He pulls away from me, bringing his teacup to his lips.

"I'm not sure I want to go back," I admit softly.

Anderson's expression widens, mouth growing slack. "Really?"

I shrug, my admission just as much of a surprise to me.

When I first arrived here, I wanted nothing more than to leave this place, return to my former life that had as little to do with being royalty as possible.

I don't feel the same urgency anymore.

In fact, the idea of falling back into my old routine is borderline depressing. Sure, I volunteer a great deal, as well as have spearheaded my initiative for human trafficking survivors. But I'm not needed. I don't feel like I serve a purpose, other than being Tristan Hughes' arm candy.

Yesterday, I felt like I actually had a purpose again.

I want more of that.

"Like you told me all those years ago. You may hate certain things about this monarchy, but it's much easier to make a change from within. So I want to be a part of that change. Here. With you. This is where I belong."

He reaches across the table and takes my hand in his once more. "I'm thrilled to hear that." A smile lights up his face for a moment before it falters. "Have you told Tristan?"

I sigh, pulling away and relaxing back into my chair. "I didn't realize I wanted to stay until now. Tristan's always been understanding. He didn't blink an eye when I told him I planned to temporarily resume my duties."

"That's true," Anderson draws out.

"But…" I say, sensing there's more.

"This is vastly different than temporarily resuming your duties. You'll be back in this life. Permanently." He narrows his gaze. "Along with everything that comes with it, the good *and* the bad. *Tristan* will have to be a part of this life, along with the good and the bad. Are you sure he wants that?"

I want to argue he'll be okay with whatever I decide. But I can't say with any level of certainty he will.

"Are you sure *you* want that, too?" he presses when I remain silent. "That you want Tristan in this life with you?" He arches a single brow.

I stare into the distance, wanting to tell Anderson I do.

But no words come.

"Before you ask him to give up everything he'll have to in order to be with you once you permanently resume your duties, you might want to figure that out, Esme."

CHAPTER THIRTY-ONE

Esme

I study my reflection in the mirror, hating everything about this.

Not because I'm forced to wear a dress and heels, as opposed to the pajama pants I've been wearing around my apartment for the past several days.

But because I'm not sure I'm ready to face the media, not to mention the upper-class society vultures who've been invited to a recognition ceremony and reception at the palace.

While I'm thrilled to be able to honor Creed with the Cross of Valor, one of the highest military honors in this country, it seems like a publicity stunt. A way for the royal household to remind the public of the attempt on my life when I'd love nothing more than to put it behind me.

Even if the nightmares that plague me every night make that impossible.

"You look beautiful."

Tristan's voice snaps me out of my thoughts, and I watch him through the mirror as he approaches, pushing my golden hair over one shoulder. His warm lips graze the spot where my neck meets my shoulder.

"Your stylists did an amazing job. I can't even see any of your bruises. In a few days, you probably won't need any makeup to hide them. It'll be like it never happened." He flashes a congenial smile.

"Except Captain Lawson will forever have a permanent reminder it *did* happen in the form of a scar." I face him, expression severe. "Those people who suffered injuries during the chaos that ensued will forever remember it did happen. *I'll* forever remember it happened, even long after every single one of my physical scars heals. The mental ones won't, Tristan. They'll always be with me."

"I know. But eventually, it'll get easier. Trust me on this, darling."

Mouth agape, I stare at him, my irritation increasing the longer he attempts to man-splain how I should feel.

"Why?" I place a hand on my hip. "Has someone ever pulled a gun on you?"

"No. I just... Fuck." He digs his fingers through his hair and tugs at the ends, messing up his stylist's hard work. "I feel like I don't know what to say to you anymore. Don't know what's going to upset you. I just want you to feel loved." He reaches for my hand and links our fingers, his thumb caressing my knuckles. "Want you to know I'm with you, no matter what."

The anguish in his voice is so raw. So real.

My unusual irritability hasn't exactly been making things easy for him. I try to blame it on the fact I haven't been sleeping much, not when every time I close my eyes, all I see is that damn gun. All I feel are the flames of the fire that took Adam's life.

But I don't think that's the only reason I've been short-tempered.

Instead, a lot has to do with feeling uncertain about our relationship.

Since Anderson's visit, I can't stop thinking about what he said. About whether I *do* want to be with Tristan. It's why I haven't brought up my plan to stay indefinitely and resume my duties. I'm not sure if I see a future with him.

"I'm sorry." I pinch the bridge of my nose. "I don't know what's wrong with me."

"It's okay, darling." He wraps me in his arms and presses a soft kiss to my temple. "I understand."

But I doubt he truly *does* understand. Doubt he ever will. Not when he seems to belittle what happened since I survived.

Tristan may not think it's a big deal, especially with the high incidence of gun violence in his home country. To me, it *is* a big deal. I can't just forget it happened. How can I when I'm perpetually reliving that split second I stared down the barrel of a gun, completely unable to move?

"Excuse me, ma'am. Mr. Hughes."

When I hear my butler's voice, I pull away from Tristan. "Yes?"

"Captain Walsh is here to take you to Lamberside."

"Thank you, Frederick."

"Ma'am." With a bow, he retreats from my private suite.

As much as I don't want to face the media, I welcome the distraction of today's event. If for no other reason than it will distract me from my increasing confusion regarding my future with Tristan.

I once felt comfort in his presence. Loved the days we

spent together doing nothing. Now all of our interactions feel stilted. Like I don't know how to act around him anymore.

Like I don't want to be around him anymore.

After a tension-filled drive, Archie pulls through the gates of Lamberside Palace and up to the grand entrance. Dozens of reporters and photographers line the walkway, camera flashes lighting up the gray sky as we crawl to a stop. I draw in a deep breath, pushing down the anxiety filling me.

"Are you ready, ma'am?" Archie asks from the front seat, concern swirling in his blue eyes.

I part my lips to respond, but Tristan cuts me off.

"Of course she is." He grabs my hand and lifts it to his mouth. "My girl's a badass."

Despite Tristan's assurances, Archie doesn't budge. He waits for my response.

"I'm ready."

He continues to scrutinize me for any sign of hesitation or doubt, his thoughtful expression silently telling me it's okay if I'm not ready.

"Promise," I tell him.

After a few moments, he nods. "Okay."

Hopping out of the SUV, he jogs around to open my door, extending his arm toward me.

Inhaling as calming of a breath as I can muster, I place my hand in his. The second I step out of the car, cameras flash around me, burning my irises. I do my best to ignore it. Focus all my attention on the entrance to the palace less than twenty feet away.

But those twenty feet may as well be twenty miles for all I'm concerned.

As I put one foot in front of the other, I remind myself no harm will come to me. But it's hard to believe it when every click from a camera echoes louder and louder, sounding increasingly like gunshots.

I know they're not. Know I'm safe here, considering this place is crawling with security.

But my brain doesn't get that message.

Needing to feel grounded, I reach to my side where Tristan typically is. But he's not there.

When I glance behind me, I find him laughing and smiling with some reporter, as if he doesn't have a care in the world. He's so engrossed in playing the part of the concerned boyfriend that he doesn't notice I'm struggling to breathe.

No one does.

Or maybe no one cares.

It's the story of my life. Always surrounded by people, but still incredibly alone.

Dizziness consumes me, my legs on the brink of giving out beneath me. Without warning, a strong arm encircles my waist, steadying me. I dart my head up, expecting to see Archie.

Instead, I meet Creed's dark eyes.

"I've got you."

I stare into his gaze, my throat heavy with emotion as I struggle to figure out what the hell's going on with me. Why can't I just put this incident behind me, like Tristan wants me to?

Like *I* want to, as well.

"Let's get you away from this."

His grip around my waist tightens, his touch providing me strength.

Despite the flashes growing even more incessant around me, I barely notice them, my sole focus on the man giving me the comfort I've needed since he left my apartment several days ago.

"Thank you, Creed."

"Anything for you, princess."

CHAPTER THIRTY-TWO

Esme

Creed steers me into the palace, his hold on me never wavering. The butler greets me with a bow, but instead of heading toward the throne room, Creed leads me in the opposite direction, ignoring everyone's protests until we're in one of the smaller reception rooms, the chaos muffled behind the closed door.

"It was the camera shutters and flashes, wasn't it?" he asks after helping me onto the couch and sitting beside me, his voice filled with concern.

I search for some sort of explanation for what happened. Play it off. Pretend it's not a big deal.

I just told Anderson I planned to resume my duties. Part of that is dealing with the media on a daily basis. How can I do that if I have a panic attack whenever a flash goes off or a camera snaps my photo?

"How did you know?"

"Bright flashes can be a trigger." There's not so much as

a single hint of judgment in his statement. Just under-standing.

"I knew they were only cameras, but every time I saw a flash or heard the click as they took my photo—"

He grabs my hand and gives it a squeeze. "All you heard was the gunshot."

I smile sadly. "Exactly."

"It's okay, Esme. What you're going through is perfectly normal. It—"

The door bursts open, and Creed quickly drops his hold on my hand as Tristan barrels inside.

"What are you doing here when the event's in the throne room?" He stalks toward me.

Creed pulls himself to his full height, his six-five stature seeming to dwarf Tristan. "If you paid more attention to your girlfriend than hawking your next movie, you'd have realized she was having a panic attack from flashbacks."

"Flashbacks? Flashbacks of what?"

"Of almost getting bloody shot. Flashbacks are common among those suffering from PTSD."

"PTSD?" Tristan scoffs. "She doesn't have PTSD. She wasn't in a war zone."

"PTSD isn't limited to those who serve in the military." Creed's jaw twitches as he balls his hands into fists. His knuckles turn white with the effort it takes to contain his irri-tation. "Anyone who's been through a terrifying situation can suffer from it, even if the nightmare only lasted mere seconds."

He leans into him, lip curling, voice growing louder with every word he speaks. "To someone who's endured a terri-fying experience, those few seconds are all it takes to change your life. Just like those few seconds that bastard pointed a gun at Her Highness changed *her* life."

"Which *you* allowed!" Spittle forms in the corner of Tristan's mouth, vein throbbing in his neck. "You were in charge of her security, and yet some guy was able to point a gun at her."

"*I know that!*" Creed roars, eyes wild, body trembling. "I've been beating myself up over it every damn second since it happened. I don't need *you* to remind me. But that doesn't change what she's going through."

"Which is *your* fucking fault! You—"

"Enough!" I jump to my feet, inserting myself between Tristan and Creed before one of them kills the other. "It's not your fault." I meet Creed's eyes, wanting him to see the truth in my words. Then I look at Tristan, stare hardening.

"You should know better than anyone that you can't control every single crowd, especially in public. He didn't want me to help at the soup kitchen because of potential security issues, but I pushed him. Refused to listen to his concerns. If you want to blame someone, blame me. If it weren't for Captain Lawson's quick actions, I wouldn't be standing here right now. I froze. Couldn't move. If he'd hesitated another fraction of a second, you'd be attending my funeral. So don't you *dare* blame him."

My chest heaves, every muscle in my body tight as I glare at Tristan, almost wanting him to fight me on this.

Instead, he hangs his head, his shoulders falling. "When I heard what happened, it felt like my heart had stopped," he says, voice choked. "Like someone had ripped my lungs out of my chest and left me gasping for air."

He looks to the ornate ceiling, blinking back his emotions. Then he steps toward me and takes my hand in his.

"I'm just...frustrated. And scared that I could have lost you. That I could *still* lose you." He brings his hands to my face and cups my cheeks, staring intently into my eyes, bright chestnut to deep green. "I don't know what I'd do without you, Esme. I love you so fucking much."

Any woman would swoon at the devotion in Tristan's words.

Several weeks ago, I probably would have myself.

Now, with Creed looming nearby, a wave of uneasiness washes over me.

Or maybe it's something else. Maybe I just don't want to share my feelings with Tristan anymore.

Maybe I don't *have* the same feelings for Tristan anymore.

Maybe I never did.

"Pardon the interruption…" A throat clears, preventing me from having to address any of this.

I pull away from Tristan and pivot toward the doorway where Pippa stands with her lips pursed into an annoyed line.

She greets me with a slight curtsy, then addresses everyone, smoothing a length of dark hair behind her ear. "You're all expected in the throne room. You were supposed to be there over five minutes ago now."

"My apologies. I just needed a minute. I'm fine now." I take a few deep inhales, adjusting my navy blue dress as I head toward the doorway, Tristan's hand on my back every step of the way.

As we're about to slip into the hallway, Creed booms, "No cameras."

"Excuse me?" Pippa whirls around, aghast. "We specifically invited the press to cover this story. It's a public relations dream, especially with the referendum."

"I don't give a fuck about that," he snarls. "So you can either un-invite them or tell them to leave their cameras at the door."

"And what will they take photos with?" She crosses her arms in front of her chest, Creed's size not seeming to intimidate her in the slightest.

"Their mobiles will have to suffice."

"I don't—"

"Do what you want, but I'm not going in there unless I have assurances that every single camera has been left at the door. No exceptions." He pins her with a glare, then slowly shifts his gaze to mine, his expression softening.

"This is absolutely ridiculous," Pippa mutters under her breath, but unlocks her mobile and types feverishly. After several silent moments, she looks back to Creed. "It's taken care of. Are you satisfied?"

Creed doesn't respond, looking my way with a single brow arched.

It's a simple thing, but the fact that he went above and beyond to remove any potential source of stress from today's event means a lot. More than I think he realizes.

"Yes," I tell Pippa.

"Let's be on our way then." She spins and heads in the direction of the throne room, heels clicking against the marble tile.

I'm about to follow, but stop, meeting Creed's gaze. "Thank you."

"Of course… Princess."

I fight to reel in my smile, especially in front of Tristan, but I can't hide the effect his nickname has on me. It's almost like a secret code between us. All he has to do is call me princess and I know I'll be okay. Know I'm safe.

"Princess?" Tristan interjects, pulling my attention away from Creed. "I thought you hated that nickname."

"I do," I respond, which only increases Tristan's confusion. But I don't offer him any explanation.

We follow Pippa into the throne room, Creed and Tristan entering with her before I'm announced. As I walk down the long red carpet weaving from the door to a raised platform containing three ornate velvet chairs, the one in the center larger than the other two, everyone bows or curtsies, a stark silence filling the room. Every other time I've walked this path, I was overwhelmed with flashes from cameras and echoes from their shutters.

Not today.

I step onto the raised platform and stand in front of one of the smaller chairs while my brother makes his entrance, followed by my father. As photographers fight to get a decent shot of me with their phones, Creed glances my way from his place to the right of the platform and flashes a smile.

Over the next several minutes, even after I take my seat and am supposed to pay attention to my father's remarks, my attention keeps floating back to Creed.

I try to fight it, focus on Tristan instead. But the more my father talks about Creed's quick thinking and self-sacrifice, the more I can't stop admiring him, especially considering he's in his military dress uniform.

I've always loved how damn sexy he looks in it.

And today's no different.

I'm so lost in my thoughts, I don't realize my father's finished his speech until he approaches and touches his hand to mine.

"You're up," he says with a smile.

I stand, allowing my father to press a soft kiss to my cheek. Then I move toward the center of the platform, stopping mere inches away from Creed. A member of the palace staff appears, opening a small box to reveal a medal sitting on black velvet, an intricate cross hanging on blue silk.

Normally, my father bestows these types of honors, especially ones of this magnitude, but the palace PR team thought it would be a nice touch if I did it, considering it was his actions in protecting my life that prompted him to be awarded this honor.

Taking a clasp in each hand, I slowly raise the medal toward his neck. His eyes lock on mine, the heat in his stare causing my pulse to increase, a fluttering erupting low in my stomach.

"For exhibiting exceptional courage, extraordinary decisiveness and presence of mind, and unusual swiftness in action, regardless of your own personal safety, I'm honored to bestow on you the Cross of Valor."

He bends down slightly, allowing me to secure the medal around his neck. I take my time, not wanting to stop touching him just yet. My fingers brush against his nape and I inhale, his woodsy scent reminding me of early morning sunrises on the beach. Of secret meetings. Of happiness.

Once his medal is in place, I step back and we share another look. It probably only lasts a matter of seconds, but it seems so much longer.

So much more…intimate.

Hundreds of people fill the room, but right now, it feels like it's only us. Like we're the only two people in the world.

When polite clapping cuts through, I turn from Creed and plaster a fake smile on my face as photographers descend on us. Pippa takes charge, arranging for the official royal photographer to snap the photos he needs.

Again with his phone.

After what feels like an eternity, I'm released from the photoshoot and make my way through the room, everyone mingling and enjoying polite conversation. I scan the area for Tristan, but before I see him, a sudden movement catches my attention, Jameson rushing toward me and wrapping me in a hug.

I inhale a sharp breath, taken aback by his sudden display of affection, especially in a room full of people.

Or maybe that's precisely why he's hugging me. Because he wants everyone to see his concern.

"I was so damn worried about you," he confesses, voice strained. Then he pulls back, frantic eyes raking over me. "Are you all right? Everyone said you were fine, barely a scratch, but…" He blows out a breath. "It brought up some memories."

I tilt my head, studying him for a moment.

There's nothing in his words or demeanor to indicate he's being anything less than a concerned ex. It doesn't matter he was never technically my boyfriend. After the roles we were forced to play, we formed a bond. Two pawns taking on the queen.

Still, I can't shake this strange premonition in my gut that there's something contrived about his behavior.

"It brought up some memories for me, too," I finally say, noticing Silas Archer watching our interaction with interest. "For instance, when I stared into the barrel of that gun, it reminded me of glancing out the back window of the SUV right before Adam and I were forced off the road. And the man holding the gun looked exactly like the driver."

Jameson remains relatively impassive, but not completely. He inhales a subtle quick breath, the corner of his mouth ticking slightly before settling back into a firm line.

Why would he have this reaction? *Is* there more to my dreams? *Are* they connected?

And is Jameson the missing link?

"But that's crazy," I say finally, laughing in an effort to break through the tension. After a few seconds, Jameson joins in, as well. "Hayes Barlow's been presumed dead for years. And Charles Thacker looks nothing like him."

"Precisely, Your Highness," Silas says with a small bow before giving Jameson what appears to be a look of warning. "No need to worry." His lips curl into something resembling a smile, but it falls short on his face. "The man responsible is dead and you're still in one piece."

I hold my head high, despite the unease filling me that neither Silas nor Jameson seem all too happy about that fact.

"Yes. I am."

CHAPTER THIRTY-THREE

Esme

I scan my laptop screen as I bring my teacup to my lips, the world quiet in the predawn hours.

This has become part of my routine lately.

Crawl into bed utterly exhausted, only to be woken up a short time later after having that same dream yet again. Toss and turn for hours, then eventually get out of bed and make a tea.

Normally, I disappear into the den and watch a movie or show with lots of humor and low drama. These days, my life has enough drama.

But after Jameson Gates' strange behavior during the medal ceremony today, I wanted to do some digging. So instead of spending a few hours watching TV in the den, I slipped into my office and opened up my laptop to run a search on Charles Thacker.

As expected, thousands of hits come back. While some are from his news site, the top results are all stories about the assassination attempt, as they're calling his attack. It's the first time I've looked into him on my own. I re-live the few seconds this man held a gun in front of me every minute of every day. I haven't felt the need to torture myself further.

But as I click on the first article, a part of me wishes I had. Because there's something off about the photo of Charles Thacker displayed in the article.

Sure, his features are mostly the same. Taken as a whole, it looks like him. But his eyes are lacking that sinister quality that left me frozen. That haunt my dreams every night.

"This is ridiculous," I tell myself as I run a hand over my face. "It's a photo, for crying out loud. Not like his eyes can be threatening in a goddamn photo."

I return my attention to the article in the hopes of learning a bit more about Charles Thacker than I've been told. The column details the events that led to the assassination attempt. How I gave a speech encouraging people to give back during this difficult time of year. How I surprised everyone by volunteering at the soup kitchen.

How I took a few minutes to talk to reporters as I left.

How a man known for his vocal anti-monarchy stance pulled a gun on me.

How a brave member of my protection team was shot when he tackled me to the ground, saving me from what would have been my death.

The article goes on to talk about the Cross of Valor ceremony earlier today, complete with a photo. It stops me cold, my gaze fixated on the image in front of me.

The heat and hunger in Creed's eyes as he admires me jumps off the screen. It's the way all women hope a man will look at her. So much affection and devotion. As if I'm the only woman who matters to him.

"There you are."

At the interruption, I suck in a sharp breath, darting my head up as Tristan steps into my office, hair disheveled, eyes reflecting his lack of sleep.

My chest tightens, heat crawling up my face. It's not like he caught me doing something I shouldn't have been. I was simply reading a few articles about my attack.

But I still feel guilty.

Probably because I was thinking about another man when Tristan walked in.

Another man I almost kissed mere days ago.

Another man who's become the only person I feel comfortable around.

"I couldn't sleep." I give him a half-hearted smile.

"Again?"

"Sorry if my insomnia inconveniences you," I bite out as I shoot to my feet, slamming my laptop closed. "I'll be sure to have a discussion with my subconscious, ask it to delay any nightmares until you've gone back to California."

I grab my tea and push past him, my aggravation increasing as I storm into the kitchen. I'm surprised the tea cup doesn't shatter when I practically throw it into the sink.

Placing my clenched hands on the counter, I draw in deep breath after deep breath.

It's probably just the lack of sleep making me unusually irritable, but with every passing second, I feel like Tristan understands me less and less.

I feel like I'm seeing a side of Tristan I've been content to ignore until now.

Or maybe I just *want* to see this side of him.

I don't even know anymore.

"It's not an inconvenience at all, Esme."

He pulls me toward him and envelops me in a hug, his

voice gentle and soothing. His fingertips trace the length of my arms, warmth radiating from his touch.

"I'm just worried about you. You can't go on like this."

I squeeze my eyes shut, a wave of regret washing over me. "I don't know what's wrong with me. I'm normally calm and even-tempered, but lately—"

"Hey." He touches my chin, forcing my gaze up. "You have nothing to apologize for. You've been through a lot. Coming back here. Then nearly being killed." His voice wavers slightly. "It's enough to push anyone to their limits. But we'll get through it." He lowers his lips toward me. "Together."

My eyes flutter shut as his mouth touches mine. I let out a soft sigh, hoping his kiss holds the same spark it once did. That it will jumpstart my heart into feeling something for him.

Instead, I feel as empty as I have all week.

He brings the kiss to an end, his gaze tracing over my face. I expect him to call me out on the lack of desire in our kiss when it used to be fiery and full of passion.

"Come to California with me," he says after a beat.

"What?"

"You deserve a break. You can relax by the pool when I'm on set. Read all those romance novels you love so we can try to recreate some of the hotter scenes. And I won't have to come home to an empty house. We can find some sort of normalcy again." He takes my hand in his. "Find some semblance of happiness again. I don't think I've seen you smile once since you've been back here. Haven't heard you laugh. I miss that. Miss how you used to be in Paris. Miss who *we* used to be in Paris. How happy we were. How easy—"

"What if I'll never be that person again?" I pull away and cross my arms in front of my chest.

"Of course you will. I get that you've been through something traumatic, that it won't happen overnight. But eventually, you'll work through all of this and be back to your normal self."

"What if I don't *want* to be that person again?" I hesitate. "What if I don't want to go back to Paris?"

He blinks, uncertainty flickering in his expression. "I thought you were happy in Paris. I thought *we* were happy in Paris." His shoulders tense as he widens his stance.

"I thought so, too."

I chew on my bottom lip, a myriad of thoughts and emotions warring for attention in my brain. I didn't anticipate having this conversation now, especially at four in the morning after yet another sleepless night. I could brush it off, pull him back to the bedroom. Surrender to him so he can't see the turmoil in my mind.

But that hasn't solved anything so far. It won't fix anything now, either.

It won't fix us.

"In the beginning of *The Wizard of Oz*, do you remember how Dorothy wishes more than anything to find a place where her troubles won't find her? Somewhere over the rainbow?"

He nods, the movement subtle.

"But when that tornado transports her over the rainbow, all she wants to do is go back home, especially when she learns there's no place far enough away where her troubles won't find her?"

He gives another slow, deliberate nod, his Adam's apple bobbing up and down.

"I think Paris was my version of going over the rainbow.

At the time, I wanted to get away from this place and the reminders of…everything. Thought by doing so, I'd find the peace I desperately needed. The *happiness* I desperately needed. But now that I'm back here…" I shake my head before slowly returning my remorse-filled eyes to his. "I realize Dorothy was right.

"I went to Paris in search of my purpose, only to learn it's been right here all along. I've never felt as useful as I did in the soup kitchen. Seeing the gratitude on all those people's faces made me realize that this is where I belong. Right here. With the people of this country doing whatever I can, no matter how small, to make their lives a little better."

"What… What are you saying?" Tristan's voice cracks, his face contorted in confusion and hurt.

I do my best to keep my expression firm, lips pressed together tightly. "I'm staying."

"Just for now, right? But at some point, you'll eventually—"

"No." I shake my head. "Not just for now. I'm staying here. Indefinitely. It's where I belong."

"But what about us? I get that you're a princess. I knew that almost from the beginning of our relationship. But that was when you claimed to have no desire to return to this life."

"I didn't think I did. But things change. *People* change. *I've* changed." I point to my chest. "My circumstances have changed. I can't just abandon Anders. He's doing better now, but that won't always be the case. There will be times when he needs me to step in, especially with my father retiring in a few years."

Tristan eats up the space between us, fingers pressing into my biceps as his gaze burns into mine. "And you can still do that without sacrificing yourself for all of this. I grew up in this kind of life, and I hated it. Hated not having freedom. Independence." He pulls his lips between his teeth. "I don't want that for my kids. Or myself."

I stare at him for several long moments, trying to feel something. *Anything.* His words should hurt me. Should break my heart. They don't, though. Maybe I'm still too numb from almost dying that the seriousness of the situation hasn't yet sunk in.

Or maybe it's a sign that Tristan isn't the one I'm supposed to be with.

Hell, I struggled to even tell him I loved him. Took me almost a year of dating him to finally say those three words. Even when I did, I'm not sure I meant it.

I still don't.

"Then you don't want me," I say with a shrug.

"That's where you're wrong." He clasps my hands in his with a gentle but urgent grip. "I do, Esme. I want you so fucking much. I *love* you so fucking much."

"Just not enough to accept this part of my life." With a sad smile, I pull away from him and stare into space before returning my gaze to his. "Years ago, Anderson said something that resonated with me. His opinion of all the bullshit we've endured is the same as mine. Hell, at times it's probably even worse. But do you know why he's never turned his back on his role? His duty to the crown?"

"Why's that?"

"Because of the people of this country. We may have been raised to believe that we need to put our duty to the crown above all else, but Anderson's always put his duty to the people even higher. He's stayed because it's much easier to fight for change on the inside than from the outside. So I'm going to stay. Help him continue to make some much-needed changes in this country. Not keep running from my problems."

"And with you officially becoming a senior royal once more, what does that mean for us?"

"It wouldn't have to change anything for us. Not unless——"

"Not unless we were to be married."

I snap my mouth closed and nod.

"And if that were to happen? What then?"

"You'd also become a senior member of the royal family."

"What about my career? And my pharmaceutical company? What would happen to——"

"Senior members of the royal family aren't allowed to hold jobs outside of the royal household. And any boards you serve on need to be approved."

He nods, not showing any signs of emotion, apart from resignation. After several heavy moments of silence, he states, "My mother was miserable."

"What do you mean?"

He lifts his gaze toward mine. "When my father was elected president. To anyone on the outside, they'd think she had it made. She got to quit her teaching job with the paltry salary and be First Lady, married to the most powerful man in the world. But teaching was the one thing that brought her joy. When that was taken away from her…" He shakes his head. "She lost her soul. I can't lose my soul, too."

My heart aches at the despair in his tone, so raw and real. We've been together for five years, yet this feels like the first genuine conversation we've ever had.

I always assumed he shunned following in his father's footsteps because he hates how the political system in the United States works, something he's told me repeatedly.

Maybe it's bigger than that.

Maybe it's because he saw how it destroyed his mother.

Now I'm asking him to put himself in the same position. Asking him to risk it all for me when I'm not even sure I love him. Not like I should.

"I won't ask you to do that. Just like I know you wouldn't ask me to lose *my* soul. And the people of this country *are* my heart and soul. It just took me a few years to realize that."

His body deflates, head bowed as he exhales a deep, sorrowful sigh. The moment stretches painfully until he slowly lifts his eyes to meet mine.

"Where does this leave us?"

"At an impossible impasse," I say through the tightness building in my throat.

Over the past several years, he's become such a huge part of my life. Walking away from him feels like I'm walking away from part of myself.

But it's part of myself I *need* to walk away from. The woman I was in Paris isn't who I really am.

The woman Tristan fell in love with in Paris isn't who I really am.

"Is this how it ends?" His voice cracks with his question, tears rimming his eyes.

"We both want two different things. We both *need* two different things. And those things are in direct conflict."

"I thought you were the one," he chokes out.

My vision blurs with my tears, chest constricting. "Maybe I was the right one, but at the wrong time."

He squeezes his eyes shut, trying to swallow down the despair engulfing him. When he pulls me into his embrace one last time, it takes everything I have to breathe through the boulder in my throat. My feelings may not amount to the soul-fulfilling love I once shared with Creed, but I still care deeply for Tristan.

Still hate hurting him like this.

"You will always be the right one for me." He presses a soft kiss to my forehead, lingering there long enough to make me wonder if he's about to change his mind.

Then he releases me and steps back. "Goodbye, Esme."

PART III

Absolution

"It is the confession, not the priest,
that gives us absolution."

~ Oscar Wilde

CHAPTER THIRTY-FOUR

Creed

Polite conversation and subtle jazz music surround me as I stand in the middle of an art gallery in the SoHo section of New York. Every few seconds, I glance toward the door. I tell myself it's part of the job.

But that's not entirely true, not when the door's being watched by two of my best guys, ensuring no one suspicious enters this space.

Instead, I keep looking at the door for another reason altogether.

Because I know Esme will walk through it at any minute.

After not seeing her for the past several weeks, I'm anxious to be in the same room as her again.

I hated leaving Belmont so soon in the first place, especially after Esme's panic attack before the medal ceremony. Anderson asked if I wanted to stay and heal, but when he told me he'd reached out to one of his contacts in the art world and arranged an exhibit featuring his photography, I knew I needed to be here for him.

And not as his chief protection officer, although that certainly played a huge part in my decision.

I wanted to be here as a friend, especially after he confessed he'd secretly talked with a reporter from a magazine here in New York about his MS diagnosis and the article would be published this week.

As I look around the upscale yet intimate gallery, dozens of people commenting about what an incredible eye Anderson has for finding beauty in the ordinary, I can't help but marvel at how different he seems from a few months ago when he was at the lowest he'd ever been. I can only hope he's made peace with his diagnosis and realized it's not the end of the world, like he once thought it was.

I'm about to head toward the back office to check on my guy manning the cameras when I sense a shift in the energy. The hairs on my nape prick up as electricity passes through the room.

I turn around, warmth filling me when my eyes fall on Esme in a form-fitting black dress that shows off her incredible curves, the hem ending at her mid-thigh. A pair of knee-high black boots make her already long legs look like they extend for miles. Couple that with the dark shadowing along her eyes and the deep red lipstick she wears, I have to fight the urge to rush to her and crush my lips to her.

As if sensing my stare, the second she shrugs off her wool coat and hands it to the woman at the front desk, her gaze finds mine, mouth curling into a flirtatious smirk.

I try not to read into it, but I can practically feel the weight lifting off her. Like she can breathe again.

I feel like I can finally breathe again, too.

She saunters toward me, her golden blonde waves

brushing against her shoulders with every sway of her hips.

"Captain Lawson," she greets me in a throaty voice that borders on being sultry.

A few weeks ago, there would have been animosity and perhaps resentment when she addressed me as such. Not anymore.

I thought I was doing the right thing by remaining cold and aloof. Not just because Anderson asked me to keep my distance, but because I thought it was for the best.

She's with Tristan. I have an obligation to Rory and AJ.

That shifted when I saw Charles Thacker point a gun at Esme.

I've seen a lot of shit during my military service. I can say without a doubt that I've never been as scared as I was in the fraction of a second when he pressed his finger to the trigger and fired. I will never forget that moment for the rest of my life.

"Your Highness." I bow, but keep my eyes trained on her. It's impossible to lower my gaze when she looks as stunning as she does right now.

Then again, I'm just as drawn to her when she wears an oversized t-shirt, pajama pants, hair piled on her head, face devoid of makeup.

"H-How have you been?" My voice shakes slightly, evidencing the nervous energy dancing in my stomach as her addictive scent wraps around me. I feel like a teenager talking to a girl for the first time.

"Hanging in there, all things considered." She smiles, but unlike mere seconds ago, this one feels forced. As if she's hiding something from me.

"Any more incidents?" I ask in a low voice as I lean toward her, her body wash becoming even stronger. Making me want to bury my nose in her hair and breathe her in.

"I've been fine." She straightens her spine, lifting her head. But she doesn't look directly at me.

I part my lips to press the issue, but before I can, she turns from me.

"This is incredible," she exhales, sweeping her gaze around the refurbished warehouse that's now home to the art gallery.

"Your brother is rather talented."

"Yes, he is."

A server wearing a white tuxedo shirt and black pants walks through the gallery, a silver tray with flutes of bubbling champagne perched in one hand.

Esme grabs two glasses, the light from the gallery's overhead fixtures cascading across her face as she extends one toward me.

"I'm on duty," I remind her.

She shrugs. "More for me." She brings one of the glasses to her full lips, my gaze fixated on them as she takes a sip.

I've never wished I were an inanimate object as much as I do right now.

"And where is the guest of honor?" she asks, forcing my attention away from her mouth.

Clearing my throat, I nod toward the small alcove where Anderson's spent quite a bit of time tonight.

"That's her in the photos," Esme says, a cross between a question and a statement.

I nod.

They may not show her face, but there's no mistaking that the subject of the black-and-white photos surrounding Anderson is Nora. Even if I didn't follow him along Route 66 and watch him fall in love with her a little more every day, I would know it's her by the way he admires each photo with a combination of regret and hope.

"Has she—"

"No," I interject before she can finish her question. "He still hasn't heard from her."

She pulls her lips between her teeth as she studies her brother. "If it's meant to be, I'm sure they'll find their way back to each other." She shifts her gaze toward mine. "Regardless of any complications."

Her words linger in the air for several protected moments, something in her tone making me think she's not just talking about her brother, but us, too. That maybe we'll find our way back to each other, regardless of any complications.

"Excuse me," she says when I remain silent.

Giving me a small smile, she makes her way toward Anderson. They talk for several minutes, and Esme even manages to get a laugh out of him. But I can tell it's laced with a hint of sorrow, especially when he turns his eyes back to the photos of Nora.

Esme eventually leaves Anderson to peruse the rest of his work, stopping occasionally to talk to a few people who recognize her.

My focus should be on Anderson, keeping him in my sights. But I can't stop myself from glancing Esme's direction every few seconds, drawn to her in a way I've never been able to explain.

As I watch her pose for a photo with a few twenty-something women, a hush spreads through the gallery.

I shift my eyes from Esme and toward the front door, dozens of people looking between the photos Anderson's still staring at and a woman in a black dress with strawberry blonde hair who just entered. She weaves her way through the gallery, the crowds parting to make way for her, all of them knowing exactly who she is. She doesn't even have to stop to ask where Anderson is. She just knows.

Just like I never have to ask where Esme is. I can always feel her. Like she's another part of me.

The room seems to hold its breath as Anderson slowly turns around, his eyes locking on Nora's for the first time in months. I may be several feet away, but I can feel the anticipation buzzing between them.

I want to know what they're saying, but at the same time don't want to do anything to interrupt this moment that's been two months in the making.

As I watch Anderson wrap his arms around her and lean down to kiss her, a strange sensation stirs inside of me. Something I haven't felt for a long time.

Hope.

Despite all the obstacles facing them, Anderson and Nora found their way back to each other. All because he never gave up hope.

I steal a glimpse across the gallery, finding Esme looking at me with a hint of longing, a sad smile tugging on her lips. But she quickly fixes her expression, gliding through the throngs of people and toward her brother.

I stay at my post, giving her space to meet the infamous Nora. She doesn't linger too long, politely excusing herself after only a few minutes and slipping out of the gallery before anyone can notice. I doubt anyone would with the excitement of seeing the woman in dozens of Anderson's photos make a surprise appearance, a fairy tale taking place in front of their very eyes.

But I notice.

I also notice she left without her coat.

In December.

In New York.

I dart toward the front desk and yank her coat off the hanger, hurrying out of the gallery.

"Everything okay, boss?" Kylian, one of the guards stationed out front, asks.

"Of course. But can you keep an eye on things inside for me?"

"Sure thing." He ducks into the building, leaving just one guard at the door, but it's nearly eleven and things are winding down.

I scan the sidewalk, searching the sea of people for Esme, finding her as she's about to climb into her car, Archie holding the door open for her.

"Esme!" I shout, my voice echoing in the night air.

She pauses, her shoulders rising and falling. Then she glances my way.

"You forgot this." I hold up her coat.

Archie looks like he's about to come grab it, but Esme places a hand on his forearm, stopping him. I jog down the sidewalk, meeting her halfway.

"Thanks." She extends her arm to take the coat from me.

"Allow me."

She gives me a subtle nod, and I help her into her coat, struggling to ignore how my body buzzes to life from being so close to her. It takes everything I possess to resist the temptation to push her hair to the side and drag my lips against her neck.

"Thanks again," she says when I step back, lips curving into a gentle smile.

She's about to start back toward Archie when I say, "Hey, Esme?"

"Yes?" She arches a brow, hope and expectation swirling in her emerald eyes.

"Do you want to do something?" I blurt out before I can

stop the words from leaving my mouth.

"Do something?" she repeats, just as surprised by my offer as I am.

"Why not?"

"Aren't you supposed to be running point on Anderson's detail?"

I shove my hands into my pockets. "The opening is technically over. Chances are he's not going to want to stay around." I give her a knowing look.

"But what if someone sees us together?"

If I didn't know any better, I'd think she was trying to make up excuses not to spend time with me. But I *do* know better. And I know her questions come from a place of concern.

Especially considering our past.

"Look around you." I gesture to everyone passing us on the sidewalk. "We're in New York. There are millions of people in this city, yet not once has anyone looked our way in the past several minutes. Hell, most people couldn't be bothered to even look up from their damn mobiles to realize the most beautiful woman I've ever known is standing right in front of them."

A blush blooms on her cheeks as she averts her gaze.

"This may be the only place in the world where you can be invisible in plain sight. It would be a shame to waste such a great opportunity. Plus, the pizza here is to die for."

She bites her lower lip, hesitating. It makes me want to bite her lip, too.

Finally, a smile teases her mouth.

"I'll never pass up an offer of food, especially something as bad for me as pizza."

I playfully waggle my brows. "Then let's go be bad, princess."

CHAPTER THIRTY-FIVE

Esme

"Are you sure your feet are okay?" Creed asks as we stroll through Central Park, the combination of snow-covered grass, illuminated trees, and festive decorations exuding holiday spirit.

For the first time in years, I feel in a holiday mood, too.

Feel all the things the Christmas season is supposed to be about — joy, togetherness, hope.

When I walked into that gallery earlier tonight, the last thing I expected was to leave with Creed. But I couldn't ask for a better person to explore this city with. I've been here numerous times, but I've never seen New York like I have tonight with Creed at my side.

After he ran back into the gallery to grab his coat and informed Archie he'd make sure I made it safely to the hotel, he took me to one of his favorite pizza places. Then we roamed Times Square, everything about it cheesy and over-the-top. After that, we decided to walk back to our hotel at the south end of Central Park, stopping by Rockefeller Center on the way. Now, we're wandering through the park, in no rush to actually get to the hotel, despite it being after midnight.

"I'm not sure those are the most conducive in which to walk around New York."

"I walk in much worse on a regular basis," I remind him.

"We can grab a cab."

"I told you. There's no need." I look to the sky and inhale a deep breath, a few snowflakes landing on my face. "I like the fresh air. Reminds me I'm still alive."

Creed nods as he shoves his hands into his pockets, a brief silence settling between us. It doesn't feel awkward or stilted, not like it once did. It's comfortable.

"So how have you *really* been?" he asks as we pass by life-size gingerbread houses, people stopping to take photos in front of them.

I open my mouth, about to brush off his question, much like I did earlier tonight. Before I can, he holds up a gloved hand.

"And don't give me the response you think I need so I'll stop pestering you. I won't. I'll never stop making sure you're okay. So…" He arches a single brow, his voice dipping low. "How are you?"

I pull my coat tighter against me as I look forward.

How much should I tell him? That I've never felt so alone? That I wonder if I made a mistake in choosing this life over Tristan? That every time I close my eyes, I still see that damn gun? That I heard a door slam the other day and nearly had a heart attack as I ducked for cover?

That I worry I'll never be normal again?

"I'm struggling," I admit without going into too much detail. "Especially at night."

"Are you still having the same nightmare?"

I nod. "It hasn't changed."

"Why didn't you reach out? I get things between us are complicated, but if you're having trouble, you can always call me, Esme. I told you that. Told you not to go through this alone. Told you—"

"I know," I exhale.

I had considered calling him on several occasions, especially once Tristan left. There have been countless times I had his contact pulled up on my phone, but I resisted the urge. I can't let him become a crutch. Can't let him burrow even deeper into my soul than he already is.

"All my life, I've been brought up to just handle things. Not show any weakness. And part of me thinks I should just be able to handle this too. There are thousands of vets who've endured far worse than me. I should be able to put it all behind me. Not still be having these stupid nightmares and waking up in a cold sweat weeks later."

Creed halts in his tracks, yanking me to stop. His gentle grip on my arms forces my eyes to meet his concerned stare.

"That doesn't matter. Like I said before the medal ceremony. You endured something that could have an impact on the rest of your life. You may never get over it completely. Will things eventually get easier? Absolutely. As I'm sure you learned after the car crash." When he raises a single brow in question, I respond with a slight nod.

Those first few months after Adam's death, I went through the same thing. Had nightmares I was still in that car, struggling to get out.

But this time feels different, like my subconscious is trying to tell me something, especially when every time I have this dream, Charles Thacker ends up being the same man who lights the SUV on fire.

All reason tells me he wasn't. Creed repeatedly assured me as much. Even reached out to one of his friends at a private security firm and asked them to see if he could verify where Charles Thacker was on the night of Adam's death. He wasn't even in the country. He has the passport stamps to prove it.

My subconscious hasn't gotten the message, though, still determined to torture me every night.

"This won't last forever." He moves his hands to my cheeks, his touch reassuring. "But these things you're going through are normal. You experienced something that made you question your security and safety. I can't make any of the anxiety or trauma go away, but I can promise that whenever you're with me, I'll do everything to make sure you feel safe. Okay?"

"Okay." I push out a long breath.

It's refreshing to be around someone who understands what I'm going through. Who doesn't tell me to just get over it, as it seems most people in the royal household want me to do, especially when I've refused to sit down for interviews with the media to discuss the attempt on my life. It's bad enough I relive those few seconds every night in my sleep. I'm not sure I can talk about it with the press so they can exploit it for their own gain.

"Good." He smiles softly, his eyes crinkling in the corners before he releases me.

Snow continues to fall around us, becoming increasingly steady, leaving more than a dusting on the path. Despite it, we don't walk any faster, enjoying this stolen moment together.

"Do you plan to go to California after this?" Creed asks after several minutes. "See Tristan?"

My steps falter, but I recover quickly. It's a reasonable

question. If we were still together, that's exactly what I would have done.

"We broke up."

Creed darts his wide eyes to mine, mouth agape. "When?"

"A few weeks ago."

"I'm sorry. I hadn't heard."

I blow out a small laugh. "You're actually the first person I've told. No one knows yet. I'll eventually reach out to him so we can discuss how we're going to handle the PR part of this, but I figure it's the last thing he needs to think about right now, since he's trying to wrap filming on his current project."

"What happened? If you don't mind me asking."

"I told him I planned to stay in Belmont. Resume my duties permanently."

I glance his way, gauging his reaction to this news. Something else I haven't shared with anyone, apart from mentioning it to Anderson.

This time, Creed's the one who falters in his steps.

"You're staying?"

"The day at the soup kitchen changed me. Not what happened after, but when I was helping." I shrug, giving him a small smile as we continue walking. "It reminded me of what's important. I want my legacy to be more than being some movie star's girlfriend."

"And Tristan didn't like the idea of you staying? Seems a bit selfish."

"Perhaps," I respond dismissively, not telling him I'd been having reservations about Tristan even before I made this decision. "I don't fault him for wanting to leave, considering I essentially changed the rules in the fourth quarter, so to speak."

"How so?"

"You know his father is a former President of the United States, right?"

"I know everything I possibly can about Tristan Emerson Hughes," he admits, his tone even. "Probably more than *he* does."

"You do?"

Archie was required to look into Tristan's background when we started dating, but that's because he's my chief protection officer. Creed isn't.

"I needed to make sure Anderson was safe when visiting you."

"Is that the only reason?" I tease, playfully nudging him.

"I also wanted to make sure he's good enough for you. Although, if you ask me, there's no man on this planet good enough for you."

The way he looks at me makes my heart skip a beat, my body buzzing with electricity from the intensity of his admission.

He shouldn't say things like this to me, but my god, I love hearing them. Love knowing I still have as strong of a hold on Creed Lawson as he has on me, regardless of the fact we can never be more to each other than what we are now.

Although with each passing day, I become more uncertain of what that is.

"Growing up how he did had a lasting effect on him," I continue.

"So much that he refused to support you in fulfilling your duty? Your birthright?"

"It's not as simple as that. When we first started dating, I'd insisted I had no intention of returning to this life. And I hadn't. I was still angry about everything the royal household put me through. Everything my *father* put me through."

"And now?"

"Now things are different. At least my father is. I'm willing to put up with the bullshit if that's what it takes to make a positive change in other's lives. But Tristan…" I shake my head. "He'd have to give up his career if we were to ever marry."

"And he's not willing to do that?" Creed asks hesitantly.

"*I'm* not willing to ask him to do that. He loves what he does. Loves bringing a story to life. Watching him on set…" A small smile curves my lips from the memory. "You can tell how passionate he is about it, despite how stressful it can be. There's also his pharmaceutical company and other charitable foundations. I can't take that away from him."

"So it was a mutual thing?" Creed asks as we emerge from Central Park, honking horns and sirens surrounding us. Even after midnight, the chaos of New York City shows no sign of slowing down anytime soon.

"More or less," I respond noncommittally.

As we enter the luxurious hotel, Creed touches a hand to my elbow, eyes scanning the lobby, obviously back in body-guard mode. Or maybe it's just a habit with him. He lives most of his life constantly looking for any and all threats. I doubt he can turn it off simply because he's not technically on the clock.

My heels click on the marble tile as we walk toward the elevator bank and step inside a waiting car. The second the door closes with a soft whoosh, I'm instantly aware of how tiny this space is with Creed's overwhelming presence, the air between us crackling with an electricity potent enough to power Manhattan for the next century.

It would be so easy to pull him toward me and press my lips to his, giving me a taste of what I've imagined for too long now.

What I've missed for too long now.

My god, I want to. I've thought of little else since I nearly kissed him the morning after the attack. Hell, since I first arrived back in Belmont and learned the chemistry between us was still there. If anything, it's even more intense, a wildfire burning brighter with every sly glance and thoughtful declaration shared between us.

With a sudden jolt, the elevator dings loudly, ripping me out of my fantasy. A faint crease forms between Creed's brow and he narrows his eyes on me.

"You okay?"

"Of course." I hurry off the elevator, making my way down the hallway and toward my room. "Was just daydreaming for a minute," I add in the hopes he doesn't press the issue.

The last thing I want is to confess I startled because I was imagining him pinning me against the elevator wall and kissing me like he did all those years ago, leaving me breathless. Thoughtless. Mindless.

"Thanks for tonight," I tell him once we reach my room. "It's exactly what I needed, even if I didn't realize it."

"It's exactly what I needed, too."

With one last nervous smile, I unlock the door and step inside.

But before I can shut the door, he darts out his hand, keeping it open. I suck in a sharp inhale, snapping my gaze toward his.

Indecision flickers in his dark orbs, an internal argument waging in his mind. I can physically feel it. The fight between duty and our hearts. Responsibility and redemption.

Legacy and love.

I know what should win. What all reason tells me he should choose. What he's chosen time and again.

But this once, I want him to follow his heart.

Because this once, I'm willing to follow *my* heart.

After a few seconds that feel like an eternity, he sighs and hangs his head, resignation washing over him.

I squeeze my eyes shut, pushing down the ache in my chest.

I shouldn't be surprised. This is the game we're destined to play. Getting so close to finally allowing ourselves to be happy, but retreating instead.

When I open my eyes, that's exactly what he does. He turns from me and retreats.

But he only makes it a few steps before he whirls around, his swift motions stealing my breath. Before I can process it, he advances on me, hands gripping my cheeks as he pushes me farther into my room, pinning me against the wall.

He stares at me, chest heaving, pupils dilating, fingers digging into my skin.

"Fuck it," he growls.

Then he crushes his mouth to mine.

CHAPTER THIRTY-SIX

Esme

Shock flies through me, momentarily freezing me in place as I try to determine whether this is real or yet another dream.

Creed's kissing me.

Hell, I'm not sure that's the correct term for what he's doing. This is so much more than a kiss, the way his mouth moves against mine, tongue sensually caressing mine with a mixture of affection and dominance, reminding me of the duplicitous nature I craved all those years ago. The pressure of his hand on my face pulls me closer, as if he's desperate to consume me in one passionate bite.

No. This isn't just a kiss.

It's a sensual communion. A carnal confession. A wanton sacrament.

I didn't think I'd ever taste his lips again. Didn't think I'd ever lose myself in the feel of his tongue as it tangles with mine. Didn't think I'd ever feel his body pulse against mine, lust and desperation colliding together in a riotous combination, pushing me to the verge of combusting.

Panting, he tears away, his turbulent brown eyes searing into me, as if fighting the urge to pull me close again.

A battle he loses when he lowers his mouth back to mine.

"We shouldn't do this," he murmurs as he brushes a soft kiss to my swollen lips, his actions a stark contradiction to his words.

"You're right," I exhale, writhing when he rocks his hips against me. "We're not supposed to kiss like this."

"Like this?" He pulls back for a fraction of a second before he slams his mouth to mine once more, tongue plunging past my lips, hand roaming my frame.

I wrap an arm around his broad shoulders, urging him to keep going. To keep kissing me. To keep touching me. To keep consuming me.

"Exactly like that," I whimper once he brings our kiss to an end. Then I pull my bottom lip between my teeth, playfully waggling my brows. "You also shouldn't kiss my neck under any circumstances."

"Oh, really?" he teases as he slides his tongue along his lips.

"Absolutely. It's completely off limits."

One side of his mouth quirks up in a devious grin. "Duly noted."

With a gleam in his eye, he dips his head toward me. But being the cruel bastard he is, he takes his time, each drawn out second making me squirm with anticipation.

Finally, he peppers soft kisses to my neck, his unshaven jawline harsh against me. I tilt my head to the side to give him better access, and he clamps his teeth onto my skin. A combination of a whimper and a moan falls from my throat as I pull him closer, nails digging into his scalp.

"What else shouldn't I do?" he asks once he releases me, leaving me a panting mess.

I want to tell him he shouldn't fuck me so he'll speed things up. But I like this game.

During our secret courtship, we never got to take our time. We always had to rush to get our fix before our time was up. I have no idea what this is or what it means. Regardless, I want to enjoy every second of it. Not rush to get to the good part. With Creed, it's all the good part. Especially foreplay. He was always a master at turning me on with his words. I can only imagine he's even more talented now that he's matured.

"You shouldn't take off my coat."

Not saying a word, he unfastens the buttons, pushing the heavy material down my arms. He drapes it over a chair in the sitting area before removing his and doing the same.

"What else?" he asks as he returns to me.

"You shouldn't kiss me again, this time slow."

His eyes pierce my soul as he lowers his mouth, the warmth of his body radiating through me. His lips are soft yet demanding, commanding my attention and stirring a flurry of emotions, each spine-tingling caress of his tongue making my heart squeeze.

"I forgot how much I loved kissing you." I place my hands on the lapels of his suit jacket, gaze trained on his chest.

"I haven't." He touches my chin, forcing my eyes up. "I've thought of little else for the past nine years." He pushes a tendril of hair behind my ear.

"Then kiss me again, Creed." I lift myself onto my toes. "Don't stop kissing me until we have no choice but to stop."

"Gladly, princess."

This time, there's nothing soft or gentle about the way he

slams his mouth against mine. It's not a kiss as much as it is a claiming, hunger dripping from every inch of him as he grips my hip and steers me toward the bed, not pulling away until the back of my legs hit the mattress.

"What else shouldn't we do?" He leans his forehead against mine.

I lick my lips, swallowing hard to catch my breath. "You definitely shouldn't take my boots off."

"Your wish is my command."

He helps me sit on the bed, eyes intense as he kneels in front of me. He smoothes a hand up the inside length of my boot, stopping at the zipper before slowly lowering it. Every drawn-out second is an exercise in patience, my pulse increasing with every brush of his fingers against me. Finally, he removes the boot and sock, tossing them onto the floor.

But instead of immediately taking the other one off, he lifts my leg, trailing toe-curling kisses from my ankle and up the inside of my knee.

I moan, gripping the duvet below me as desire floods through my veins. I want to squeeze my thighs together to release some of this mounting pressure, but that would mean not feeling his mouth on me.

That's the last thing I want, especially as he inches up my thighs and toward my center.

"How about this?" he asks, his unshaven jawline scraping my skin. "Should I be doing this?"

"Fuck no."

"Good."

He moves to my other leg and makes quick work of removing my remaining boot and sock. Then he drags his tongue along my ankle, traveling the same path as he did on the other leg.

I pant, desperate to feel his face buried between my

thighs, but at the last minute, he retreats, torturing me in a way I didn't think possible.

"Creed," I moan, attempting to squeeze my legs together. But he won't let me, gripping my knees and pushing them apart, depriving me of any sort of release.

"And what's your opinion on this?"

He grazes his hand up my thigh once more, heat flaming in his stare as he ghosts his thumb against my panties.

"Should I lick your pussy? Tongue-fuck your cunt?"

"God, no." I move in time with his motions, chasing that feeling of bliss only Creed can provide. "That would most definitely be against the rules."

"You're right. It would be."

Abruptly, he stands.

His lack of touch causes a chill to rush over me. I snap my eyes open, worried he finally realized just how dangerous this game is, at least for him.

"Creed, I—"

Before I can utter another syllable, he presses his mouth against mine, our kiss brief but still enthralling.

"If I'm going to lick your cunt, I want you naked, Esme. I want you laid out on this bed so I can properly feast on you. Want to watch you become so overwhelmed with sensation you feel like you're on the brink of exploding. I can't do that if you're clothed, despite how bloody hot you look in this dress. I need it gone. Now."

I swallow hard, pulse skyrocketing, taking a few seconds to calm myself before standing. Grabbing the bottom of my dress, I yank it over my head. Desire swirls in his eyes as I unclasp my bra and allow the lace material to fall to the floor before sliding my panties down my legs, kicking them to the side.

"Goddamn, Esme."

He yanks me against him, mouth devouring me as his hand explores my body, my breasts and hips a bit fuller than they were all those years ago.

"I didn't think it was possible for you to become even more beautiful. But now." He sucks in his bottom lip, tracing his gaze over my frame, "You're bloody breathtaking."

He slams his mouth back to mine, shrugging out of his suit jacket and loosening his tie as he lowers me onto the bed. Making quick work of the buttons on his shirt, he rids himself of it before crawling on top of me, his kiss unraveling me. When the outline of his erection presses against my clit, I moan, my core aching for him.

He tears his lips from mine, pressing hungry kisses along my jawline and collarbone before circling my nipple with his tongue.

"You definitely shouldn't do that, either." I close my eyes, reveling in the warmth of his mouth on my breast and hard length between my legs.

"Open your eyes, Esme." His demand cuts through my haze of bliss.

"Sorry. I forgot that's what you like."

"Only with you."

He softly touches his mouth to mine, then snakes down my body, leaving fiery kisses along my skin as he goes.

When he settles between my legs, he teases a finger down my slit.

"And I certainly shouldn't do this, either. Should I?" He rubs my clit with his thumb as he pushes a finger inside me.

Potent lust clouds my brain, erasing every voice in my head telling me to stop.

"Definitely not."

"Good girl," he croons in the seconds before dragging his tongue up my center.

I whimper, body briefly growing taut before relaxing into his touch.

"You're such a fucking good girl." He pushes another finger inside of me, stretching me even more.

"Creed." I dig my fingers into his hair, nails scraping against his scalp. My grip is probably too hard, but I need something to keep me grounded when it feels like the world is evaporating around me, his talented tongue catapulting me higher and higher with every swirl, every nip, every lick.

"That's it, baby. Fuck my face with this delicious cunt."

"God, your mouth is still as dangerous as it was all those years ago. The things it says. The things it does to me. Nothing's ever come close."

"And your pussy is still as delicious as it was all those years ago. Makes me want to stay right here and never leave."

"If you keep making me feel like this, I doubt you'll hear any complaints from me."

"I plan to." He thrusts his fingers inside me with more intensity. "Plan to make you feel everything you've been craving. Plan to make you scream my name so damn loud, all of Manhattan will know I'm the only one who can make you feel this way."

"You are," I pant, increasing my motions as that familiar sensation of bliss builds inside me. "It's always just been you, Creed. Always."

"Always, he repeats, pressing his tongue back against me.

That's all it takes for me to succumb to him, my cries filling the room as my body quivers and shakes around him. But he doesn't stop. He keeps licking me, keeps massaging my insides, keeps worshiping me the way only he ever has.

But I need more.

I need him.

Scrambling to a sitting position, I pull him closer to the headboard and force him onto his back, my hair falling around us as I straddle him.

"Do you know what else we shouldn't do?" I circle my hips against him, still sensitive from my orgasm, but desperate for more.

"What's that?" He threads his fingers through my hair, dragging his tongue along my neck.

"Fuck, Creed. We absolutely should *not* fuck."

I feel his smirk before I see it.

"I wholeheartedly agree."

His lips collide with mine in a searing kiss as he flips me onto my back. When he pulls away, he stands and kicks off his shoes, quickly shoving his pants and boxer briefs down his legs. My eyes instantly go to his erection, mouth watering at the promise of feeling it inside me again.

"Tell me something, Esme," he says as he strokes his cock.

"Yes?"

"That night I heard you scream my name and barged in on you… What were you doing?"

"I think you know exactly what I was doing."

"That may be so…" He climbs back on the bed and settles between my legs, teasing me with his erection. "But I want to hear *you* say it. I wouldn't want to jump to any conclusions."

"Don't worry." I wrap my legs around his waist and pulse against him. "Your conclusion is accurate."

"Tell me," he demands as he straightens, forcing me to drop my grip on him. Eyes focused on me, he strokes himself again. But he doesn't allow me to feel him, staying just out of reach.

And I know he won't give me what I need until I give him what *he* needs.

"I was using my vibrator."

"And why did you scream my name?" He brings his length back between my legs.

I brace for him to thrust inside, but he doesn't. He remains at my entrance, making me wild with need.

"You know why," I pant, squirming.

"Just say it." Resting his hands on either side of my head, he leans toward me, lips brushing mine. "I'm not going to fuck you until you tell me."

"I was imagining you on top of me. Imagining you fucking me."

"Good answer." He drives into me, the invasion sudden yet so wanted, causing me to cry out in surprise, then moan as I succumb to the sensation of him inside me again.

"Did it feel like this?" he grunts, each thrust becoming more punishing. More desperate.

"No," I say through my labored breathing.

"Oh no?" He slows his motions, but even the sensual rocking of his hips electrifies me.

"No." I tilt my head toward him, urging his lips against mine. "The real thing is infinitely better."

"Good to know I can't be replaced by an inanimate object." He increases his rhythm once more.

"You could never be replaced, Creed. By an inanimate object *or* something real." The words fall from my mouth before I can stop them. "No one can ever replace you."

He frames my face in his hands, this moment incredibly intimate. Not because he's moving inside me. But because I'm finally allowing myself to share my feelings with him, regardless of what tomorrow holds.

"You can't be replaced, either," he tells me. "You'll never be replaced."

His mouth recaptures mine, our tongues tangling in a dance they've done a thousand times over.

Even still, it feels new. Exciting. Exhilarating.

"My nipples," I tell him when he pulls back.

"What's that?"

"I was pinching my nipples. Hard. Pretending it was your teeth."

Grinning slyly, he brings his lips to one of my breasts, swirling his tongue around it before nibbling on the pert bud. He's gentle at first, but as he picks up his pace, he clamps down harder.

The increasing pain pushes me higher and higher, blinding me to everything except this intense sensation until I cry out, my orgasm taking me by surprise.

"Fuck, Esme," he groans, hooking one of my legs over his shoulder. "Please tell me you're still on birth control."

"I am."

"Thank fuck." He increases his motions, each thrust deeper and more desperate until he stills, body jerking through his release before he collapses on top of me.

"We definitely shouldn't do that," I remark after several long moments, my heart still beating an erratic rhythm.

"Definitely not." He laughs, carefully extracting himself from me and standing. "Give me a sec."

Leaving a kiss on my forehead, he briefly disappears into the bathroom. When he returns with a washcloth, I reach for it, but he shakes his head.

"Let me take care of you," he begs, just like our first time together.

I give him a small nod, and he brings the cloth between my legs, gaze steady on mine as he cleans up the evidence of what we did. Once he's finished, he stands and heads back into the bathroom. When he re-emerges, there's a hesitation about him, as if he's unsure where to go from here.

"Do you want to know one more thing you absolutely shouldn't do?" I jump up from the bed and close the distance. "You absolutely shouldn't stay the night." I drape my arms over his shoulders. "Shouldn't fall asleep with me wrapped in your embrace." Lifting myself onto my toes, I skim my mouth against his. "Shouldn't wake up next to me so we can do it all over again." I pinch my lips together. "Don't you think?"

All his uncertainty disappears, and he loops an arm around my waist, yanking me into him.

"I couldn't agree more… Princess."

I don't know where we'll go from here, especially since Creed has even more to lose than he did before.

But as he covers my mouth with his and lowers me back onto the bed, I don't care about any of that.

Years ago, we made a promise that, whenever we were together, we wouldn't think about the future. That we'd only focus on the present.

So that's what I do.

I stay in the present. In this moment with Creed.

Right now, it's the only thing that matters.

CHAPTER THIRTY-SEVEN

Creed

I blink my eyes open to sunlight streaming into the room, casting a glow over everything. Clothes are scattered like breadcrumbs on the carpet, ending at Esme's crumpled dress, her boots beside it. My gaze travels to the bed, where she lies next to me, golden hair fanned out, soft curves rising and falling with each breath.

I have no idea what came over me last night. One second, I was watching Esme disappear into her room. The next, I had my hand on the door. The next, I was kissing her.

And the next, I was *more* than kissing her.

In the light of day, I should regret my actions a little more. Should extricate myself from her, tell her this can't happen again and go on with my life. But as I pull her closer and pepper soft kisses to her shoulder blades, I can't seem to muster the will to worry about the potential ramifications. Not yet. Not when I still have her, regardless of how fleeting it may be.

Inhaling a deep breath, I smooth a hand down her stomach, my already throbbing erection hardening even more.

"I can't believe you're ready to go again," she says, her voice lazy with sleep.

Or lack thereof.

Sleep wasn't exactly at the top of my list of priorities last night. Nor was it on hers. Even when I wasn't fucking her, I didn't want to sleep. Didn't want to waste a single minute of feeling her body wrapped in my arms.

"This is what you do to me, Esme." I circle my hips, showing her how much I need her. "You make me lose my bloody mind." I bury my head in the crook of her neck as my hand inches farther down her stomach.

She props up a leg, giving me better access in an unspoken invitation. When I run my finger along her slit and find she's as turned on as me, I groan.

"Make me want to forget everything and lose all control." I nip at her neck, an odd sense of satisfaction filling me when I see the faint outline from where I marked her last night.

"Then do it, Creed." She moves with the rhythm I set, a tiny whimper falling from her throat when I push a finger inside, stretching and savoring in her. "Lose all control. Lose control with me."

I insert another finger, thumb pressing against her clit. She pulses against me with more urgency, chasing that sensation of bliss we've both indulged in countless times in the last eight hours. But I don't want her to come on my hand. Not this time.

Pulling away, I force her onto her back and hover over her.

"Creed, wha—"

I press my lips to hers, swallowing her protest.

"You know I respect you. That I care about you. That I lo—" I stop short at what I was about to confess. It wouldn't be the first time I've told her how I feel about her. That was years ago, though. I can't go down that path with her. Not right now. Not when I'm still uncertain about what this means.

If it *can* mean anything.

She cups my face, running the pad of her thumb along my cheek. "I do."

"Good." I lower my lips back to hers. "Because I'm about to fuck you like I don't."

Before she has a chance to react, I flip her onto her stomach and yank her onto her knees. Covering her body with mine, I slide my hands down her arms, linking my fingers with hers. I inhale her scent again, wanting to douse myself in it for eternity. When I nibble on her earlobe, she moans, squirming against me.

"This is going to be hard and fast. Okay?"

"Yes."

"Good." I straighten and bring my erection up to her.

But as hungry as I am to lose myself in her, I don't thrust inside her. Not yet. Instead, I take a minute to appreciate how damn amazing she looks as she waits for me. Smooth skin. Full breasts. Hair cascading over her shoulders. And right now, she's all mine.

When I don't move for several moments, she glances over her shoulder. "Fuck me, Creed."

I don't think I'll ever tire of hearing those words come out of her mouth.

I run my fingers down her back, tracing the line of her spine before clutching her hip. With my free hand, I line myself up at her entrance, teasing her with my cock.

"I'll always give you want you want, princess."

Then I slam into her, my motions fast and relentless.

She buries her head in the pillow to muffle her cries.

"You feel so damn good like this. I just… Fuck." I drive into her harder, my grip on her hips tightening. "I just want to crawl inside you and never bloody leave."

"Creed," she whimpers, meeting my motions, thrust for thrust.

"Touch yourself, Esme," I demand. "I'm ready to lose my damn mind and I need you to come." I curve over her body, scraping my unshaven jawline against her neck. "Like I promised all those years ago… I'll always make sure you come first."

Her breathing becomes ragged, her muscles clenching. But she follows my command, lowering her hand to her clit and rubbing. I could have easily done it, but I love watching her play with herself. Love watching her chase her own bliss. Love knowing she still feels comfortable enough with me to explore the deepest parts of her desires.

"Please tell me you're close."

She nods. "I'm so close, Creed. So damn close. So—"

I clamp my teeth onto her neck, licking and sucking at the same time. That's all it takes for her to cry out, her body convulsing around me. The feel of her quivering is the last straw and I let out a strangled groan as I release inside of her.

Placing my hand on her stomach to support her, I help her onto her back, lips touching hers in a gentle kiss.

The softness in our exchange is at complete odds with the way I just fucked her. But I can't imagine kissing her any other way, neither one of us breaking away as we come down from our orgasms.

"I hope you enjoyed that." I move to her jawline, wishing I could stay here with her. Kiss every inch of her body.

Even then, it won't be enough. I'll want more of her.

I'll want all of her.

"I like when you're rough with me. Like when you don't treat me like I'll break."

I brush my lips against hers. "You're a strong woman, Esme. I know it'll take a lot more than rough sex to break you." With a wink, I pull back, grabbing the towel from the foot of the bed and pressing it between her legs.

Although I'd love nothing more than to leave her marked there. Would love her to have a constant reminder of what we did as she goes through her day and feels my cum drip down her leg.

"Are you hungry?" I ask as I toss the towel onto the floor. "I'll run out and get you something."

"I can order room service. No sense sending you into the cold when I can have food delivered at the touch of a button."

"But room service doesn't have pastries from this amazing little French bakery just down the block." I curve toward her, lips seeking out hers once more.

"Damn you for knowing my weakness." She moans as she melts into my kiss. "Do you know how hard it is for me to say no to French pastries, even though you could fuck me at least once more in the time you're gone?"

"That may be true." I waggle my brows. "But I need to get you fed. Need you to have some energy for what I plan to do to you later."

I slide off the bed and head to my pile of clothes, hastily getting dressed, if for no other reason than to get back to Esme as soon as possible.

Before she realizes what a mistake this is.

Before *I* realize what a mistake this is, too.

"And what did you have in mind?" Her green eyes narrow on me, sultry and sensual as they skate over my body.

"You'll have to wait and find out." Returning to her, I cage her between my arms. "But it will most certainly involve you." I press a kiss to her cheek. "This bed." I leave another kiss on her opposite cheek. "And possibly the filling from a cream puff." I cover her mouth, swiping my tongue with hers.

"Well, then, you'd better hurry back."

"Yes, ma'am." With one last kiss, I turn from her and step into my shoes before heading toward the door, shrugging on my coat.

"Creed?" she calls out.

My hand on the knob, I pause, glancing at her. "Yes?"

"What does this mean for us?"

My shoulders falling, I shake my head, wishing I had an answer for her. "I don't know."

She nods in understanding.

"What do you want it to mean for us?" I ask after a protracted pause.

"I don't know, either."

I give her a reassuring smile. "Then we'll figure it out. But not on an empty stomach."

I open the door and scan the hallway for any sign of life before slipping out of her hotel room undetected.

I should have told her it can't mean anything, not with who we are to each other.

But I *want* it to mean something.

Hell, I want it to mean everything.

Because Esme *is* everything to me.

She always has been.

But I don't know if that will ever be enough.

CHAPTER THIRTY-EIGHT

Esme

The second the door closes, leaving me alone in my hotel room, I already miss Creed, especially with his scent surrounding me.

I still struggle to wrap my head around last night. Exploring New York City. Walking through Central Park. Hating to say goodnight after he walked me to my room. Him kissing me like he used to all those years ago.

Hell, *better* than he did all those years ago.

Then spending all night indulging in each other, both of us on a mission to make up for lost time.

And did we ever. I lost count of the number of orgasms he treated me to last night. I probably only slept an hour or two. But even when I *did* sleep, the nightmares stayed away.

As I ruminate over everything that happened yesterday, a ping sounds on my phone. I grab it off the nightstand, my stomach dropping when I see a text from my brother. I navigate toward the message, praying he doesn't know I spent last night with his chief protection officer, especially since Creed left his exhibit early.

But as I read the text, relief floods through me. I should have known my brother would be too distracted by Nora to pay much attention to anything else.

ANDERSON:

Just wanted to let you know I'm planning to stay in New York a few more days. Maybe another week. Thanks for coming out last night. Love ya.

ME:

Am I to assume things are going well with Nora?

ANDERSON:

They certainly are. I want to stay here a little while longer to reconnect and figure out where we go from here.

ME:

Reconnect? Is that what they're calling it these days?

ANDERSON:

You know what I mean.

ME:

I do. Enjoy your time "reconnecting". I love you.

I wait for a few minutes to see if he responds, but he doesn't. After all the downs my brother has endured these past few months, he deserves having a win in his column. Based on my conversation with Nora last night, I have no doubt she's exactly what he needs. She doesn't treat him like he's special or the heir to the crown.

She treats him like he's anyone else.

He needs that. Needs someone willing to fight for him, yet put him in his place when necessary.

In desperate need of a shower after spending the better part of the past eight hours having more sex than I have in the past eight weeks, I throw the duvet off me and pad into the bathroom. I start the shower and am about to step under the water when someone knocks on the door.

I thought I had at least another ten or fifteen minutes before Creed would be back, but I won't complain. Maybe he'll be interested in joining me for a quick shower. Then again, I doubt it would be all that quick. Creed's a master at prolonging things, making sure I experience every ounce of pleasure possible.

And boy did I experience pleasure last night. The mere thought of it causes my skin to prickle, my pulse increasing.

Grabbing my robe from the closet, I pull it on and wrap the sash around my waist. Then I hurry to the door and open it, not wanting Creed to stand outside my room any longer than necessary in case anyone walks by.

"That was quick, they must be closer than—"

I snap my mouth shut when I realize it's not Creed.

It's Tristan.

But he doesn't look like the Tristan Hughes I spent the past several years with. There's a weariness about his, his hair disheveled, eyes red.

"Tristan." I pull my robe tighter. "What are you doing here?"

"I'm sorry for barging in on you like this. I just…" He runs his fingers through his hair and tugs at it. "I needed to see you."

"How did you know I was here?"

He shoves his hands into his pockets. "Based on the fact

that I'm still getting emails with your daily itinerary, I can only assume you haven't told your private secretary we… ended things."

I briefly close my eyes.

When you're a royal, ending a relationship isn't as simple as dividing the flatware and bedding. There are people who have to be made aware of it, too. Something I simply haven't wanted to deal with yet.

"I haven't."

His shoulders fall in what looks like relief. "Can we talk? Five minutes. That's all I'm asking. Just five minutes so I can get this off my chest."

I chew on my bottom lip, unsure I want to hear what he's about to say. But he came all this way to see me. The least I can do is give him a few minutes of my time.

With a subtle nod, I step back and allow him to enter my room. He comes to a stop when he sees the pile of clothes by my bed, my lace bra and panties on the top of my dress. I nervously scan the space for any inflammatory evidence of last night's activities, namely my vibrator that Creed begged to use on me at one point. Thankfully, it must have rolled underneath the bed.

"Just give me a second. I was about to jump in the shower." I grab a t-shirt and yoga pants from the dresser and duck into the bathroom, steam filling the space from the running shower. I turn off the water and dress quickly, then rejoin Tristan, stomach heavy as I contemplate why he's here.

Actually, I'm pretty sure I know why he's here.

I just don't know how I'm supposed to respond.

I gesture to the couch in the sitting area, and he lowers himself onto it.

"What would you like to discuss?" I sit on the opposite end.

"Us," he responds without a hint of hesitation.

"Us?"

"Yes. Mainly the fact I was a — how do you put it — a bloody wanker."

I crack a smile at his attempt at mimicking my accent. "That's one way."

"How about twat? Pillock. Git. Arsehole. Just a plain stupid tosser."

"You didn't do anything wrong. I changed the rules. Spun the table on you. You had every reason to walk away. I made you promises, and broke those promises. I don't blame you at all."

He slides closer and grabs my hands. "But I should have supported your decision, especially once you shared your reasons for choosing this path. Instead, I was a fool, Esme. A goddamn selfish ass. These past few weeks have been the worst of my life. I thought I was doing the right thing. I had a front-row seat to how miserable my mother was all of her life. How miserable she *still* is. I didn't want that for myself. At least I didn't think I did. But then I realized something."

"What's that?" I ask, even though a part of me doesn't want to hear his answer. Doesn't want to feel anything for him.

But I do. I may not love him like I do Creed. But there are degrees of love. I still care deeply for Tristan.

Is it enough, though?

"What's the point of having a career I enjoy when I must sacrifice the woman I love in exchange? Who does that? Who chooses their career over someone they love? That's what I realized these past few weeks while I was on set. At first, I welcomed the distraction of filming. Thought it would make things easier. Thought it would reaffirm I made the right choice. Instead, all being there taught me was that I fucked up. That I don't want that life anymore. Not if it means losing you."

He inches closer, bringing his hands to my face, urging my lips toward his. "And I don't want to lose you, Esme. You're the love of my fucking life. If I have to give up acting to spend every day of the rest of my life with you, that's exactly what I'll do. Because I know you're worth it. *You* are my life. Nothing else. Just you."

His mouth skims mine, the gentleness in his touch making my heart ache. Not because I've missed him.

But because of what I'm about to do to him, especially after his heartfelt declaration.

"There's something you need to know." Pulling away, I meet his eyes.

"Uh oh." He laughs nervously. "In my experience, nothing good ever follows a statement like that."

"I know. But the thing is—"

A loud knock rips through the space, and I dart my gaze toward the door, my heart plummeting to the pit of my stomach.

Creed.

I squeeze my eyes shut for a moment, then pull myself to my feet, praying this doesn't become as awkward as I fear it will.

I pad across the room and place my hand on the knob, drawing in a deep breath before opening the door. The second I do, Creed's eyes light up, a sexy smile crawling on his full lips.

"God, I—"

"Thanks so much for running to get my breakfast for me," I say louder than necessary, hoping Creed picks up on my demeanor.

He furrows his brow, studying me for a protracted beat. Then his gaze widens as he focuses just past me.

"I thought I heard your voice," Tristan says as he approaches, grabbing the bag and tray of coffee from Creed. If he wonders why there are two cups, he doesn't say anything. "Let me take those off your hands."

"Mr. Hughes." Tone clipped and rough, he looks between Tristan and me, eyes hard. "I wasn't aware you'd be here."

"It was a last-minute trip. But I had to see Esme." He glances my way with nothing short of adoration in his gaze. "I'd be an utter fool not to."

I quickly lower my head, every word he speaks like another punch to the gut. I technically didn't cheat on Tristan, but I hate that I can't tell him the truth. Not without putting Creed's livelihood at risk.

"You certainly would be," Creed says through gritted teeth as he turns toward me, stance rigid, shoulders square. His jaw clenches, nostrils flaring in an attempt to reel in his anger.

Or perhaps disappointment.

"Enjoy your breakfast, Your Highness. I hear the cream puffs are to die for."

With a curt bow, he spins on his heels and marches down the hallway, his strides quick and powerful, as if determined to put as much distance between us as possible.

CHAPTER THIRTY-NINE

Creed

My hands shake as I stalk down the hallway, barely registering the room numbers zooming past me. My stomach churns with a bitter mix of animosity and regret. Not because I learned Tristan flew across the country to surprise Esme.

But because of what it made me realize.

Something I happily ignored last night.

And this morning.

But I can't ignore it anymore.

"Creed!"

When I hear Esme's voice, I hesitate, not wanting to torture myself further.

But I can't avoid this forever.

Pausing in my tracks, I glance behind me as Esme hurries toward me on bare feet, her hair a mess, not a lick of makeup on her face.

Regardless, she still looks so damn beautiful it makes my

heart squeeze. Makes me want to drag her into my room, push her against the wall, and fuck her so hard she'll forget Tristan Hughes ever existed.

That won't fix anything, though.

It never does.

"Can we… Can we talk?" Her wide eyes plead with me.

Sighing, I face forward and unlock my door, holding it open for her.

As she steps into my room, she gives me a small smile, the combination of her body wash and my scent on her wrapping around me.

"I'm so sorry about that, Creed," she blurts out once the door clicks closed. "I didn't know what else to do. I didn't intend to make you feel like nothing more than the staff charged with delivering my breakfast. I just—"

"But isn't that what I am?"

She stiffens, breath catching, lips parting.

"Of course not. You're so much more than that. You always have been." She drags herself within a whisper of me, lips skimming mine. "You'll *always* be so much more to me."

I close my eyes, savoring in the light touch of her mouth to mine. So full. So warm. So bloody perfect.

But there's one thing her lips can never be.

They can never be mine.

She can never be mine.

I snap out of her hypnotic trance, increasing the space between us. "*You* may not see me as just the staff, the hired help. But that's what I am. That's all you *should* see me as. Nothing more."

"Is this because of Tristan? We broke up. He came to apologize, but that doesn't mean anything. Not when I don't want him." She touches my hand. "I want you."

"But I can't want you, Esme," I tell her through the

boulder in my throat, ridding myself of her touch, despite craving it more than I do my next breath. "As much as I wish I could, I just…" I hang my head. "I can't."

"What about last night?" She crosses her arms in front of her chest, the pain my words cause her visible in the subtle quiver of her chin. "And this morning? Were you just horny and knew I'd be an easy lay?"

I bark out a laugh. "Nothing about you has ever been easy. Nothing about you ever *will* be easy."

"So that's it? You're walking away because it won't be easy?" Her voice grows louder with every word, the passion and determination in her expression making me want to sweep her into my arms. "I didn't take you for someone to run when things got challenging."

"They're not just challenging, Esme!" I roar, my voice louder than I intended.

When she flinches, I squeeze my eyes shut and draw in a deep breath to calm myself, attempt to have a somewhat civilized conversation without everyone in this hotel finding out the truth.

Especially her brother.

And Tristan.

"They're not just challenging," I say again, this time much softer. "They're impossible. Last night…" I shake my head as I fight to get my thoughts in order. "Last night was bloody incredible. I'd thought about what it would be like to fall asleep next to you again for years. Since you came back, I wanted to keep my distance. Fought to do so. Because I knew if I allowed myself to get close to you, I'd want more. I'd want all of you. And I. Can't. Have. You."

I struggle to even get the words out, my body fighting me every step of the way. But they're true. Sleeping with Esme wasn't just a bad idea, like it was all those years ago. It's forbidden. I could lose everything.

Worse, I'd be letting my father down. Letting Rory down. Letting AJ down.

Letting Adam down.

When he learned Rory was pregnant, I promised I'd take care of her and his unborn child if anything happened to him.

This isn't doing that. Not when it could put our livelihoods in jeopardy.

"We both needed this wake-up call. Needed the reminder that we're from two different worlds. While it may feel bloody incredible in those moments when our two worlds collide, it's not reality. It can never *be* our reality, Esme. We need to leave the past in the past. Look toward the future. And I can't be your future," I pause, voice unsteady as I add, "But Tristan can."

"Tristan?" she chokes out. "Wha—"

"He's a good person, as much as it pains me to say. From the first time I saw you together, I could tell how much he adores you. That's what you deserve. To be with someone who will look at you as if you're the only woman he sees. Who will hop on a plane and fly across the country to tell you what a dolt he's been. Who will give up his career to be with you."

I don't know for sure if Tristan has agreed to do that, but if he's here to apologize and set things right, I assume that's what he's willing to do.

It's what *I* should be willing to do.

But our circumstances are vastly different.

"And you won't do that?" she asks in a barely audible voice, chin quivering.

Last night, we were in a bubble. I ignored the real world.

Now that the cloud of lust has evaporated and we've been yanked back to reality, I can see clearly again.

Can see the truth again.

And the truth is that Esme will forever be my greatest love, the one woman who ignited a fire in my soul that will never die. But my love for her can only exist in the shadows. *We* can only exist in the shadows.

I can thank Tristan's surprise appearance for helping me realize that.

Pulling my lips together, I shake my head. "I can't."

She doesn't say anything. Simply stares at me, as if waiting for me to change my mind. But I won't. Not about this. Not when other people depend on me.

Every sound in the room seems to be amplified. The whirring of the heating unit. The traffic of the New York City streets thirty floors below. And the pounding of my erratic heart.

Finally, she turns and heads for the door, but hesitates before opening it. When she glances over her shoulder and parts her lips, I swallow hard, sensing I'm not going to like whatever she's about to tell me. That it's only going to make this situation hurt more than it already does.

But instead, she snaps her mouth closed and shakes her head, as if deciding it doesn't matter.

Then she disappears into the hallway, the door closing with an echoing thud behind her.

CHAPTER FORTY

Esme

I stare out of the floor-to-ceiling windows in the bedroom of Tristan's penthouse apartment in Paris. The Eiffel Tower and Seine are visible in the distance, the morning sky painted a cacophony of purples and blues.

It's been one week since Tristan showed up in New York.

One week since he made a heartfelt plea for me to forgive him, that his career was pointless if he no longer had me in his life.

One week since Creed pushed me into another man's arms, insisting we could never be together.

I know we can't. Not unless he's willing to walk away from his legacy. But it's more than that now. There's also AJ and Rory to consider. And Adam. He may not have come right out and said it, but I know Adam's ghost is still influencing most of his decisions.

I want to hate him for what he did. Hate him for

reminding me what true passion felt like. Giving me a taste of heaven.

Then yank me back to reality.

And the reality is that Creed will never choose me.

It's ironic to think it was Adam who forced me to break Creed's heart all those years ago.

And it's Adam who caused Creed to break mine last week.

When I returned to my hotel room that morning, I had every intention of telling Tristan it would never work. Not when my heart belonged to someone else.

But as I stared at him, at this amazing man who was willing to give up the career he loved to be with me, I couldn't manage to find the words I needed.

Not when it brought into sharp focus the fact that Tristan was willing to do the one thing Creed wasn't.

I was too numb to fight it, so I agreed to give him another chance.

I convinced myself it would be okay. Thought if we came to Paris, I'd be reminded why I fell for him in the first place.

Instead, all I can think of is Creed, especially when Tristan circles his hips, his erection noticeable, even through his pajama pants.

"Good morning, beautiful," he croons in a raspy voice.

"Morning." My response comes out somewhat clipped.

"How did you sleep?"

"Fine," I tell him, although it's as far from the truth as possible.

All night, I tossed and turned after having that same nightmare yet again.

In fact, they've gotten worse.

Now, when I look into the front seat, Creed's with Adam.

I know it's just a dream, a result of something in my subconscious, but it feels so real.

To the point where I nearly pick up the phone and call Creed to make sure he's okay.

But I don't.

"God, I've missed this," Tristan says, hand exploring my body, his touch becoming increasingly sensual. "Missed waking up next to you."

He kisses a line from my shoulder blades to my neck, nibbling gently.

I want to tell him to bite me. Mark me. Anything to make me feel *something* again. Anything other than this intense longing for Creed.

"Miss feeling your body against mine."

He pulses against me, and I try to melt into him. Try to think of only him. Try to remember how turned on I once was whenever he touched me.

But nothing works.

"I need you, Esme." He pushes me onto my back and crawls between my legs. "Need to make love to you." His lips move along my collarbone before he snakes down my body, hooking his fingers into my panties.

But before he can lift my hips and drag them down my legs, I push away from him and sit on the edge of the bed, wracking my brain to come up with yet another excuse.

Like I have every other time he's tried to initiate things between us since New York.

He sighs, running a hand over his face, his frustration obvious. It's not about the lack of sex. Tristan isn't like that. It's about the lack of connection.

"Is everything okay?"

"I'm just still dealing with some…stuff." I flash him an apologetic smile, hoping he doesn't press the issue.

"I don't want you to think I'm pressuring you." He moves to sit beside me. "I just… I'm trying really fucking hard here, Esme. I know I screwed up."

I grab his hand in mine. "It's not that."

"Then what is it?" he asks in a pained voice. "I'm trying to rebuild what we lost when I was a complete idiot. Thought coming to Paris would help." He licks his lips. "Instead, all I feel is the divide between us widening. Like you're not even present. I'm not blaming you," he adds quickly. "I just…" He brings his hands to my cheeks. "I love you, Esme. I want that to be enough for you."

"I want that to be enough for me, too," I quiver, the heartache in his voice nearly splitting me in half.

"But it's not, is it?" He pulls back, dropping his hold on me.

I *want* to love him. Part of me does in the only way I can love someone other than Creed.

But the other part of me is still clinging to my past.

Maybe I need to stop thinking about Creed. Do everything to forget he ever held a piece of my heart. Like my mother often said… *We can't live in the present if we're still held captive by the past.*

I made the decision years ago not to remain held captive by the past.

Maybe I can make the same decision again.

Creed is my past. He insisted he needed to remain precisely that.

Tristan could be my future. But only if I finally come clean about my past. About everything.

Even if he hates me afterwards.

"The reason I haven't wanted to be intimate is because I slept with someone after we broke up."

A hush falls over the room as his shoulders sag and he

rests his forearms on his knees. Several painful moments pass as he processes this information. Then he looks my way.

"I can't fault you for that, as much as I want to cut off the bastard's hands for touching you." His jaw ticks, fists clenching and unclenching. "But I'm not mad, Esme. I said things that made you think we weren't ever going to get back together. I don't blame you for having some revenge sex, more or less. If I blame anyone, it's myself for being an idiot."

I run my hands down my legs and worry my bottom lip.

Noticing my reaction, he remarks, "But it wasn't *just* revenge sex. Was it?"

I slowly shake my head. "It was someone I had feelings for a long time ago. Someone I've tried to forget. I thought I had, especially once I met you. But when I returned home and our paths crossed again—"

"It's Jameson Gates, isn't it?"

I part my lips, then pause.

I can easily say it was. After all, most of the world still believes we were once in love but tragedy tore us apart. I can simply continue the lie.

But Tristan deserves better than that, especially if he's willing to give up everything for me.

"I was never in love with Jameson Gates," I confess in an even voice.

He scrunches his brows. "But I saw the videos and photos of you together. Heard the rumors you were about to get engaged."

"My entire relationship with Jameson Gates was a publicity stunt. A ploy by the royal household to garner positive press since everyone loves a royal wedding. None of it was real. I had no choice but to go along with it. At least, that's what I thought. All my life, my grandmother continually told me there was no place for love in a monarchy, and I believed her. Didn't think I was strong enough to fight centuries of tradition."

"If you weren't in love with Jameson, who *did* you have feelings for?"

I swallow down the lump in my throat. "Someone I could never be with. Someone who didn't have remotely close to the social standing required for the royal household required to approve."

"What happened?" he asks hesitantly.

Drawing in a deep breath, I steel myself to split open the wounds I thought had healed long ago. Then I confess everything. How I was upset after learning I was being married off to someone I didn't choose like a piece of property. How I took matters into my own hands and propositioned this man to take my virginity as an act of defiance. How he initially refused, but eventually changed his mind. How it was only supposed to be one night, but we couldn't keep our hands off each other. How we decided to continue our fling until the end of the summer.

How I fell in love.

How my former chief protection officer learned about us and begged me to end things.

How I eventually relented and broke this man's heart, making him hate me.

How my chief protection officer eventually realized his actions were about to sentence me to a lifetime of being miserable.

How he was taking me to make things right when our vehicle was attacked.

How I never told this man the truth.

How I left for Paris because I couldn't stand to be around reminders of everything I'd lost.

How I thought I'd put it all behind me until I returned home and realized I still had strong feelings for him.

How I *still* have strong feelings for him.

How I fear I always will.

When I come to the end of the sordid tale, a silence settles in the room, heavy and thick. I study Tristan, but his expression doesn't give anything away. I wish it did. Wish I could see some sort of emotion, even if that emotion is anger.

"This man who still owns your heart…" His voice catches, tears welling in his eyes. "Who is it?"

I hesitate, not wanting to get Creed into trouble, since he was with me mere weeks ago. While he was a member of the royal guard.

"Someone who stands to lose everything if anyone learned we were together. Especially this recent."

"I'm not going to…" He trails off, his face draining of color as realization sinks in. He briefly closes his eyes, posture slumping. "It's Creed Lawson. Isn't it?"

I don't even have to respond. He can tell just by my apologetic expression.

"How did I not see it all before?" he says softly, although I'm not sure if his question is directed at me or himself. "I was so worried about Jameson Gates. I just…" He digs his hands through his hair, tugging at it in frustration. "And he was assigned to be your CPO on that trip? No wonder you were—"

"No!" I interject, voice echoing in the room. "My history with Creed had *nothing* to do with what happened. Hell, at that point, we were still at each other's throats. We wanted nothing to do with each other."

"Then what changed?"

I shrug. "He took a bullet for me."

Tristan parts his lips, probably to argue he'd do the same, but I hold up my hand, cutting him off.

"It was more than just that. He understood what I was going through. He was the only person who really did. The only person who never told me to get over it. The only person who didn't make light of it because I wasn't harmed, so what if some guy pointed a gun at me."

"Like I did," he says dejectedly.

I remain silent, not agreeing with him.

But not disagreeing, either.

As wonderful as Tristan is, he *did* downplay things. Made comments that had me questioning my sanity. Made me think I should be able to forget some guy was less than a second away from killing me.

"Do you still love him?" Tristan asks after a beat, his eyes like bottomless pits of sorrow.

"I don't want to," I confess, throat aching.

"But you do."

I squeeze my eyes shut, hating to hurt Tristan like this, but he deserves the truth.

"I do."

He pushes out a long sigh as my confession seems to echo in the quiet of the morning.

"Answer me this. If there was nothing preventing you from being together, who would you choose?"

"Tristan…" His name is like a plea on my lips as I beg him not to ask this of me.

"Tell me, Esme. I need to know where I stand. Will I always come in second place in your heart?"

I want to tell him he won't. That I love him. That I'm happy with him.

But he deserves better than this.

He deserves someone who will love him without restraint.

Who lights up the instant he walks into the room. Who can't imagine a future without him. Who will fight for him. Who will *burn* for him.

That's not me.

It never was.

"I'm sorry," is all the response I can give him.

My words are like a punch to the gut, all the strength disappearing from his body as he deflates in front of me.

I hadn't expected this morning to take such a drastic turn. But as much as I hate hurting Tristan, this needed to happen. I need to stop pretending.

"Okay then." He pushes to his feet, his defined muscles tensing and stretching with the motion. "I'm going to hit the gym. Try to…process this."

I stand, awkwardly pulling my t-shirt to cover my bare legs. "I'll pack my things and be out of here by the time you get back."

My eyes trace over his frame as I take in every detail about him. From the light dusting of stubble along his jawline, to his disheveled hair, to his plaid pajama bottoms that fall so perfectly from his hips.

"I really am sorry," I say for what feels like the hundredth time in the last ten minutes. "I didn't mean for this to happen. Thought I could leave the past in the past."

"Even if you could, I'm not interested in being anyone's consolation prize."

"I'm sorry I made you waste all these years waiting for me."

He cups my cheeks, his grip on my unwavering. "No time spent with you will ever be a waste." His lips touch mine in a soft but full kiss. Then he pulls back, red-rimmed eyes meeting mine. "Take care of yourself, Esme."

"You, too."

He gives me on last smile, then turns, making his way across the bedroom. Just as he's about to slip into the hallway, he pauses, eyes meeting mine.

"She's wrong, ya know."

"Who is?"

"Your grandmother. Love can exist anywhere if you're willing to fight for it." He holds my gaze for another beat before disappearing from view.

CHAPTER FORTY-ONE

Creed

I sink into the deep leather couch, admiring the Christmas tree standing in the bay window. Tiny lights adorn each branch and glitter against the backdrop of soft white snowflakes falling outside. The sweet aroma of nutmeg and cinnamon fills the living area as our Christmas Eve celebration winds down.

Sipping on my scotch, I can't help but smile as I watch AJ play with his gifts from my parents, who spoiled him, as they always do.

This is what I need. A reminder of what truly matters. I'd forgotten for a bit. Allowed myself to fall into my old patterns.

Between acting as Esme's temporary CPO, as well as Anderson's extensive travel prior to that, I hadn't been home much. Hadn't been around Rory and AJ much.

Had forgotten about the promise I made to Adam.

Never again.

This is where I belong.

This is what's important.

Nothing else.

No *one* else.

"Look at this, Uncle Creed!"

AJ's voice forces me back to the present, and I glance toward the dining area, the table that previously held the roast beef, potatoes, and green beans Rory prepared for us now turned into a construction zone for all the LEGO bricks my parents bought him.

"That's great, buddy," I say, taking in the start of an intricate pirate ship. "I guess I know how you plan on spending your school holiday."

"You've got that right," he shoots back with a gleam in his eye.

He may never have known his father, but there's no mistaking he's Adam's son. Not just in appearance, but also in his mannerisms. The older he gets, the more I feel like I've gone back in time thirty years and am seeing a younger version of Adam.

He loved building LEGOs, too.

I can only imagine the hours he would have spent with AJ, constructing as many complicated sets as possible.

When you lose someone you love, their absence always seems more pronounced around the holidays. Today's no exception. But I refuse to dwell on that. This needs to be a happy time. For AJ's sake.

"Don't forget you have to start researching topics for your social studies project," Rory reminds him as she lowers herself onto the couch beside me and takes a long sip of her wine.

"Yes, Mum," AJ groans, then gives Rory a playful wink.

"How are you doing?" I ask in a soft voice once AJ refocuses his attention on his pirate ship, my mum and dad seeming just as interested in building it as AJ.

While my father and I still have a somewhat strained relationship, he's been making more of an effort since Adam's death, especially once AJ was born. When he was younger, he would stop by and take him to the park. Or out for ice cream. Or to a big football match.

I think Adam's death brought into focus everything he missed out on with us. Opportunities he'll never get back. Opportunities he regrets wasting.

"I'm good, actually. I think I've finally come to terms with the fact that I'll never *not* miss him. But I think it's okay to miss him."

I give her hand a squeeze. "I miss him, too." I glance past her at AJ. "Especially when I see him building LEGOs. Adam loved doing that when we were kids. He'd be right in the middle of it. Hell, he'd probably encourage AJ to put off his school project so they could keep building together."

"He absolutely would," my mum chimes in. "There were quite a few times your brother claimed to be sick, so I allowed him to stay home from school, only to find him hours later making an entire village with his LEGOs. The next time he attempted to pull one over on me, I said I needed to use a rectal thermometer on him. That made him change his tune rather quickly. He was dressed in his uniform in a matter of seconds."

We all erupt in laughter, the sound welcome in this place that's typically filled with sorrow and loss.

"What other things did my dad do?" AJ asks after a beat, his question slightly hesitant.

It's silent as we exchange glances.

For years, Adam's been the elephant in the room. We've told AJ bits and pieces about his father, did everything to make sure he knew he died a hero, but we haven't gone into too much detail.

And AJ never asked.

Until now.

"He would watch your Uncle Creed sleep," Mum says after a few moments. "He was so excited about having a little brother. But he didn't understand why he slept all the time, so he would always sneak into his crib and watch him." Her eyes glisten with unshed tears, a nostalgic smile tugging on her lips as she meets my gaze. "From the beginning, he always watched out for you. Always wanted to keep you safe."

I swallow hard, pushing down the new wave of remorse filling me. My mum doesn't mean anything by it, but it makes me regret my actions even more.

Solidifies I made the right decision in New York.

"He would make a mess in the bathroom whenever he took a bath," my dad says, his voice wistful. "I lost count of the number of times I told him the point of a bath was to keep the water *in* the tub. Not out of it." He shakes his head and chuckles. "He would bring all these toys in with him. Army figurines. Dinosaurs. Stuff like that. He always had a rather active imagination. Would make up these stories as he splashed around." He pauses, pulling his lips between his teeth. "I wish I was home more to watch that." His gaze lifts to mine, an apology within.

I give him an understanding smile. My dad may not be perfect, but at least he's trying to do better.

"How about you, Uncle Creed?" AJ looks my way. "What's your favorite memory of my dad?"

I fix my eyes forward, searching my brain for one memory of my brother I'd consider my favorite. It's harder than I thought. My brother and I may have had our differences, but we also had a lot of good times together.

Like when we rode our bikes to the local market on the "busy street", as we called the road with slightly more traffic than our sleepy residential neighborhood.

Or when we built a fort out of bent trees in the wooded area behind our house, complete with a "No Girls Allowed" sign.

Or when I called home during my training for special teams, ready to give up, only for him to remind me I was stronger than this and to persevere.

But there's one memory that will always stand out.

"The day he told me your mum was pregnant with you. He wanted to go to the shops and start buying baby clothes, even though he had no idea if you were a boy or a girl."

I look into the distance as I remember how ecstatic my brother was, the memory of that day playing like a movie in my mind. I didn't think he could get any happier than when he first told me about meeting Rory. That was nothing compared to the unbridled joy he exuded when he told me he was starting a family with her.

"But he was also a little scared."

"Scared?" AJ presses.

"Worried he wasn't going to be a good dad. I assured him he would. He was always an amazing older brother to me." I lift my lips into a smile. "Still, I promised I'd always be there for him, as well as you and your mum. And it's a promise I'm happy to keep for the rest of my life."

Rory reaches for my hand and squeezes, eyes awash with gratitude.

"How about you?" I ask her guardedly.

She chews on her bottom lip as she stares at the red liquid in her wine glass. Then she pulls her hand from mine.

I worry I overstepped. That she's not ready, even all these years later.

"He always brought me coffee in the morning," she finally says. "It was such a small thing, but every morning when his alarm went off, he prepared two cups and we spent twenty minutes drinking our coffee in bed, talking about our hopes for the future. Even when he was on assignment, he made sure to FaceTime me each morning so we could still have our coffee together." She swipes at a few tears falling down her cheeks. "It just shows how thoughtful he was. He always made time for those he cared about, regardless of how busy he was."

Another silence settles in the room, the only sound that of Christmas music playing in the background. Then my father stands, raising his scotch glass. "To Adam."

We all follow suit. Even AJ lifts his glass of water, all of us toasting the impact Adam had on our lives. It's bittersweet to share these memories. But also freeing. Like we're finally allowing ourselves to put our past behind us.

"I'll be right there," Mum tells Dad as they start toward the door after Rory's taken AJ up to read with him before bed.

"Sure thing." He gives me a brief hug. It's a change from the typical handshakes we once limited ourselves to. "Happy Christmas, son."

"You, too, Dad."

He pats my back, then slips out of the house. I grab my mum's coat off the rack in the mudroom and help her into it.

"How are you, Creed?" she asks as she pulls on her gloves.

"Good," I respond, although I can tell her question is deeper than a polite inquiry.

She studies me for a beat, her analytical stare sweeping over my face. Other than Adam, she was the only person who could figure out what I was feeling or thinking.

"He wouldn't want this life for you. You know that, right?"

"What are you talking about?"

"Adam," she says softly. "He wouldn't want you to sacrifice your happiness like this. Don't get me wrong. What you've done for Rory and AJ is remarkable. You put your life on hold to give them the support they need. But you did so at the expense of your own happiness."

"Mum, I—"

"The story you told tonight. About how happy Adam was when he told you Rory was pregnant."

"What about it?"

"He'd hate to know you never got to experience that same happiness." She places her hand on my arm. "You need to stop punishing yourself. Because that's what you've been doing since Adam's death, Creed. You've been punishing yourself."

"I'm not punishing myself," I insist, although my words lack even a modicum of conviction. "I'm just fulfilling my promise to Adam. He asked me to look out for Rory and AJ if anything were to happen to him."

"He'd take it back in a heartbeat if he knew about all the sacrifices you've made in order to fulfill that promise." She grabs my hands in hers. "You know how much your brother loved you. He was willing to lose everything so you'd be happy. He wouldn't want this life for you. He *didn't* want this life for you. I don't want this life for you, either. I know things are…complicated. I wouldn't count yourself out just yet."

She hoists herself onto her toes and presses a soft kiss to my cheek. Then she turns and makes her way out of the house, leaving me with even more questions.

Was she talking about Esme when she mentioned things being complicated? And what did she mean by saying Adam was willing to lose everything so I'd be happy?

Once my parents' car pulls out of the driveway, I head up the stairs, my thoughts consumed by my mother's words. Until I peek into AJ's room and admire his sleeping form.

While I appreciate my mother's concern, AJ needs to be my priority. He's nearing an age when he's going to need a positive male influence in his life. Since my father was never around much for me, Adam filled that role for me.

And now I need to repay that favor.

Not chase something as fleeting as happiness.

CHAPTER FORTY-TWO

Esme

"Happy New Year!" Harriet greets me with a lopsided hug when I step into her townhouse, making me think she's already been hitting the bottle pretty hard today.

"Happy New Year to you, too."

When she releases me, Marius envelopes me in his embrace. "I've missed you."

I sigh against him. "I've missed you, too."

It feels like I haven't seen my friends in ages. Between resuming my duties, going on the goodwill trip in my brother's place, flying to New York before heading to Paris in the hopes of rekindling what I once had with Tristan, then coming back to Belmont for the traditional holiday events, the past few months have been a whirlwind.

While I've seen Harriet and Marius on occasion, it's typically been at a formal event. Not when I could relax and be who I really am. Even when they visited me after the attempt on my life, I didn't feel like I could be myself, not with Tristan lingering nearby.

That should have been the only sign I needed to realize it would never work between us.

"Where's your plus one?" Marius glances over my shoulder for any sign of Tristan.

I push out of his embrace, taking off my coat and draping it over a barstool. "He won't be making it."

"Is he still filming?" Harriet hands me a glass of champagne.

"I'm not sure."

This piques Marius' interest and he darts his furrowed brow my way, studying me for several long moments.

Then he exhales, "You broke up."

It's not even a question. He knows without me saying anything.

I force a smile and shrug. "We did."

"Oh, Esme." Harriet pulls me into her arms, her hug nearly suffocating me. "I'm sorry. I thought you were happy. You always told us how perfect he was."

"He may have been perfect," I begin as I extract myself from Harriet. "But he wasn't perfect for me. It just took…" I trail off, not wanting to go into all the details right now. "Well, it took me a few years to realize that perfect doesn't mean it's working."

"Did something happen with Creed?" Marius asks in a hushed voice, even though we're the only ones here, at least for now.

"It doesn't matter." I wave him off. "Can we not talk about this tonight? Tristan and I have agreed to keep it quiet until after the holidays. We plan to inform our publicists next week so they can put together a joint announcement. For now, the world thinks we're still together, so I'd like for you both to conduct yourselves tonight as if we are. I just didn't want you to learn the truth from the bloody tabloids."

"Your secret's safe with us." Harriet gives me an exaggerated wink, then pretends to zip her lips together.

Despite the fact she's had a bit to drink, I know she'll keep it to herself. They both will.

"Thank you. For everything."

"You know we love you." Marius envelopes me once more. Harriet joins us, all our arms intertwined in a group hug as we bask in this friendship that's survived the past three decades.

And I have a feeling it will survive the next three decades, too.

"I do believe this calls for shots," Marius announces as he steps back, a mischievous grin on his face.

"I'm not sure I can do shots anymore." I playfully grimace. "Not now that I'm in my thirties."

He rolls his eyes and heads toward the kitchen island where a makeshift bar has been set up. "If there's any time shots are called for, it's when you're nursing a broken heart."

"And if I'm not heartbroken over this break up?"

He hands me a glass filled with a clear liquid. "I didn't say you were." He gives me a knowing look.

It doesn't matter that I haven't mentioned a single thing about what's happened between Creed and me these past few months. Marius senses something. He's always had an uncanny ability to read between the lines.

"A toast." He clears his throat, handing Harriet a shot before raising his own in the air. "Here's to good friends. Never above you."

"Never below you," Harriet chimes in.

"Always beside you," I finish, having done this toast with them more times than I can count.

"Always beside you," Marius says, eyes locking with mine.

"Always beside you," Harriet repeats, the three of us clinking our glasses together before tilting back our shots.

It takes everything in me to get the tequila down. I don't normally do shots like this, preferring to drink wine or champagne. Perhaps the occasional beer when at a football match. But like Marius said… If there's any time shots are called for, it's when you're nursing a broken heart.

And I've been suffering from a broken heart for close to a decade now.

"If I end the night next to the bloody toilet, I'm blaming you, Mari." Harriet scowls as she slams her glass on the counter, wiping her mouth.

"And not the bottle of champagne you consumed as we were setting up? I thought by now you'd know the importance of the one-to-one rule." He swipes a bottle of water off the counter. "One water for every drink."

"I started out with orange juice in my champagne. Does that count?"

"No."

"Bugger." She pulls her lips together, as if giving consideration to Marius' recommendation. Then she shrugs, lifting a glass of champagne to her lips. "It's the last day of the year. May as well go out with a bang."

"Cheers to that." I lift my glass.

"I had a feeling I'd find you up here."

At the sound of Marius' voice, I snap my gaze toward the rooftop door, watching as he trudges a path through the snow that's accumulated over the past few weeks, a bottle of champagne in each hand.

"I just needed a minute." I force a smile, then shift my eyes forward once more. The city surrounding me pulses with excitement as the clock ticks closer to midnight on New Year's Eve.

I'd hoped spending the last few hours with my oldest friends would help me keep my mind off Creed. It was impossible, though, considering everyone Harriet invited to her annual New Year's Eve celebration was at the villa with us the week Creed and I began our secret tryst. Everyone apart from Anderson, that is. But I didn't expect him to be here.

These days, he spends as much time as he can in the States with Nora.

Which is good for me, since that means Creed also spends a great deal of time in the States.

I'm not sure my heart could handle seeing him on a regular basis. Not after New York.

"Want to talk about it?" Marius hands me a bottle of champagne that I happily accept and bring to my lips. My grandmother would lose her head if she learned I was currently drinking champagne straight from a bottle. At least it's expensive champagne. That should count for something.

"Not much to talk about." I lean against the railing on Harriet's rooftop terrace. "Tristan and I both wanted two different things. With my decision to stay—"

"That's not what I'm talking about, Ezzy." He narrows his gaze on me. "I'm talking about Creed."

I part my lips, about to argue there's nothing going on with Creed. But Marius already senses there is. I may as well come clean.

Turning from the ledge, I walk toward one of the patio chairs, the snow crunching under my shoes. Marius follows and we both sit, our breath foggy in the chilly air. I bring the bottle back to my lips and take a long sip of liquid encour-agement.

"We slept together in New York."

He briefly closes his eyes, not a hint of surprise covering his expression. "I had a feeling."

"I thought this might be it," I continue. "Thought this was our chance to finally be together."

"What happened?" he asks cautiously.

I turn my eyes forward as I attempt to get my jumbled thoughts in order. Then I tell Marius everything I've kept to myself since returning to Belmont, starting with Creed and me nearly kissing at the opera, and ending with Tristan showing up in New York and everything going up in flames.

"Did he walk in on you two together?" Marius asks, eyes wide as he hangs onto my every word.

"Thankfully no. Creed had gone to get us some coffee and pastries. When I heard a knock on the door, I thought it was him."

"It was Tristan."

I nod. "He begged me to give him another chance. Said he'd give up his career to be with me if that's what it took. Then Creed knocked on the door, and things just spiraled down from there, especially when I acted like his only role in life was to fetch me breakfast. But I only did that so Tristan wouldn't realize what we'd done. And not because I felt guilty about it," I add quickly.

"But because of the potential ramifications Creed would suffer," Marius states, able to put the pieces together without me spelling it out.

"Exactly." I pull my coat tighter around me as I stare up at the night sky. When I do, my eyes float to Pegasus, as always seems to happen.

I have a feeling it always will.

"I guess it all forced Creed back to reality. Reminded him of who we are to each other. And who we shouldn't be to each other. Who we can *never* be to each other."

Marius is silent for a moment, his unblinking eyes fixed on me. Music from a nearby bar thumps in the night, the excited chatter of late-night revelers echoing from the street four stories below.

"I can see why he'd think that."

"I know," I say with a sigh. "And I knew that when he kissed me. Things aren't like they were last time. He's in the royal guard now. He could lose so much. He—"

"Not that," Marius interjects, and I whip my gaze toward his.

"What do you mean, Mari?" I furrow my brow.

"Have you ever told him how you felt about him? How you still feel about him?"

"I told him I wanted to be with him," I respond, but know that's not what Marius is asking. The admonishing look he gives me confirms as much.

"But have you told him that you love him? That you've loved him for years now?"

I part my lips to argue that I don't see why that matters, but clasp my mouth closed as I shake my head. "No," I reply softly.

Marius wraps an arm around my shoulder. "I get that you don't have the best relationship with love. How could you with your grandmother constantly telling you there's no place for love in a monarchy?" He pulls away, meeting my eyes. "But maybe if Creed knew how you felt, that you were willing to put your heart on the line for him, he'd be willing to do the same."

"And if he's not?" I say around the tightness in my throat from the mere thought. "If it still doesn't make a single difference? If he still insists on burdening himself with guilt about the past?"

Marius shrugs. "Then maybe you need to finally help him unburden himself." He gives me a knowing look. "You may be the only person who can do that."

"Or he'll feel even more guilty if he knew the truth about where Adam was taking me the night he died."

"True. But that's a risk you need to be willing to take. Life's all about taking risks, Esme. You took a risk on Creed all those years ago. I think it's finally time you take a risk on him again." He meets my gaze. Then his lips lift into a playful grin. "And if it all goes to hell, I'm still more than chuffed to be your plan B."

I burst out laughing at the memory of sitting in that café with Marius and Harriet as they developed a plan for me to lose my virginity to Creed. He'd offered to be my plan B back then, too.

"Plan B? What do I possibly need a plan B for now?"

He shrugs. "Life." His light expression falls, becoming more serious. Thoughtful. He grabs my hand. "If you need someone by your side to navigate any stormy waters, I'll be there for you."

On a long sigh, I snuggle back into his embrace, finding comfort in its familiarity as I contemplate whether I can really come clean with Creed, not just about the night of his brother's death, but also my feelings for him.

"I know you will."

He presses a kiss to the top of my head as fireworks erupt in the sky, the entire city lighting up.

"Happy New Year, Esme."

"Happy New Year, Mari."

CHAPTER FORTY-THREE

Creed

"I'm not sure this is a good idea," I mutter when Lieutenant O'Kelly pulls up to Harriet's row house across from the canals in the downtown area of Montrose.

It took everything I had to get into the SUV with Anderson, and in the back seat. I can't remember the last time I've ridden back here with him. Probably before I was sworn in.

But he went around my back tonight, insisted Kylian be on duty so I could have the night off to celebrate his birthday.

Any other year, I would have refused. After he reminded me of everything he'd been through the past twelve months, I couldn't deny him, not when he said all he wanted was to celebrate with the people he cares about the most.

"Why the bloody hell not?" Anderson retorts.

What do I tell him? That I'm still in love with his sister, even after I promised him I'd stay away so she could be happy? That I broke that promise and slept with her, which led to the destruction of her relationship with Tristan, the breakup having been headline news for a solid week after it was announced?

That I wish I could be with her, but it's just not possible?

I've successfully avoided Esme since New York. Three months ago.

With Anderson spending more time in the States, it's been easy to keep my distance, considering there's often an ocean separating us.

Even when I'm in Belmont, I've assigned someone else to Anderson's protection detail whenever Esme was slated to be at the same event. Not because I didn't think I could control myself around her. But I didn't want to make things difficult for her.

I didn't want to make things difficult for me, either.

Tonight, I have no choice but to see her again. Spend hours with her. Stare at a living reminder of my greatest love... And my biggest regret.

"Things aren't the same as they were when we were teenagers. I'm your chief protection officer."

He pats my leg. "Not tonight, you aren't. Tonight, you're my friend. Kylian's in charge of keeping me safe. Isn't that right, mate?" He looks toward the front of the SUV.

"Sure is," Kylian replies.

"Good. Now let's go celebrate my birthday."

Kylian jumps out of the SUV and runs around to open Anderson's door. I meet him on the sidewalk, scanning the area out of habit.

"Enjoy your night, Lawson," Kylian says. "You deserve a night off once in a while."

"I don't know what that even feels like anymore."

"All the more reason to have some fun." He winks, then

addresses Anderson. "I'll be standing by for when you're ready to leave."

"Thanks, Kylian."

As I follow Anderson up the front steps, I'm about to renew my argument that I shouldn't be here when the door swings open, Esme standing in the doorway.

I blink, my pulse kicking up of its own accord when I take in her short black dress and those same boots she wore in New York that I've fantasized about digging into my back far too many times to be healthy.

"Hey, Ezzy."

"Happy birthday, Anders." She offers her cheek to her brother, purposefully avoiding looking directly at me. As if that will make me disappear.

"Thanks for planning all of this," he responds, kissing her.

"You only turn thirty-six once."

"I lost count after thirty, if I'm being honest."

"Haven't we all." She rolls her eyes. "But this is an important one. For many reasons." Her light expression falters.

She doesn't have to say why it's such a significant birthday for Anderson. Their own mother didn't make it to her thirty-sixth birthday, having succumbed to the disease that now plagues Anderson when she was only thirty-five.

But Anderson's been doing great, all things considered. He still can't overexert himself, but he's finally taking his diagnosis seriously, especially once he reconnected with Nora. No more drinking alcohol or coffee. And he follows his nutritionist's diet to the letter.

"Come on in. I have quite the feast planned for you." Esme steps aside, allowing us to enter.

"Your Highness," I say with a slight nod as I pass, her

scent wrapping around me in the small space of Harriet's entryway.

"Captain."

"Don't you two start with that bullshit," Anderson snips out. "Not tonight. He's not my CPO. I'm not heir apparent. And you're not the bloody Princess Royal. We're all just normal people celebrating the fact I survived another trip around the sun. Got it?"

"Of course," Esme says with a forced smile.

Anderson arches a brow in my direction, waiting for me to agree.

"Sure."

He looks between Esme and me, and I'm confident he's about to call us out on the tension growing thicker with every passing second.

"Jesus Christ." He throws his hands up in frustration. "I'm starting to think we'd all be happier if you two would just bang it out." He spins on his heels and heads into the open living area, a chorus of happy birthday greetings filtering into the foyer.

"Too bad we tried that. It didn't exactly work." Esme shoots me a glare. "Did it?"

"I—"

"Sorry." She winces. "I shouldn't have said that."

"It's true, though."

"I know. I just…" Briefly closing her eyes, she draws in a deep breath. Then she plasters a congenial expression on her face.

I hate everything about it.

Because it's the one she wears when in public. When pretending to be anyone other than who she really is.

"I know this is probably quite awkward for you. It's awkward for me. But we're both adults, correct?"

I nod.

"And we both adore Anderson, right?"

"Without a doubt."

"Then let's get through tonight and pretend there's never been anything between us. Can you do that?"

"Of course," I say, even though the idea of being nothing to Esme is like a knife to the heart.

But that's the decision I made. I can't regret it now.

"Thank you." She holds my gaze for a beat, then spins from me, making her way into the living area.

I run a hand over my face and give myself a mental pep talk that tonight won't be too bad, not with all of our other friends here.

But like that week we spent at the beach villa all those years ago, no amount of people can be a distraction, considering we're at the same townhouse where I once planned a surprise birthday celebration for Esme. Where I was able to spend a full twenty-four hours with her. Where I made love to her.

I try not to think about any of that, though. Try to only think about the reason I'm here — celebrating Anderson's birthday.

But as the night goes on, it becomes increasingly difficult. Especially every time I glance toward the kitchen and watch Esme cook, the sight bringing back memories of cooking with her on her birthday. Of walking up behind her and kissing that spot where her neck meets her shoulders. Of her teasing me by rubbing her body against mine, knowing how much I craved her.

How much I *still* do.

Which is why I find Anderson after we've had dessert and tell him I've ordered an Uber to take me home.

"You're leaving? It's not even eleven o'clock yet."

"I have an early day tomorrow. I've been doing a lot more advance work lately with all your trips to the States."

I feel like an arse making him think he's the reason I'm leaving early.

With him splitting his time between Belmont and New York, my workload *has* increased, especially with his recent hunt for an apartment to purchase in Manhattan. Regardless, that's not the reason I'm ducking out early.

"You stay and enjoy yourself. I'll see you tomorrow." I give him a bro hug, something I haven't done in a while. "Happy birthday, Anders."

"Thanks, mate."

I wave a quick goodbye to everyone else, then make my way out of the townhouse and down the block, no longer suffocated by memories of Esme.

Until I hear a door open and close behind me. I don't even have to look to know it's Esme. I can physically feel her, awareness causing goosebumps to prickle my skin.

"Creed, wait."

I pause, silently cursing under my breath. Then I turn around as Esme jogs toward me to the best of her ability in her boots.

"Thanks for coming tonight," she says once she catches up to me. "And for being so good about everything, all things considered."

"Like you said earlier. We're both adults."

"Yes, we are." She chews on her bottom lip as silence descends on us.

I faintly make out the low thumping of music from one of the clubs a few blocks away. Other than that, it's quiet.

Awkwardly so.

"Sorry about Tristan," I eventually say to fill the void, then immediately cringe.

It's probably not the best thing to bring up right now. But I can never manage to keep my head on straight when I'm around her. Can never think clearly with she's so close, my thoughts a jumbled mess.

"No, you're not," she says with a subtle laugh.

"If you're upset over it, of course I am. I still care about you, Esme. Despite…everything."

She crosses her arms in front of her chest as she peers into the distance. A gentle breeze ripples through the air, causing a chill to rush over me, even though I'm wearing a jacket. Esme must be freezing in her short-sleeved dress that barely covers her ass.

"I shouldn't leave my ride waiting," I say and start to turn, regardless that I haven't actually ordered an Uber yet.

"I wanted to love him." Her voice stops me in my tracks and I spin back around, my fists clenching at the mere idea of her giving her heart to another man.

It's precisely what I asked her to do when I turned her away. It's different when I hear her talk about it. When it's not just an abstract idea but something real.

"I thought I could do it." She tilts her head back, eyes tracing over the stars before returning to mine. "I thought I could forget the past. Only focus on the present. And the future. A future with Tristan. He was willing to give up so much for me."

"Which is what you deserve."

She steps toward me, a vulnerability about her I haven't seen before. "But I couldn't let him do that, Creed. Not when someone else still possesses my heart."

My chest tightens, becoming increasingly painful with every word she speaks. I can't stomach hearing her feelings for me. Not when there's nothing either of us can do about it.

"Esme, I—"

She holds up her hand, cutting me off. "I understand you've made your choice, and it's not me. I've spent all of my life keeping my feelings locked up tight for fear they'll be used against me. Or worse, not returned. But I'm not going to do that anymore.

"I didn't tell you this in New York. And it may not make a difference, but if there's anything I've learned in my life, it's that everything's fleeting. I may not get another chance to tell you."

"Tell me what exactly?" I ask hesitantly, unsure I want to know.

But at the same time, desperate to find out.

"That you haven't left my mind for so much as a second in the past nine years. Even when I was with Tristan, it was *your* hands I imagined touching me. *Your* lips I imagined kissing me. *Your* body I imagined loving me. Even if I lived nine lifetimes, I'll never stop thinking about you. I'll never stop wanting you." She pulls her lips between her teeth to stop her chin from quivering. "I'll never stop *loving* you. You own my heart, Creed Lawson. Regardless of what our future holds, you always will."

I stare at her, the weight of her admission crushing me.

I want to go to her. Sweep her into my arms. Kiss her and promise her we'll find a way to make it work. Tell her *she* hasn't left my mind for a second during the past nine years. That she still owns my heart. That she always will.

But it won't change anything. Choosing her would mean breaking my promise to Adam. I can't do that.

So instead of telling her how I feel, I simply say, "I'm sorry."

The air between us thickens, and I shift my weight from foot to foot, waiting for her to say something.

But she doesn't. Just stares at me with resignation, as if she fully expected me to respond this way.

Feeling my resolve crack the longer I remain in her presence, I force my legs to move and turn from her, continuing up the street. With each step, the heat of her stare burns hotter, even though I wish it were nothing more than an icy chill.

"We weren't going to my mother's grave."

At the sound of her voice, I halt in my tracks and glance over my shoulder, brows furrowed.

"The night Adam died," she clarifies. "He wasn't taking me to my mother's grave. I just…" She briefly looks to the sky once more before returning her gaze to mine. "I just thought you should know."

She spins on her heels and hurries up the street, disappearing into Harriet's townhouse, her statement repeating in my mind.

What does that have to do with anything?

CHAPTER FORTY-FOUR

Esme

My steps are sluggish as I walk into my apartment after midnight, this part of the city much more quiet compared to the bustling nightlife near Harriet's townhouse.

Or maybe it's just my apartment that's too quiet. Too empty. Especially after I finally poured my heart out to Creed, only for him to shatter it all over the sidewalk.

To be honest, I hadn't planned on sharing my feelings with him tonight. Over the past few months, I'd convinced myself it didn't matter, despite Marius insisting it might. But some outside force took over, causing me to finally tell him everything I'd kept locked inside for years now.

Well, *almost* everything.

I just couldn't bring myself to come right out with the truth of the night Adam died, not after how anguished Creed looked when I told him we weren't going to my mother's grave. He was so distraught. So tormented, like every word was another boulder crushing his chest. I couldn't add any more weight to that.

So I left it at that, allowing him to draw his own conclusions from my statement.

I knew there was a chance he'd respond this way. That sharing my feelings wouldn't make a difference.

It still stings, though. Because now I have no choice but to face the truth that Creed will never choose me.

Pausing in the formal living room, I lean against the bookshelf and unzip my boots, my feet screaming in relief once I kick them to the floor. I leave them there, and start toward the wet bar to pour myself a heaping glass of scotch when a knock cuts through the silence.

Considering Archie left less than a minute ago, I assume it's him and make my way toward the door. But when I glance at the security monitor, Archie isn't standing in the foyer.

Confusion knitting my brows, I open the door. "Creed, wha—"

"I couldn't go home," he interrupts as he pushes past me, walking into my apartment without an invitation.

"Okay…" I draw out, closing the door and taking a timid step toward him. He's normally calm, not much getting to him.

There's nothing calm about him right now. He seems agitated. Unsettled. Conflicted.

"I thought I had it all figured out," he says, pacing the length of my living room. "Thought I was doing the right goddamn thing. What *Adam* asked me to do. He specifically made me promise I'd look out for Rory and AJ if anything happened to him. So that's what I've done. I've made them my priority over everything else. Including my own happiness."

"Adam wouldn't——"

"Adam wouldn't want that for me, right? Is that what you're going to say?"

I nod.

"That's what my mum tried to tell me." He runs his hand over his face. "I tried to pretend everything was okay. That I wasn't spending every fucking minute convincing myself I didn't make a colossal mistake in New York." He lifts his eyes to meet mine. "But mums just know these things, I guess. Told me Adam wouldn't want this life for me."

"He wouldn't."

"I know." He slowly nods as he peers into space. "Do you know what else Mum told me?"

I swallow hard. "What's that?"

"That Adam was willing to lose everything for my happiness."

"He loved you, Creed. He——"

He holds up his hand, expression pinched, as if my words physically pain him. Just like earlier tonight.

He takes a few moments to collect himself before pinning his stare on me once more.

"Tonight, you said Adam wasn't taking you to your mother's grave, like the royal household claimed following the attack."

Emptiness settles in the pit of my stomach, my mouth growing dry. "That's correct."

"Right." He turns, digging his hands through his hair as he paces once more. "At first, I had no idea why the hell that mattered. It made no bloody sense how that could be relevant to what we were discussing. To *us*." He stops in his tracks. "Until I remembered what my mum told me."

My heart thrashes in my chest as he stalks toward me, a

myriad of emotions swirling in his eyes. Heartache. Despair. Confusion. Grief. Fear. Hope.

But through them all, I see the love he still has for me, regardless of how much we've hurt each other over the years.

"I'm going to ask you a question. And I'm begging you to give me the truth. Not avoid answering for fear of what it will reveal."

"Okay," I answer with a tremble.

"The night my brother was killed, where was he taking you?" He can barely say the words, his voice choked, eyes welling with tears.

"To your apartment," I whisper.

His shoulders slump, all the tension in his body disappearing.

"But I don't want you to—"

"Why?" he interrupts before I can say another word, that same intensity returning as he moves toward me, his expression begging me to give him the answer he's desperate to hear. "Why was he driving to my apartment?"

I draw in a deep breath, bracing myself to share the last few moments of Adam's life with Creed. I've kept it from him for years, not wanting to burden him with any more guilt.

But as I stare into his eyes, I'm hit with a new realization. By keeping the truth from him, I added to that burden. Every decision Creed has made over the past decade has been with his brother in mind in the hopes of making things right between them.

If he knew Adam's final act was selfless, one born out of love for his brother, perhaps he wouldn't continue punishing himself like this.

Maybe he'll finally realize he *does* deserve to be happy.

That he doesn't have to keep making sacrifices for a man

who wanted nothing more than for his brother to have the same happiness he'd found.

"When Adam picked me up to take me to the gala, he asked me something."

"What's that?" Creed asks, muscles in his face tight.

I have to bite on my lower lip to stop my chin from quivering. The memory's still so raw, it feels like it was just yesterday. I can still see his pained expression. Still remember the strain in his voice. Still recall the way his shoulders fell out of remorse.

"He asked me if I wasn't who I was and you weren't who you were who I'd choose." I swallow hard. "Jameson Gates or you."

He steps toward me, barely a breath separating us as his stare bores into mine. "Who did you choose?"

"You, Creed," I sob. "I told him that I would choose you today and every day forward, no matter what."

With every word I speak, the weight that's been crushing me for the past decade disappears, the truth I didn't think I'd ever be able to admit flowing so easily.

"Told him that the royal household could dictate who I marry, but they didn't get a say in who I loved. I told him I loved you." I pause, blinking back my tears as I peer into those dark eyes that have always been my anchor. My salvation. My true north. "And I still do."

"Still?" he asks, even though I essentially confessed as much earlier tonight.

"Yes, Creed. I love you today. Tomorrow. And always. Nothing will ever stop me from loving you. Not time. Not distance. Nothing. I'm sorry I didn't tell you all those years ago. I guess I was scared. After constantly being told there's no place for love in a monarchy, you start to believe it. When everything fell apart, I didn't think it mattered anymore, especially when I learned you'd been sworn into the guard. I knew how guilty you felt about everything. I didn't want to add to that. Didn't want you to place any more blame on your shoulders. But I realized something tonight."

"What's that?"

"You've spent the past ten years trying to do right by Adam. But if you knew his last act on this earth was in furtherance of *your* happiness, maybe you'd finally allow yourself to be happy. Maybe you'd finally realize you *deserve* to be happy. Even if I don't picture into that happiness, I—"

Before I can utter another syllable, he cups my cheeks, his grip on me firm and determined.

"Do you really think I could even attempt to find happiness with anyone but you?"

His stare locks on mine, smoldering and intense as his lips descend toward me. Barely a whisper separates us, but with how much I've craved this man over the past several months, there may as well be an entire continent between us.

"It's you, Esme. Today. Tomorrow. And always."

He crushes his lips against mine, kissing me with more intensity and fervor than he ever has. I loop my arms around him, pulling him as close as possible, not wanting so much as a breath between us. Not now that we've finally made it to this place. Finally unburdened ourselves from a decade worth of regret, avoidance, and grief. Finally laid ourselves bare, put all our cards on the table. Despite it all, we managed to find our way back to each other.

"I can't stop kissing you," he rasps, eyes tracing over my face. Then he covers my mouth with his again. "Each one makes me want another. And another. And another."

"Then don't stop," I murmur against his lips. "I don't want you to ever stop kissing me."

"As you wish." He coaxes my mouth open, tongue tangling with mine as he breathes into me, giving me life.

Sliding a hand to my waist, he steers me backward through my apartment, barely coming up for air until we reach my bedroom. I've gone so long without losing myself in Creed's kisses. I never want to go another second without them.

When he brings our kiss to an end, we just stare at each other, as if wanting to take a mental picture of this moment. Remember it for the rest of our lives. The moment *we* finally begin.

Then he lunges for me again. But instead of kissing me, he spins me around, pushing my hair over one shoulder as his fingers find the zipper of my dress.

"Too bad you've already taken the boots off," he murmurs as he leaves soft kisses along my nape. "Do you have any idea how often I imagined fucking you while you were wearing them?"

My core clenches, a shiver rolling down my spine. All the tiny hairs dotting my body stand on end, a delicious tremor rushing through me as he slowly slides my dress down my arms, allowing it to fall to the floor.

"I can put them back on if you'd like."

When I face him, his eyes flame as they take in my lace bra and panties. It doesn't matter this man's seen me naked countless times. The appreciation in his gaze is still as strong as it was all those years ago when we stood in this same room about to have sex for the first time.

When I made him agree to one night and nothing more.

Now I want to give him the rest of my nights.

"As tempting as that sounds…" He loops an arm around my waist. "I'm not going to fuck you tonight, Esme." His lips softly touch mine. "I'm going to make love to you."

I whimper, melting into his kiss. The world disappears around me as I lose myself in this man and everything he is to me. Everything he'll always be to me.

His mouth moving against mine, he walks me the few feet toward my bed, kicking off his shoes and loosening his belt as he goes. When the back of my legs hit the mattress, he pulls away, shoving his jeans down his legs before ripping his shirt over his head. Not wanting to waste a single second, I reach behind me and unclasp my bra, tossing it onto our growing pile of clothes.

"God, I've missed these." His pupils flame with desire as he cups my breasts.

When he pinches my nipples the way he knows I like, I throw my head back and moan. "And I've missed your hands on them. On me."

He slams his lips back to mine, supporting me as he lowers me onto the bed and crawls on top of me. His hands roam my frame, every touch igniting an inferno inside me until he grips my panties. I lift my hips and he slides them down my legs. When he returns to me, he pushes my thighs wide.

Then his mouth is on me, tongue swirling, fingers thrusting as he murmurs how much he craves me. How much he can't live without me.

How much he *loves* me.

Finally being free to confess our feelings during this intimate moment makes it even more intense. Even more vibrant. Even more powerful. So much so that it takes no time at all for my orgasm to overtake me.

I pull him to me, not ready to come down from this high anytime soon, and cover his mouth, the taste of me on his lips making me burn hotter still.

"I need you inside me, Creed. Need to feel you. Need you to make love to me."

He returns my kiss with even more fervor, and I wrap my legs around his waist, his erection against my core making me whimper.

"I love that sound," he remarks, taking my bottom lip between his teeth. "Love the way you move." He circles his hips, teasing me with what I want. Then his expression falls, becoming more serene. "I love *you*, Esme."

Emotion swells in my throat, my heart so full I fear it will burst through my chest.

"I love you, too, Creed."

He closes his eyes, briefly hanging his head. "I thought I'd go to my grave without hearing you say those three words to me."

"I should have told you years ago."

"I'm glad you didn't." He frames my face in his hands. "If one thing were different, we may not be right here. Right now. And I've finally realized that this is all that matters. In New York, I begged you to leave the past behind you. All along, I've refused to do the same thing. I thought by focusing on Rory and AJ, I *was* doing that. But nothing could have been further from the truth. They're not my future. They're a past mistake I thought I needed to fix. Now, the only future I see is one with you."

His eyes sear into me as he eases inside, everything about this moment bigger than I ever expected it could be. From the way he worships me with his body. To the way he links his fingers with mine, each thrust and retreat hitting places I didn't know existed. To the way he continues to murmur how much he loves me.

And for the first time in my life, I'm happy to return that love. To admit my feelings, to hell with the consequences. To allow Creed to possess all the tiny pieces of my heart I swore I'd always keep locked up tight.

But I could never keep them from Creed. He's always been the exception to the rule.

"Don't fight it, Esme," he grunts as he buries his head in the crook of my neck, picking up his pace. "Let me feel you. Let me worship you. Let me love you." His dark eyes meet mine, affection and need combining within. "God, I love you so bloody much."

His declaration shatters my last shred of resistance. I cry out, my body no longer under my control. It belongs to Creed. *I* belong to Creed.

He joins me in my bliss, moaning through his own release as he holds me tight. Then he collapses on top of me, pulling me into his arms.

As we struggle to catch our breath, I rest my hand against his chest, savoring in the rapid beating of his heart.

"It's yours," he says breathlessly.

I lift my eyes to his.

"It's always been yours, Esme. Even before you realized it."

"And my heart is yours, Creed." I take his hand and press it to my chest. "Today. Tomorrow. Always."

"Today." He brushes his mouth against my cheek. "Tomorrow." He moves to the other cheek before hovering his lips over mine. "Always."

"Always."

CHAPTER FORTY-FIVE

Creed

My mobile buzzes on the nightstand, jolting me awake. I fumble around for a few moments before silencing the alarm. The room is still shrouded in darkness, the small gap in the drapes indicating the sun hasn't yet risen.

When I feel an arm wrap around my torso, I sigh, basking in Esme's touch. It doesn't matter how many times I made love to her last night. Or the fact I slept with her in my arms. I doubt I'll ever tire of feeling her hands on my body.

I turn in the bed, pushing a few tendrils of her hair behind her ear to admire her. No makeup. Hair a mess. Eyes droopy from sleep. But she's still the most beautiful woman I've ever seen.

"It wasn't a dream," I remark as I brush my lips to her forehead.

"It wasn't a dream."

I run my fingers up and down her back, replaying the last twelve hours in my mind.

When I showed up at Harriet's and saw Esme for the first time since New York, waking up in her bed was the last thing I expected. I'd spent the past several months convincing myself of my place. And it wasn't here. It was with Rory and AJ.

But last night, something inside me snapped.

Or maybe the lightbulb finally went off, especially after Esme told me Adam wasn't taking her to her mother's grave the night he died.

At first, I didn't understand why that mattered. Not when it was nearly ten years ago.

But as I walked the city streets, probably looking like I was absolutely crazy, all the puzzle pieces locked into place, showing me the truth that had evaded me for years.

And the truth is that Adam wouldn't want this for me. He'd want me to be happy. Would want me to stop living in the past.

I'd convinced myself Esme *was* my past.

In reality, she's my everything. Past. Present. Future. Eternity.

"So…" Esme's voice pulls me back to the present. "How is this going to work?" Her question comes out timid, as if she's not sure she'll like my response, especially after the way things blew up in New York. "Or are we back in that gray area again?"

"I don't think we have any choice *but* to be back in that gray area. At least for a little while." I pull her closer, hoping the kisses I leave on her head reassure her I'm not going to push her away again.

But I'm not sure *how* this is going to work. I haven't wanted to think about it, even though the thought's been in the back of my mind since I jumped into my SUV and drove over here in the late night hours. It almost had me turning around and returning to my life.

"Things are complicated," I sigh.

"I'm more than aware of that."

I pinch her chin, forcing her gaze to mine. "But I still want to be with you."

She touches her hand to my cheek. "And I want to be with you. But you can't be with me if you're—"

"Still in the royal guard. I know."

"And leaving will mean also leaving my brother."

I push out a breath, squeezing my eyes shut.

This is the hardest part about our situation. I feel like I have to choose between my friendship with Anderson and the love I have for his sister. I worry he'll see it as a betrayal of his trust, especially after he begged me to stay away from her.

But that was when he thought she was happy with Tristan, something she's admitted she never was. After everything Anderson's been through with losing Nora and finally winning her back, I'd like to think he'd understand. At the very least, he'd support my decision to make a change in my current situation with Rory.

Pretty sure *everyone* would support my decision to make a change in that situation, especially my mum.

"At the end of August, I'll have eighteen years of service under my belt," I tell her. "Four in the infantry. Four with special teams. Then ten in the royal guard. With the consideration I get from my time on special teams—"

"You can retire two years early without a mark on your record for early discharge."

I nod. "Exactly."

"So we wait until August?"

A knot forms in my chest at the mere idea. I don't want to wait five months for her to be mine. So much can happen in that time. What if she realizes I'm not worth it? Or meets someone else?

But what other choice do we have?

Even if I wasn't close to being able to retire with full military honors, I can't just abandon Anderson without giving him appropriate notice. The bond between chief protection officer and the royal we guard isn't one that can be formed overnight. It's why I was chosen to be his chief protection officer in the first place. Why Adam was chosen for Esme. Then why Archie took his place.

Not to mention, it's going to take time for me to separate myself from Rory's life. I don't plan on removing myself entirely. AJ's my nephew. And Rory's still family. I want to be there for them as much as I can. Want to be a positive influence in my nephew's life.

But I'm no longer going to sacrifice my needs to do that. It's just going to take some time to break the news to Rory, especially since she still has abandonment issues. This isn't something I can just spring on her overnight. It'll be a process.

"I hate that idea," I say honestly. "But—"

"But after last time, it's for the best."

"I don't want this to blow up in our faces. I want to do everything I can to make sure it works this time."

"So do I." She wraps an arm around me, mouth seeking out mine.

I sigh, losing myself in her kiss, wanting to remember everything about the way her lips feel while I can still enjoy them.

The idea of having to walk away again makes my heart physically ache. The only silver lining is the fact that it won't be forever. It's been five months since she first returned to Belmont, and it seems like it was just yesterday. I can only hope the next five months will pass just as quickly.

But with much less drama.

"It'll be okay," Esme assures me, although I get the feeling she's also saying it for her benefit. Then her expression brightens. "It'll be like in *An Affair to Remember*."

I throw my head back and laugh. "What is it with you and your brother and that movie?"

She playfully punches my chest. "It's a great story about two people finding their way back to each other, regardless of all the obstacles. Maybe you think it's cheesy, but I love it, if for no other reason than the message it contains."

"And what's that?" I push her onto her back and settle between her legs, her warmth against my erection causing desire to pool low in my stomach.

She threads her fingers through my hair. "To never give up hope."

"I haven't given up on you in the past nine years, even if my actions made you think I had. Even if I *wanted* to." I lower my mouth to hers, reveling in the soft flesh of her lips. "I have no intention of giving up on you now. Not when we're so bloody close."

I coax her mouth open, tongue dancing with hers.

"Just promise me one thing." I pull back, hands cupping her cheeks.

"What's that?"

"That you won't stand me up on our agreed-upon meeting day, like in the movie."

"She didn't stand him up. She was hit by a car. She—"

I erase her protest with a kiss. "Then promise you won't get hit by a car. Or do anything else that will prevent you from being in my arms the second I sign my discharge papers."

"I'll be there." She holds up her pinky, like we used to do as kids. "Pinky Promise."

I link my pinky with hers. "Pinky Promise," I repeat as my mouth reclaims hers, our pinkies still linked.

As I sink into her one last time, all I can do is pray that these next five months will be the last ones I ever spend without her.

CHAPTER FORTY-SIX

Creed

By the time I pull into my driveway after taking a detour to the gym, then the office, Rory's car is gone.

I hate avoiding her like this, but I need time to figure out how I'm going to handle things. It doesn't help that Adam's birthday is coming up in a few weeks, which is always a difficult time. Hopefully, she'll understand why I need to start extricating myself from this situation. That she'll see I'm not abandoning her, but moving on with my life.

Maybe this will give her the freedom to move on with *her* life, too.

When I step into the house, everything's quiet. The kitchen's a bit of a mess, dishes scattered across the island, a stack of dirty pans piled in the sink, evidence of a rushed breakfast. On the refrigerator is a hastily scrawled note, reminding me about AJ's football game in thirty minutes, giving me just enough time for a quick shower.

I grab a banana from the fruit basket and quickly eat it.

Just as I toss the peel into the garbage bin, my phone buzzes. I pull it out of my pocket, secretly hoping it's Esme. Instead, I see my father's name.

While we're much closer than we once were, he still doesn't call me out of the blue like this. Whenever he needs to discuss something, he typically stops by my office. Or calls my work mobile. Not my personal one.

"Is everything okay?" I ask, dispensing with a normal greeting.

"Did you see the news?"

Heat rushes over my face, my worry increasing.

Were paparazzi stationed outside Gladwell this morning? Did they catch me leaving Esme's apartment and try to make a quick buck by selling a photo to the media? We'd just agreed to wait until August to avoid this kind of thing. Did we screw ourselves over already?

"I haven't. I—"

"A car was pulled from Sufford Lake in the Brimford Recreation Area. A fisherman discovered it yesterday evening."

I blow out a breath, shoulders falling in relief that this isn't regarding Esme and me.

"What does this have to do with—"

"It was registered to Callie Sloane. Her remains were found in the trunk."

Silence falls over the line as I squeeze my eyes shut. I can't say I'm surprised. She's been missing for ten years. Regardless of any evidence of foul play, I'd assumed she was dead. At least her family will finally get some closure.

If she has any family.

From what I remember, Hayes Barlow was the only person who seemed remotely interested in finding her.

"Were they able to determine the cause of death?"

"Evidence of sharp force trauma was found in her ribs, indicating she most likely died from a stab wound to her lower right abdomen."

"Stab wound? Wasn't Gianna Vale *also* stabbed in the lower right abdomen?"

"I won't lie and tell you I didn't immediately think the same thing when I heard, but as of right now, the authorities are treating them as two isolated events. At least until they can investigate things further."

"Any idea who's responsible?" I ask.

"Right now, their lead suspect is Hayes Barlow."

"Really?" I blink repeatedly, taken aback by this revelation. "What led to that conclusion?"

"Her car was found just a few miles away from a lake house Hayes Barlow owned."

"Why?" I scrunch my brows, a heaviness settling in the pit of my stomach.

"The working theory is that he was infatuated with her. That—"

"No. Not why he'd kill her. Why would he go through the effort of bringing her disappearance to the public's attention, even after the police refused to do so, when it could potentially backfire on him?"

My father sighs. "I'm not an expert in these types of things, but according to a forensic psychologist the bureau brought in, he displayed signs of being infatuated with Callie Sloane. Obsessed, really. When she didn't return his affections, he killed her. In his mind, if he couldn't have her, no one could. When no one would look into her disappearance, he was probably irritated. He was often ignored as a child, which shaped his need for attention as an adult, both positive and negative. The idea that his crimes weren't being displayed all over television most likely angered him. So he took matters into his own hands and made sure everyone knew what he'd done, even if he didn't come right out and confess his involvement."

I look into the distance, ruminating this theory over in my mind. It *is* plausible. But something about it doesn't sit right with me. It seems too clean.

Too easy.

"I just wanted to make sure you knew, given who Hayes is, and what not." My father's voice forces me back to the present.

"Thanks," I respond, still somewhat in a daze.

"Of course. I'll see you at AJ's game."

"See you then," I say before ending the call, unable to shake this premonition that there's more to Callie's death than the police believe.

But what?

Running a hand over my face, I push down my unease so I can get ready for AJ's game. At least that will be a good distraction. And right now, I can certainly use a distraction.

I trudge up the stairs and am about to slip into my room but stop in my tracks when I glance at the door to Adam's office and notice it's slightly ajar.

If it were any other room, I wouldn't think twice. But this room is different. This door is always sealed tight, no matter what.

It could be nothing, but I can't shake the feeling in my gut that something's not right, especially after my father's phone call.

And Adam taught me to always listen to my gut.

Lifting my hand to the knob, I take a deep breath, the hair on my nape standing on end. Then I push the door open, my blood spiking when my eyes fall on a figure standing by the windows, his head lowered as he flips through one of Adam's files.

With all the military precision I've been taught throughout my career, I reach into my coat and grab my pistol, aiming it at him.

"You have exactly two seconds to tell me what the fuck you're doing in here before I decorate the walls with your brain."

My voice echoes in the silence, jaw clenching, nostrils flaring.

"Now!" I yell when he doesn't move, completely ignoring my presence.

As if he belongs here more than I do.

Finally, he sighs and slowly turns around.

The air whooshes from my lungs as I stare into the eyes of the man who killed my brother.

Whose boat had been attacked on the North Sea.

Who everyone thought was dead.

But he's not.

How could he be when Hayes Barlow is currently standing in my brother's office, looking very much alive?

"Good morning, Captain Lawson," he says with a sly smile, tossing the file onto the desk. "You look like you've seen a ghost."

Thank you for reading *Fallen Knight*! Will Esme and Creed's love survive when ghosts of their past resurface? To find out how it all ends, grab Broken Crown today.

https://www.tkleighauthor.com/brokencrown

Thank you so much for taking the time to read this book. If you enjoyed it, please let your friends know by leaving a review so more people can fall in love with Creed and Esme.

BROKEN CROWN

After a decade of allowing his guilt to burden him, Creed Lawson is finally ready to move on from his past and only focus on his future. A future with Esme.

Until a ghost from his past shows up and makes him question everything he's believed to be true.

Makes him question *everyone* he's believed to be true

When a shocking revelation comes to light, he'll not just have to risk his legacy in order to be with Esme.

He'll have to risk his life.

Scan above or type the address into your web browser to grab your copy.

https://www.tkleighauthor.com/brokencrown

ACKNOWLEDGMENTS

Thank you so much for picking up *Fallen Knight*. I hope you enjoyed reading this next chapter of Creed and Esme's story! Their journey has been so much fun for me to write. There's just something I love about weaving a love story as well as a suspenseful story. It's one of the most difficult yet fulfilling things to do. With more mainstream contemporary romances, you only have to worry about the romance arc, more or less. But with romantic suspense, you almost have two different storylines you're trying to weave together into a seamless experience for readers. It can be challenging at times, but I absolutely love it. And I hope you're enjoying the ride, too! Don't worry. All will be revealed soon!

But first, I want to take a minute to acknowledge everyone who helps me behind the scenes in making these stories come to life.

First and foremost, a huge thanks to my husband, Stan, and my daughter, Harper Leigh. I couldn't do this without their support.

To my wonderful PA, Melissa Crump — I can't tell you how much I appreciate everything you do for me.

To my fantastic beta readers — Lin, Melissa, Sylvia, Stacy, and Vicky — thank you so much for offering your feedback.

To my admin team — Melissa and Vicky. Thanks for keeping my reader group and page running. Love you ladies!

To my review team — Thank you for always not only reading my books but also taking the time to write reviews. Your support means the world to me.

To my reader group — Thanks for being my super-fans and giving me a place to go when I need a break from writing.

And last but not least, a big thank you to YOU! My amazing readers. I'm so grateful for your support.

Can't wait to share the final chapter of Creed and Esme's story with all of you!

Love & Peace,
~ T.K.

ABOUT THE AUTHOR

T.K. Leigh is a *USA Today* Bestselling author of romance ranging from fun and flirty to sexy and suspenseful.

Originally from New England, she now resides just outside of Raleigh with her husband, beautiful daughter, rescued special needs dog, and three cats. When she's not writing, she can be found training for her next marathon or chasing her daughter around the house.

facebook.com/tkleighauthor

instagram.com/tkleigh

tiktok.com/@tkleigh

bookbub.com/authors/t-k-leigh

pinterest.com/tkleighauthor